Celebrities in Disgrace

Also by Elizabeth Searle

My Body to You
A Four-Sided Bed

Celebrities in Disgrace

A Novella and Stories

ELIZABETH SEARLE

Graywolf Press

Publication of this volume is made possible in part by a grant provided by
the Minnesota State Arts Board through an appropriation by the Minnesota
State Legislature, and by a grant from the National Endowment for the Arts.
Significant support has also been provided by the Bush Foundation; Dayton's
Project Imagine with support from Target Foundation; the McKnight Foundation; a grant made on behalf of the Stargazer Foundation; and other gener-
ous contributions from foundations, corporations, and individuals. To these
organizations and individuals we offer our heartfelt thanks.

Graywolf Press
250 Third Avenue North, Suite 600
Minneapolis, Minnesota 55401
All rights reserved.

www.graywolfpress.org

Published in the United States of America

Some of these stories appeared in a slightly different form in the following
magazines: *Boulevard, Chelsea, Five Points, Michigan Quarterly Review,
Ontario Review.*

The story "Celebration," published as "Birthdays," received the *Michigan
Quarterly Review*'s Lawrence Foundation Prize for 2000.

David Foster Wallace quote from *Infinite Jest*, a novel, used by permission of
Little, Brown & Company (Boston, New York, Toronto, London) Copyright
1996, First edition.

Matthew Gilbert quote from *The Boston Globe* used by permission of author.

ISBN 978-1-55597-324-7

2 4 6 8 9 7 5 3

Library of Congress Catalog Number: 00-105091

Cover design: Christa Schoenbrodt
Cover art: Artville, Paul Gilligan

Acknowledgments

My thanks—first, to my first reader, all ways: John Hodgkinson; to Elaine Markson; to my two Girl Groups for countless readings and priceless advice: Debra Spark, Jessica Treadway, and Joan Wickersham; to Gail Donovan and especially Ann Harleman & her magic red pencil; to Elizabeth Sheinkman; to my ever-encouraging parents and family; to Sara Al-Doory; to the great Graywolf staff, especially the leader of the pack and founder of this feast: Fiona McCrae.

to two stars
my sister Kate
&
my son Will

i.e., If you worried at all about how you looked. As in to other people. Which all kidding aside who doesn't.

—David Foster Wallace

. . . he could not quite give up on trying to meet the dare to be extraordinary.

—Henry James

Contents

Memoir of a Soon-to-Be Star

I first began acting, I'll tell you when you ask, in dress-up games I played with my sister Mol till I was—body-wise—a woman. Till Easter Break, 1977; the week Mol and I broke up. Something I never thought could happen between sisters. Our last game, like all our games, was my inspiration. On our ratchety Brownie camera, we'd shoot the pig-blood prom scene from *Carrie*. Pretend-directed by Mol; starring four-teen-year-old me. Showcasing my range: wary shy-girl joy at being crowned prom queen; knew-it-all-along shock when—splat!—John Travolta's girlfriend dumps a bucket of pig's blood onto Carrie; pur-est fury as Carrie, with only her telekinetically electrified eyes, zaps her whole hateful high-school class dead. BamBamBam! See, though you'd never guess it (here I'll give a wry actress-looking-back laugh), *my* Greenville High School–self was as bad off as witchy, spit-upon, tampon-pelted Carrie. Only I didn't have telekinetic—but I've got some other kind—powers.

Me: Em O'Moore. Whom you and the world will know as Emma-line Moore.

And when did you first sense your special powers? you'll ask. *Your talent, your*—(you will hesitate, shy like I used to be)—*much-celebrated sex appeal?*

That last Saturday night of Break. When we—not Mol and me but a new *we*—performed that pig-blood scene. (Uneasily, I'll recross my long legs; avidly, you'll scribble on your pad). The night I stood in my old cardboard Miss South Carolina–crown and my new spaghetti-strapped prom dress under a wobbly bucket of Hunt's Tomato Ketchup, lit by our Brownie camera light. Hidden on the lowest level of our split-level house. My shyly widened prom-queen smile shone with the same LIP-SMACKIN' lip gloss that makes the mean mouths of Greenville girls look as drooly as my big brother Kenny's mouth. His thick lips. Which, when he's watching something too hard, he forgets to shut.

But, see, I don't want to talk about that night.

Oh? you ask, pen poised. Sometimes lately, I picture you not as a big-time magazine reporter but as an altogether different kind of interviewer. A shock-faced principal from my brother's Special School. Or even—please God, no—a scornfully slow-voiced Greenville cop. Either way, you want the history of my game-playing. How it all started, where it all led.

So: what were Mol's and my first, as we say in my profession, parts?

Simple. (I will seem to relax.) Mol played the man; I played everyone else.

Mol wore our dad's old square-shouldered floppy-sleeved candidate's jacket, still bearing its still-shiny button, the name I will remake: O'MOORE. Back in Penn Wynn, PA, Dad ran for Congress and Mol played hapless First Man to my all-powerful Lady President. After Dad quit what he called—like there's only one—The Game, after he moved us out here to SC, to the sticks, Mol played devoted Darrin-Donald to my *Bewitched* version of *That Girl.* An Aspiring Actress who wriggles her nose to make magic, make herself a star. Then in early '77, when I got my period and Mom began asking, "Aren't you getting a little old to play pretend?" I made myself an Aspiring Actress for real.

We—Mol and me—began shooting the Home Movies you will view as my Early Works. Silent movies. I wore Mom's old Basic Blacks and her oldest waxiest '50s lipstick. Labeled, simply: RED. One weekend, when he was home from school, we recruited tall Kenny from the sidelines, draping him in a cape.

Kenny the Villain tied me to our dogwood tree with clothesline.

2

He ran round and round me, still running when the rope ran out, my brother's body a blur obscuring my made-up face. I scissored my throat with my hand, signaling to Mol, the entranced cameraman: Cut, cut!

And why, you will ask, *did you stop making movies after your* Carrie?

No comment, I'll say. But I'll tell only you only this. Off the record.

The end of Easter Break, 1977, I stood in the bathroom in my red-spattered prom dress. Sticky-skinned sticky-haired sticky-lipped with pretend pig-blood. Hunt's Ketchup mixed with scared-sweat smells like real blood. I pulled off my dress, knocking off my stop-sign framed glasses. Blindly, I stuffed the bloody-looking dress down our laundry chute. Heard it fall, weightless as an angel.

"Em-my?" Kenny called through the chute, his newly deepened voice incredulous. As if I, not my dress, had wafted down over him. I clanked shut the metal chute door. Then rattled open the sliding shower door.

Isn't it only natural, I ask you, that a soon-to-be star like me needs—even when I'm, especially when I'm naked—an audience?

Scratch that last, OK? Start all over, OK?

Not even Molly O'Moore knew how much Emma O'Moore had been looking forward to Easter Break, 1977. Or how miserably freshman Em had walked the halls of Greenville High. How, the week before Break, she'd kept singing to herself, "There's Got to Be a Morning After." One of those self-consciously pathetic facts Em told the imaginary interviewer inside her head.

"Look, Mol. This's what I'm changing *into* tonight."

On the last Saturday of Break, the day they'd set for their pig-blood shoot, Em finally showed Mol the prom dress that not even Mol knew she'd bought.

"Holy moly." Mol gaped down at it, standing on an uncushioned den armchair. Mol had just balanced the bucket on a makeshift ply-wood shelf. She'd rigged that shelf above the curtain rod of the drapes hanging over the den's glass doors. Outside on Dad's screened porch, workmen swore and stomped, wiring the house with an Alarm System. "You bought that, Emmy?"

Em nodded, draping it over her arm. A pink slip of a dress, like Carrie's.

"Did anyone *see* you buy it?" Mol demanded from above, as if it might be against the law to buy a prom dress when you're not going to the actual prom.

"*Mai oui!*" Em shook back her Cher-length hair. She considered her long hair and long fingernails to be her only beauties. "Bunch of Greenville High girls saw me. Giggled their panties wet over me. And ya know what I did? I zapped 'em with my Carrie-stare. I reduced 'em all to smoking rubble!"

"*Em-* my." Mol widened her Bette Davis eyes so whites surrounded the blue. The little-sister stare twelve-year-old Mol hadn't given Em in ages.

"Anyhow, I bought zee *robe de soirée* with my library-job money. Plus—" Em lay her dress on Mom's desk and reached in her jeans' pocket. "Lip *gloss.*"

"Lemme see." Mol hopped down, landing solidly on her feet. She seized the fruity tube as if she wanted to try it on her own small plump-lipped mouth.

"*Pour moi!*" Em pursed her lips like Brigitte Bardot, playing Sullen Star.

"Keep yer mouth shut, schweetheart," Mol answered in her man-voice, playing Gruff Director. She knitted her brows and dabbed Em's frozen-kiss lips, deftly smearing the thin upper then the full lower. "There!" Mol stepped back.

Dramatically, Em pulled off her stop-sign glasses. Mol's round pink face blurred. "So how do I look?" Em demanded, her strawberry-flavored lips slick.

"Different." Mol sounded grudgingly impressed—enough to make Em dare think, *Sexy?* "Stand on this X for a sec." Mol gripped Em's bony shoulders and pushed her onto the masking-tape X she'd fixed to the floor. "Yep. The blood oughta hit you just right." She sighted from

Em's head to the empty bucket. Anyone watching might think Mol, the pretend-Director, was truly in charge.

"Let's not wait till tonight." Em popped back on her glasses, raising her voice above the workmen's hammers outside. "Let's do a dry run now."

"But we gotta get going to Sky City. Mom said we'd leave by noon—"

"So?" Em asked, watching Mol give an unconvincingly casual shrug.

"I just wish those Alarm guys'd hurry *up* so's we can go buy our *blood*."

The den door exploded open. Crack: it banged the already scarred paneling. *"Way—"* Kenny bounded down the short flight of steps that made their house a split-level. "Way for *me!*" He began bouncing on his heels, fully wakened from his nap. His face blurred above his tall body, strong legs. *"Don' go,"* Kenny pleaded to Em like he was six, not sixteen. Like she'd vanish in a greeny pink puff of *I-Dream-of-Jeannie*-Starring-Barbara-Eden smoke.

"You're going too," Em reminded him. "But you gotta keep your pants on."

Kenny guffawed. His last weekend home from school, he'd pulled his sweatpants down in Sky City Supermarket. The bologna packages behind him had seemed a pale dead pink compared to Kenny's floppy cock.

"Next thing, you'll be streaking at the Oscars," Em added now. Kenny crowed with laughter. Em smirked, remembering the naked man darting across the Oscar stage on TV. When David Niven quipped, "Some people can't resist displaying their own shortcomings," Em had wondered why it was laughable to have a short neat man-cock instead of a limp-club cock like her brother's.

"He all-way makin' th' news, wearin' just his ten-nis shoes!" Kenny jogged round the den's half-circle of worn armchairs. He loved best the worst songs. "Oh yeah, they call him th' Stree-eak; th' fastes' thing on two fee-eet—" Circling behind Mom's desk, he snapped the waistband of his sweatpants. His hipbones stuck out like Em's, only his bones were bigger.

"Simmer down, Kenny," Mol scolded like Dad. "Or you can't come with us."

Automatically, Kenny folded his arms, pinning his man-sized hands under his elbows. Straitjacket pose, Em thought as he looked to her for approval.

"Good boy," Em began. And the phone rang. They all jumped without moving. *"Mom,"* Em shouted toward the glass doors, the muffled drills.

"No; *I'll* get it!" Mol bolted for the phone as if—could she be? Em worried—expecting a call.

Why? you will demand, unable to picture me unpopular. *Why did I have no friends? And,* you might dare to add, *what did I mean about needing an audience when I'm naked?* Oh, I might answer teasingly, I'm playing a whole new kind of game these days. Age fifteen, sixteen. Not "dress-up" anymore but—the opposite. I imagine your tell-me-more interviewer face. Then I shift subjects, listing to you the reasons why I at fourteen had no friends.

(1) Because Dad moved us down here to SC, tearing us away from our home outside Philly. A super-conservative district where no Democrat ever won, including our dad. Out here, instead of working all hours for the Dems, Dad cemented bricks on his porch or weeded the zucchini that no one—not even he, who heaps his supper plates, saying O'Moores always want more—ate.

(2) Because, see, for all my dad's talk, he couldn't stay on the sidelines like Mom'd like; he had to write to the *Greenville Sun*, supporting the bussing that everyone else's dads hate and suggesting that kids like Kenny—*my own son, born with what is called Mental Retardation*—might be fully "integrated," too, into our public schools. I couldn't imagine why Kenny'd be any happier in Greenville High than I was. Than the black kids there seemed to be. But I nodded solemnly when Dad asked: Did I understand why he wrote that letter? Combined with Mom being a teacher, the letter made kids stare sideways at me. Then when Dad gave his case before the School Board, we

got Hate Mail that I overheard Mom mention but that I never found in any of our trash baskets.

(3) Because, unlike Mol, I hate back. Invisible rays shoot out of my Carrie-stare. I am an equal opportunity hater; I hate Jo Jo and her band of blonds, waving at me all friendly-like so I'll lift my hand in my own stiff wave that they, two steps down the hall, can collapse in spasms of giggles, imitating. And I hate, though maybe a little less, Lugenia and her separately but equally mean girlfriends who at least are up-front about hating me, Lugenia decreeing straight to my pale face: "Girl, you look like a *dog* in them glasses."

Stop-sign framed glasses that I wear though I know they're uncool. But STOP is all I want to say to all of Them, especially Miss "Jo Jo Parkins," whose name I will give you whole because I've vowed to make it—Jo Jo's name—mud.

(4) Because my brother Kenny is and always will be—at least Mol and I can dream of being someone different someday—Kenny.

"O'Moore's," Mol answered briskly, the way their mom had taken to answering the phone these past tense weeks. Announcing to whoever was on the other end that she—they, the O'Moore's—were unfazed, unafraid. Now, Mol listened bug-eyed to the loud slurred man's voice that blared out of the receiver. Drunk or Southern or both, Em thought, stepping closer.

—*Can tell your nigger-lovin' daddy,* it was saying as Em whipped the live-wire phone from Mol—*Quit tellin' us how t' run* OUR *schools, who-all* WE *oughta let in*—Em fumbled for the steel whistle Mom kept by the phone. How did Mom do it: hold both whistle and phone, shrilling the whistle so smartly?

—YOU *oughta head on back north 'for we come an'* RUN *you-all*—

Em's whistle shrill made only a weak tweet. But she slammed down the phone so hard she thought she'd cracked the receiver.

"Jesus, Mary, and Joseph!" she burst out. Dad's oldest Catholic-boy curse.

"Who that, who *that*?" Kenny, who'd been standing as still as Mol, sprang into one of his cat pounces. He crowded Mol and Em behind the desk.

"Just some redneck son of a bitch," Em managed to answer, her slick lips stiff. Then she seized Mol into a hard hug. She wanted the comfort of Mol's solid tomboy body, wanted to whisper into Mol's short tousled brown hair: *See why I hate 'em so much, the people down here?*

"O' bitch, o' *bitch*—" Kenny repeated gleefully, opening his long arms.

"So screw 'em all." Em pulled back from Mol, bumping Mom's desk. Avoiding the hug Kenny wanted to give his sisters: always squeezing too hard. Mol blinked at Em. Kenny blinked too, both their gazes dazed and expectant.

"Just wait'll tonight—" Em climbed up onto Mom's neat desktop, towering over her little sister and big brother. "Wait'll you see me as Carrie the prom queen!" She lifted by its straps her prom dress, flourishing it like a bullfighter.

"Wan' that—" At its silky flash, Kenny shot out his arms, reaching.

"No, Kenny," Mol snapped out of her daze to tell him. As Kenny screwed up his long-jawed face in protest, Em noticed his faint beard bristle.

"It's OK; he can touch it." To keep Kenny from going off, to remind Kenny who was his favorite sister, to remind Mol who was the real boss, Em tossed Kenny the dress. He caught it and hugged it to his chest, his mouth half-open. Would he, Em tried not to worry, drool on its pink sheen?

"Look," she told Kenny and Mol, feeling like the grown-up. The one who'd protect them, distract them. "I'm Sissy Spacek, only I've *won* Best Actress for *Carrie* like she should've. And I'm giving the *best* Best Actress speech!"

Mol straightened up as if for a national anthem. Oscar night had replaced Miss America night as their biggest event of the year, TV-wise. Mol and Em tape-recorded the acting winners; they could recite their favorite speeches. One, in particular. Em drew a deep breath, balancing on the desk like she was standing before judges in Speech and

Debate. Telling herself (Mrs. Bjorklund, the coach, had block-printed it atop Em's script pages): DON'T SWAY.

"—To my mother and my father, I want to say—" This was where the 1975 Best Actress had burst into American Sign Language as if into song. "Thank you—" Em directed her blow-a-kiss "thank you" sign at Kenny. She'd learned minimal Sign Language from Kenny's Speech Therapy. He looked as transfixed now as he'd been two years before, believing the actress at the Oscar podium was signing her speech not to her deaf parents but to him. "—For teaching *me*." Em pointed a mime-finger at herself. "To *have*—" She raked in invisible poker chips. "A *dream*—" (Em's hands froze; she didn't know "dream.") "You." She pointed to Kenny. "Are see-ing." Em sign-pointed to her eyes. "My dream." Em felt her voice choke exactly like Louise Fletcher's. "Come true!"

In the beat before Mol and Kenny cheered, Em met Kenny's blank yet bright blue stare. Someday, she promised him silently, she'd sign her own Oscar speech to him, explaining later in all her interviews how her brother had always—what other word was big enough?— worshipped her.

Who was your First Love? you'll ask me, sensing in the intimate middle of our interview that you must be getting nearer to my hottest secrets.

If you mean (I'll answer, crafty too) who loved *me* first in the #1 queen-of-everything way, my answer is: I won't tell. *You may bury me twelve feet deep* (this is Catherine in *Wuthering Heights,* in my Speech and Debate performance, the judges decreeing I "crossed the line" between "Oral Interp," which uses only hand gestures and all-out "Acting," which uses the whole body, mine trembling); *You may bury me twelve feet deep and throw the church down over me, but* (these last words are my own) *I'll never give him away!*

In Sky City Supermarket, an hour after the phone call Molly had answered, Emma and Molly broke up. This, at least, was the way Em explained to herself, excused to herself, what she let happen later that night. At noon, when they set off for Sky City, Em felt herself and Mol to be united soldiers. All Easter Break week, Em had savored the home-under-siege atmosphere created by the threatening phone calls, by the Alarm System Dad had decided to install. Now, leaving their newly wired house, Mom drove their station wagon cautiously, like an armored tank. Maybe still shaken by that phone call—a shared secret, since they'd both promised Mom to yell for her if the phone rang— Mol sat close by Em in the backseat. She scribbled on a notepad, seeming intent upon their task, calculating how much ketchup they'd need to (they whispered) dump the blood.

"Dumb blood," Kenny chanted in the front seat, and in the aisles at Sky City. "Dumb blood, dumb blood," as Mom led him past other moms with buzzing eyes and beehive hairdos. Aiming their gazes at Kenny, at Mom in her pantsuit, at Em in her faded McGOVERN T-shirt pushing the cart. But no one stared outright as they'd done when Kenny had dropped his pants in COLD MEATS.

"I'm gonna scope out the jumbo ketchups," Mol told Em, taking Em's money and slipping into the CANDY AND CONDIMENTS aisle.

By the time Em and Mom got to checkout—Kenny grabbed a plastic gun—Mol was still gone. "Kenny, stay where I can see you," Mom was commanding. Em stepped out of line. Her flip-flops flapped as she passed the photo booth displaying its strips of black-lipsticked '60s faces. She picked up a whiff of Carolina candies: Red Hots and pillowy orange-powdered Circus Peanuts. She slowed to a stalk so her flip-flops wouldn't flap. So Em saw her, saw them.

Mol leaned on one leg like a boy, balancing a jug of ketchup on her hip. Her sloppy cutoffs slid past her knees. The other Junior High-aged girl slouched more naturally than Mol, her cutoffs shorter. Her frizzily permed hair and Mol's short hair almost touched, they stood so close. Em backed out of the candy aisle. She ducked into the fusty velvet-curtained photo booth where she and Mol had squeezed their light-shocked faces together. Alone, Em's face was white and warped in the black-glass LOOK HERE square.

Only Kenny noticed that Em had been gone. Mom was paying for her loaded cart. "*You* wanna be the one to shoot me tonight?" Em asked Kenny.

"Shoot you?" He waved his new pink water gun. "You two, you two!" Kenny trotted behind Mom as she pushed the cart into the sun, her glasses flashing. You two, Mom had always called Mol and Em. Mol appeared in tow behind them, lugging the ketchup jug, her pie-face both blank and smug.

In the car, Mol didn't notice Em pretending to ignore her because she was ignoring Em. For, Em realized grimly, real.

"Where were you all that time in the store?" Mom was the one to ask.

"I, um, ran into Cindy Alexander. You know, from my class? And she—" This part came in a nervous proud-sounding rush. "She's having a sleepover tonight 'cause Darla, this girl we kinda know, got invited to the High School Prom and a bunch of us wanna stay at Cindy's house and. Wait for her and all."

Mom drew in a big happy breath; Em felt Mol shoot her a sideglance. She rigidly did not return it. Mol, she guessed, must have known she'd run into that Cindy. Mol so damn anxious to leave by noon. "*Won*-derful, Mol!"

"*One*-dur!" Kenny echoed Mom. Like his Special Olympics chant: Number One! Em maintained her sullen silence as the Reedy River flowed by and Kenny fiddled with the radio and the pinewood near their house thickened. She sat so close to her window her glasses click-clicked with every bump.

As the O'MOORE mailbox jutted from the shrubbery, Mom slowed the station wagon to a sudden crawl. Between the second-floor bedroom windows of their house, the brand-new Home Alarm light— orange, oversized—was blinking.

"We've been broken *in*-to!" Mol sounded stupidly stunned.

Told you, Em thought. Mom halted atop their hill of a driveway. Told you what kind of place this Greenville is. The evil-eye light blinked and blinked.

"They probably never even got inside," Mom assured them in a halfway convincing teacher voice, the car engine still running. "Probably cracked the window, heard the alarm, left their foolish message, and ran."

They were all still just staring. Their dining-room window had been broken: one fist- or rock-sized hole. Below the window, jagged words were scrawled on the house's beige brick in black chalk. "O'MOORES GO HOME."

"The police must be on their way. Meanwhile we can wait at, at—" From the back of her head, Mom seemed to Em to be thinking: Where in Hell? At the Irvings' across the woods, their home guarded by blue-tongued chow dogs?

"*Way*—" Kenny, who'd unbuckled his own seat belt, burst from the car. "*I* shoot, *I* shoot—" He stampeded down the hill, waving his new toy gun.

"No—" Mom lunged from the driver's seat, cutting off the engine.

"Look dare, look *dare*—" Kenny had charged up to the house, to the fist-busted window. "Dare! DARE!" He swung his gun around the empty yard.

"A MAN! A MAN!" he kept insisting in his acre-wide shout as Mom half-led half-dragged him back up the hill to the station wagon. "I saw a MAN, he run a-WAY! Run from ME!" Stretching Mom's arm, Kenny leaned toward the car windows, his wildly brightened eyes seeking Em's.

"Me too," Em found herself chiming in, rolling down her window. "I saw a man running across the yard just when Kenny came running down the hill!"

"No you didn't," Mol objected but she was drowned out by Kenny.

"See?" he shouted jubilantly. "SEE? SEE?" And Em felt at first like a genuine Wizard of Oz: granting Kenny his wish, making him a hero.

"*I* didn't see any *man* and I didn't see *Em* see any man either!"

"Since when can you see what I saw, Miss Know-It-All Mol?"

In the rearview mirror, a weary-looking blue and rusted-white police car pulled up behind their station wagon, its lights and siren turned off.

"Do you want to tell him what you 'saw'?" Mom asked Em, tensely calm.

Em fixed her eyes on the rearview policeman ambling up behind

12

her mother. Would he hook Em to a lie-detector test? Book Em, book her brother, haul all the unwanted O'Moores down to the station? Em shook her head.

"I thought not." Mom turned briskly. "You two keep Kenny away from the house." Mom's hard-heeled sandals clicked toward the slow-moving cop.

In one Mom-like motion, Em climbed out of the backseat. She seized the hollow water gun from Kenny. Bending into the open car window, she waved it under Mol's nose. God; could that cop see? "Maybe you don't believe Kenny, but *I* do! And y'know what? I'm gonna use his gun in the *Carrie* scene!"

"But Carrie kills 'em all with her *eyes.* How're you gonna use a *gun*?"

"That's for us to know and you to find out," Em snapped, picturing— an odd flash—Kenny squirting the gun at her, rinsing her ketchup-drenched body.

"'Us'?" Mol asked back, pretend-dumb.

"Kenny and me. We're gonna film our *Carrie* scene tonight—with-*out* you!" Em straightened. "And I'm gonna send that film to real-life movie agents! I'm gonna be a million-to-one-shot winner like god-damn Rocky!"

"Gonna fly, fly-*eye*!" Hoarsely, Kenny burst into the *Rocky* theme song, running circles round Em on the sun-shimmery slope of lawn.

What were your biggest humiliations? you will ask near the end. A question you probably won't ask years from now, when you're really real—but since you're not yet, you do. Since it relieves me to let out some of the shamefullest stuff I keep inside, I will tell you: as of Easter Break, 1977, my biggest humiliation was not, anymore, Valentine's Day, 1977. My hopelessly well-meaning mom sending me, in Home Room, a pink carnation. The girls who'd gotten carnations from boys giggling. Jo Jo Parkins spreading word in French 101 that my own mom had sent my flower. Me at lunchtime hiding in Mom's Biology classroom, sobbing in Mom's formaldehyded lab closet, surrounded by iguanas and wolf spiders and never-got-to-live fetal pigs.

No: a bigger humiliation hit me after supper on the day Mol and I broke up. The duct-taped cardboard of our broken window loomed over our table. Mol scarfed down her meat loaf. Kenny, for once the supper-table star, kept bragging about the MAN who RAN from his GUN. Tall grave-faced Dad sat next to me, nodding and reminding Kenny to chew. Dad smelled—I couldn't look at him anymore than I could look at Mol—of bourbon and the woolly business jacket he'd shed and the red-clay garden dirt he'd been hoeing before supper. I ate my crunchy homegrown peas with a fork, shooting one at Kenny. He chortled. My fork tines clinked, impaling another pea.

"I gotta get packed." Mol stood. She and Mom left, leading Kenny.

"Now Emma," Dad murmured. "We need to talk." A stage set had shifted; Dad and I sat alone. Beard bristle darker than Kenny's showed on Dad's long Abe Lincoln jaw. Dad's gaze locked mine; his eyes darkest brown, like mine. "You didn't really see a man running across the yard today, did you?"

I smelled the beef and bourbon on his breath. I heard Mol moving above me. My mind twisted what I'd say. One beat before his sizing-up stare turned disappointed, Dad almost seemed to buy it. Because I was, technically, telling the truth. Because it was Kenny himself I was talking about, Kenny I was picturing: my brother with his own beard bristle and his Sky City penis.

"No, Dad; I *did* see—right then and there; I swear—a man."

Emma slammed into their room just as Molly was zipping her overnight bag. "Don't mind me; I gotta change for the Shoot." Shaky after her shameful talk with Dad, Em pulled off her McGOVERN T-shirt, knocking her glasses askew. She marched up to the closet, straight-backed in her training bra. Junior-sized, yes, but she had breasts while sturdy Mol didn't.

"I know you planned on running into Cindy whatsername, Mol."

"Yeah. So? Her mom shops around noon too and I knew you'd freak out if I even mentioned Cindy. Jeez Louise, you don't got to make a federal case 'bout this sleepover." Mol hefted her packed bag. Em stepped into the silky circle of the prom dress. Slowly as a stripper in reverse, she eased it over her body.

"So you're gonna make ol' Kenny believe *he* can be Director? Just like you made him believe he scared away that made-up man?"

"Jesus X. Christ. First Dad, now you." Em smoothed the cool dress, liking the way it clung to her body. "Kenny's *happy* making-believe he's a hero."

"Only it's not make-believe to him. Anything you say," Mol finished with a gratifying jealous-sounding edge, "he thinks's true." Mol stepped over to the bedroom door. She'd barely glanced at Em in the slinky pink dress.

"What's so goddamn great, Mol, about the 'real' world?"

Mol was facing the door with its *Rocky* poster but Em felt her roll her eyes. "It's no wonder," Mol muttered, "that you're all alone, Em."

As Mol swung the door shut, Em struck a Garbo pose. "I *vant* to be alone!"

Brusque as a burglar, she dug into her and Mol's shared closet, their old costume box. She bobby-pinned onto her head the cardboard crown Mol had pinned onto her four years before, their first South Carolina spring.

The One Good Thing about Greenville, they'd discovered, was that it was beauty-contest-crazed. The *Greenville Sun* printed color photos of every Miss South Carolina contestant. Ten-year-old Em acted out their Talents: Miss Greenville smiling while playing the flute, Miss Charleston belting, "Oh Babe, What Do You Say?" Kenny cheered each one, loud enough for a whole audience. Mol graded each one on Mom's old report cards. Each was called a—inside, Em called herself this—Hopeful. Along with the TV crowning, Mol crowned Em. Mol sang the Miss South Carolina song as Em walked her runway. *A figure to match her fate*, Mol crooned (though Mom insisted the newspaper's misprint was meant to read "face"). *In a land famous for beauties* (maybe that's why I don't fit in, Em thought as she waved at wildly applauding Kenny and Mom and Dad) *she's the fairest of them all! Miss South Car-o-lina is—you-oooh!*

"Kenny?" Em called softly outside his never-quite-shut bedroom door.

She wore her old terry-cloth robe over her new prom dress. Her hair was brushed, her lips reslicked with LIP-SMACKIN' gloss. Leading sleepy Kenny by the hand, Em passed the living-room archway. Mom sipped wine; Dad read his paper, sitting as still in his recliner as Abe Lincoln in his stone chair. On the eight-track tape stereo, Barbra Streisand torch-sang "Happy Days Are Here Again."

"You ready to be my Director?" Em asked Kenny in the den doorway.

"I'm Num-ber One! I chase the *man*; I—" He tried to meet her gaze, to make her confirm this new end to the story. "I *shoot* the man!"

Lowering her mascara'd eyes, wondering what Kenny did believe he'd done today, Em led him down the steps into their house's lowest level.

"You know you didn't really shoot anyone, right?" Em asked Kenny, mixing in water with the jumbo ketchup, testing for the consistency of blood.

"I shoot *you*—" Kenny pointed to the Brownie camera on Mom's desk. Em laughed at his—wasn't it? and a good one, too?—joke.

As Kenny spun on Mom's desk chair, Em positioned the loaded bucket. "I'll show you *how* to shoot me." She hopped down from the den's biggest armchair. And she held up the old-fashioned camera she and Mol had never let him touch. Cautiously, Kenny stepped close, his arm brushing her robe sleeve. He gripped the camera with both big hands. "You've gotta aim it steady and watch me through it *and* push this button hard. Not *too* hard—"

But Kenny squeezed the trigger button with both thumbs. His tensed fingers jammed the camera's ear-shaped metal dial as it began its slow spin.

"No—" Em wrested from Kenny's fumbling hold the Brownie camera, its whir already jagged. "Don't break it like you break *every*-thing—"

"I—I—" Kenny protested, stuffing his fingers in his mouth to bite them.

Guiltily, Em ducked his stricken eyes, shutting off the camera and

16

setting it on the floor. She straightened up before Kenny could go off. "You can—direct me from a Director's Chair!" She shoved the biggest armchair in front of her X; she pushed Kenny into it. "I'll do the scene 'live,' like a play. Just for us!"

"Jus' us?" Kenny gazed up from the chair, rapt as a boy. Though his face in the dim light resembled Dad's: lean and long-jawed.

Em left the shut-off camera on the floor in front of Kenny. She bolted its light on its top, wondering as she switched on the light how her sister had lifted and aimed that heavy light-and-camera contraption. How she could've expected Kenny to do the same. A spotlight burned on the glass door. "You *are* Director, Kenny." Em pulled off her glasses, tossing them to the desk. "'Cause I'm blind."

She turned her back on Kenny's face, its unreadable flesh blur. Em slipped off her untied robe. The always-cool air of the den woke her skin, her bared arms and shoulders. She faced the sliding doors, feeling her back and ass outlined by her sheer dress. Behind her, Kenny breathed open-mouthed. Em remembered two black boys breathing behind her once in the Greenville High halls. Bold, mock-panting breaths. One muttered, Hey girl, you're cute. Em hadn't turned. Scared they'd take it back if they saw who she was.

"It's Carrie's Prom Night!" Impulsively, Em slid open the glass doors to the April evening. She spun round. Kenny looked shadowy in his seat behind the waist-high camera light. A backyard breeze swelled through the screen porch behind Em, wafting the half-open drapes and scenting the stale den with cool grass, balmy Carolina air. "We start," Em told Kenny loudly above the crickets and frogs, "with Carrie happy." She inched forward onto the X, beneath the loaded bucket. Under her skirts, she set her foot in the noose loop of clothesline tied to the bucket. "OK, Kenny; they just crowned me prom queen! OK: *cheer*!"

As he'd learned to do in their play beauty pageants, Kenny let loose a throaty ferocious hoot. His clapping filled the den. Night wind billowed Em's hair; she straightened up regally. Outcast Carrie is crowned prom QUEEN!

In the hot furry light, Em gave an incredulous tremulous-lipped smile. Tears burned her eyes. If only Mol could see this, shoot this. Em waved at the doomed high-school class she heard and felt applauding her now. Kenny's hands smacked and smacked. Under her skirts, Em toe-hooked the clothesline noose. She kicked backward, feeling the line behind the drapes jerk in answer, thinking the damn thing wouldn't work without Mol here to make it.

But: *thunk.* The bucket tipped. Em startled at the sound, then—not slow-mo like in *Carrie*, but brutally fast and hard—the cold slapping *splat.* Ketchup hit her head, ketchup-blood oozing onto her bare shoulders, into her neckline. Blood dripped between her breasts, down her stomach, into her panties. Feeling the bucket swing above her, Em held out her arms in unfeigned disbelief: her dress splattered, her spotlit body nakedly outlined. Her nipples stood up under sticky cloth, sudden and sharp as her goose bumps.

"Whoa-oh!" Kenny rose now, only a few feet away. Em sensed him standing as she stared at herself. The cold bloodstain spread from the center of her dress like her body had been chopped in two. She blinked, mascara sticky.

"Whoa-oh," Kenny repeated in a deep choked voice. "Whuh-*ohh*—"

Em was remembering how when she saw the movie *Carrie* the kids all around her and Mol cheered lustily as blood-drenched Sissy Spacek began zapping to death the whole prom: slamming the EXITS shut in her classmates' smug faces, shorting the lights, torching the paper-star-decked gym! All those super-smug Greenville High-ers whooping it up like they had the right. Em raised her eyes, widened them like Sissy Spacek's lit-up skull eyes. Her bloody lashes rimmed the den in red. How furiously Em fixed her Carrie-stare on the spot where Mol should be standing with their camera. Where, right behind the camera's low light, Kenny was still standing, moving in some new way.

"Kenny?" Em asked aloud, out of character. Crickets and frogs throbbed in the silence. Em hadn't figured out how to end, she realized only now.

She squinted. The blur of Kenny's face was seconded by a flesh blur below his waist. His hands made jerky contained motions. "Stop that—" Em told Kenny, shooting a scared glance up the den steps. The den door so blurry Em couldn't see if Mom or Dad were standing there seeing Kenny's bared ass, seeing what Em with her panic-sharpened squint was only now making out.

"*Ken*-ny—" She stumbled from the light to Mom's desk. She jabbed on her stop-sign glasses. "*Stop*—" she commanded as Kenny let go of his stiffened penis. It pointed where she'd been standing. For one second, she purely stared.

"Emmy?" Kenny turned, groping for his dropped sweatpants, gaping at her in slack-jawed confusion. He yanked up his pants. She rushed back to the glass doors. Sticky-fingered, she heaved them shut, chopping off the fragrant spring night. "Em-*mee*," Kenny repeated in a deeper, more demanding voice.

"Stay back!" Em barked, ducking her head, hiding behind her sickeningly sticky hair. She stumbled past the light, the laundry room. "Stay down here!"

"*Way*-ait!" Kenny called, plaintive now. She sped up the den steps.

Only at the top did she spin round to face him. "There *wasn't* any man—" Em called down to Kenny. "No man in the yard! *No man*; you hear?"

She thumped the door shut. Herb Alpert's Tijuana Brass blared from the half-dark living room: Dad deep in his paper and bourbon; Mom dozing on the couch. Em rushed past the archway like a streaker, stumbled up the longer flight of shag-carpeted stairs, slammed into the bathroom. Its familiar mirror filled, incongruously, with a blood-splattered wild-eyed witch.

Em wrenched off her glasses. She yanked off her crown, bobby pins pinging the tile floor. She remembered Kenny's last face downstairs, slack with hurt. She scrubbed her own face hard, red water streaming between her fingers. Automatically, she put her glasses back on. But she turned from the mirror to undress. Pounding in her head were the stern words of the Speech and Debate judge who'd caught her acting, caught her using her body.

You crossed the line; you crossed the line.

What's the worst thing you've ever done? And the best?

These are your all-but-final questions. And what, I will ask you back, if I find myself feeling they were one and the same?

The shower; the first. As I stand shivering in that blast of cold water, still hearing Kenny's *Emmy?* through the laundry chute, I know I should run downstairs and wake Mom, ask her to put Kenny to bed. Then—wondering what, seeing me, *she'd* ask—I crank HOT. It scalds the skin of my back. I stay bent, mixing in enough COLD so I can stand up. In my first drenched glimpse, my body looks the same as ever: my pear breasts pointing to nothing, my stomach stretching flat between them, my kinky pubic hair dark like a beard, my legs long, my feet bony and long-toed like Dad's, like Kenny's.

I grope for the green Palmolive soap, each bar worn down quick by me and Mol and, on weekends, Kenny. As I rub the sliver between my palms, as the oily-feeling ketchupy-smelling lather froths up, I hear—something in me is expecting it—the door I left unlocked thud. Open, shut.

Kenny, I know. Not because I turn my wet head to look but because I feel him looking. Standing as still as me, facing the semi–see-through shower door. Pebble-textured Plexiglas. A silver screen of sorts, this door: Kenny staring into it more raptly than he's ever stared at any movie screen. *With a figure to match her fate,* I'm think-singing. Picturing myself, shadowy and shiny.

I cup my breasts in my hands, making them bigger in silhouette. Tentatively, running my shaky hands down my slick skin, I arch my back. Displaying, as no one's taught me to do, the curve of my ass. My eyes half-shut in the hot stream, I sneak a side-glance, sensing Kenny's sidestep.

Doubly blurred by my nearsightedness and by the shower door, he still faces me, his dark-haired head unbowed. He is standing by the toilet now, his bent arm moving. He is pumping it, the oblong flesh blur that must be his cock.

Who am I to tell him No? Shutting my eyes, I focus on the hiss. You are a man, I think toward Kenny. I, alone in all the world, see that. Hot water sluices down the divide of my back, between the halves of my ass. I run my hands over my body as if peeling off a skin-tight dress, a shimmery dress made of water. Bending my legs, I lower my hands, my outspread thumbs brushing my crotch, a moist tip of flesh standing up like a spur. I gasp at my own rough touch. The water streaming over me turns cold. A roar like man-made thunder straightens me up. As I blink open my underwater eyes, I realize—the shower shifting to luke-cool—that Kenny has just flushed the toilet. That this might mean Kenny has—but what *does* this mean, exactly?—finished. Come.

I stand still under the cooled-down shower. I'm hugging myself; I'm a statue made of flesh. I hear the bathroom door thud open and—so resoundingly I flinch—shut. I crank off both faucets. The shower hiss that filled my head like TV static stops. It leaves me bent and dripping in stony silence. My hands cup my knees; my body is braced for the beating I deserve. I blink my wet-lashed eyes at the faucets. Hot and cold; best and worst. Besides Kenny and me, only you—my audience of one—will ever even know it happened.

What is your biggest secret?

After her parents' steps had sounded in the hall, after they'd cracked open Kenny's door and—seeing Kenny, please God, safely asleep?—thumped their own, Emma sat up in bed. She faced her bed's empty twin. Not even Mol had seen the worst Em. The pervert Em who'd let her retarded brother, as they'd say at Greenville High, get off on her. The self-pitying Em who carried on—she swung her legs off the mattress—silly pretend-interviews inside her head.

What do you most want to hide?

Em bolted out of bed. She shoved open the door, plunging into the dark hall. No glasses, she realized as she stumbled past Kenny's door onto the stairs. But she needed to clean it up: the dumped ketchup-blood. Her damp hair swung against her face as she groped down step by step. You two, Mom must've called Kenny and Em back before Mol came along. Were she and Kenny the more alike, really? Em's foot skipped the last step. She fell onto the landing.

Did Kenny hear the thud? Would Kenny bound downstairs to see her again? Em crawled to the den door. It must've scared Kenny, for reasons he couldn't understand, to see his sister naked. She pulled herself up, unsteadily. Had it also made him, like her, feel for the length of the shower less alone? More alone and less alone, both at once. Em opened the door and stepped down, chilled in her sleeveless cotton nightgown. She groped toward the sliding doors, glimpsing the new Alarm light, wondering what she'd say if her parents caught her. A born liar, Mol called her. A born—what was the word for people who played with other people like puppets? Dictator? Director? What I'll be, Em decided as she inched forward. She'd make up for her ugly self by shooting beautiful movies. Scenes she'd completely control. She sped her blind steps.

And she slipped on the ketchup, tripped over the camera and light. Em fell hard, ramming her shoulder against the sliding door. The glass gave a muffled crack. Will it show? Em thought, pulling herself up, squinting at the spiderweb crack. The Alarm light lit that crack, blinking mute beats of warning.

The buzzer, giant-sized, woke the house. *MM, MM, MM—*

A harsh bone-jarring buzz like—Em clapped her hands over her ears, her nails broken—a robot's cry for help, for its mom. *MM, MM, MM—*

Em wheeled around to face the steps, the door she'd left open. None of which she could see. No movie, she assured herself as she heard them all moving above her. She peered down toward the tipped-over camera, its film unshot. And Kenny wouldn't—well, he couldn't—describe what had happened. Could he?

"Kenny?" Mom called out from above. "Kenny, Em?" *MM, MM, MM—*

Under the all-surrounding buzz, they trooped down the long stairs, Dad leading the charge. "Who the Hell's there?"

"I shoot 'em!" Kenny shouted, his steps surging ahead. *MM, MM, MM—*

"Wait!" Mom's cry cut through the buzz. "*Give* me that," she pleaded, as if the gun Kenny must be waving might be real. "Stay where we can *see* you!"

Someone flicked on the kitchen light, the den doorway illuminated. Em squinted hard. Three hulking adult shapes. The second-tallest Kenny. A man, all right; body-wise. Em hugged her bare goose-bumped arms. Her shoulder ached. She felt like a stranger inside her own suddenly buzzing house. In a new stage-sized voice, she called up to her brother, "It's OK; it's only me."

What It's Worth

date: Tues. Aug. 12, 1999; 11:58PM
from: brigfly@brown.edu
to: flynn@oldecraftshoppe.com
subject: gunk & more gunk

hi Mom—found a diamond in her icebox. no joke: the ring
was sealed in an ironed-looking envelope, stowed amidst
ice-age ice crystals. i emptied her fridge this PM; couldn't
sleep for worry over my dissertation, its/my *big day* (tomorrow, in case you care). you can get the rock *valued* at
your next antique to-do. but don't go hoping i'm *engaged*
if you spot it on my finger.

incidentally, Mom—i may not stop & see you, en route
to ann arbor. i'll know after i contact my friend in syracuse,
one who might intro me to *useful* profs @ Syracuse U (a
FEMALE friend). diamond ring or not, infamous diamond
tattoo or not, i'm a *spinster* like Great Aunt B—or maybe
not quite *like.* do you still nix my theory that Aunt B
might've found romance w/ the Lady Next Door? or that she
might've earned her own PhD if she hadn't wasted her life?

(no doubt you think it's ME who's *wasting* my life/our
$. no doubt that's why you won't come help your #1 & only
daughter clear out this crazy house).

tonight—i try tackling Aunt B's bedroom nightstand.
what do i find in its top drawer but another sealed yellowed

envelope, this one labeled, BRIGID, AGE 8, 1928. all ginger-
fingered, i pull out limp locks of her—young Aunt B's—HAIR!
fine and jet-black like mine (how'd it keep its color all these
years?). then, after i drop the hair into my THROW AWAY
box, i grope out Aunt B's reading glasses. the cat's-eye ones
she'd wear re-rereading Dickens.

speaking of whom: i've got the first half of my *final* dissertation printed; i'll turn in the whole thing tomorrow afternoon. then there'll be the traditional *surprise* farewell
party—a bunch of fellow lit. crit.ers will nab me on the library
steps & sweep me off to a bar on Thayer St.

meanwhile, the Jaworski bros will clear out the last of
Aunt B.

to answer your latest Guilt-Gram, Mom: OF COURSE
i feel bad that i stayed on at MLA the week she died (though
i think Aunt B might've understood better than you WHY i
skipped her funeral & stayed). anyhow, amidst her GUNK—
a.k.a. glorified junk—i haven't found the leather-bound
Dickens Aunt B wanted me to have. believe it or not, she also
WANTED to read my 100-plus pages on OUR MUTUAL
FRIEND. i told her she could, when/if i finished.

(don't worry, Mom; i won't even ASK if you want to read
it). i'll keep you posted if Jaworski or i unearth anything
else—NOT likely, i suspect—of value.

  b

Waking in the hot Providence night, in the 99-year-old house her great-
grandfather had built, Brigid Flynn rolled over blindly and pulled on
her glasses. The muggy close-walled bedroom blurred, submerged in a
substance thicker than water. Aunt B.'s glasses? Bolting upright, feeling her headphone cord pop loose, Brigid whipped those glasses off.
They whirled like a boomerang, cracking against the wall. Oh God,
I broke Aunt B.'s glasses, Brigid thought as if she were a girl again,
tucked into the guest room with its glittery wallpaper.

Then, blinking: What difference does it make? She's dead.

Brigid switched on the lamp. 3 A.M. Here I lie, she thought, tugging off her silent headphones. Twenty-seven years old; guarded by the pineapple-carved posts of Great-Aunt B.'s bed. Dying, myself, in this heat. Brigid wiped her forehead. Why had she bungee-corded her dorm air conditioner into the center of her packed Honda Civic? *Not a practical bone in your body,* Great-Aunt Brigid had decreed, not critical like Mom but companionable. *So you'll be lost in this world, like me.*

Brigid hooked on her own wire glasses. Through the warped thickly poured windowpane and Irish lace curtains, she made out her Honda, parked askew at the curb as if she were paying her great-aunt one of her hasty visits.

If I'd stopped on the way to MLA, Brigid told Aunt B., I would've been the one to find you. Brigid swept back her blunt-cut hair as she'd kept doing in her tense Oral Defense. She had Aunt B.'s black hair, blue eyes, high forehead. *A highly evolved forehead,* Jarvis told Brigid on their one night together. Even in postsex languor, he'd sounded intelligent, discriminating.

Brigid stretched, her bare thigh nudging her Walkman. She'd fallen asleep listening to Joni Mitchell, "Case of You." Rolling on her side, facing Aunt B.'s dusty nightstand, she popped open her shiny black laptop. Sideways, Brigid began typing another unsendable e-mail to calutz@syracuseu.edu.

> Casey: is it too corny to say that when i hear Case of You, i think of you?

Rolling her eyes like Casey Lutz would at that line, Brigid sank back onto the mushy 1940s mattress. Her great-grandpa had died on this bed, tended till the end by his eldest daughter. The mattress's tea- or blood- or piss-stains were covered by Brigid's own silky Calvin Klein sheets. Her bed, one of her one-night men had commented, the only hospitable spot in her nun's cell of a dorm room. *The room I'd expect you to have,* this naked loquacious Semiotics student had gone on, *but not the bed.* At least Jarvis had shown no ridiculously predictable surprise when she'd shed her Brigid the Brain glasses and clothes, stripping to her blue diamond tattoo. Her biggest turn-on that night: Jarvis bending her over his knee to rub the tattoo with his thumb, see if it was real, Jarvis alone knowing it matched Casey's birthmark. Same shape, same place.

> is it too late to say Jarvis isn't worth losing the friendship we had/have?

Brigid sat up. Rereading this last, she rewiped her sweaty forehead. Foolishly, Brigid had confided to Jarvis what she'd told no one but Casey: how she'd always imagined her forehead to be a sign of some higher calling. *Ha,* Jarvis had muttered as he did in seminars, quietly derisive. Whereas Casey—pre-Jarvis, girl to girl—had confided in turn that she'd imagined the diamond-shaped birthmark on the small of her back marked *her* as special.

Brigid hugged her slim bare legs, gripping her hands to keep from sending the e-mail. She couldn't afford another dumb mistake with Casey.

In that first seminar Jarvis had TA'd, she and Casey had competed for his rare nods of approval. Brigid had gazed at Casey as Casey had brazenly gazed at him. His eyes half-lidded, like Casey's olive eyes. His sullen lips promising—Casey predicted—Four-Star Eating Out. H. Jarvis: Brown's lit-crit. boy-genius; Casey's semester-long love. Brigid's night with Jarvis no doubt no longer a secret. Why else would Casey leave for Syracuse without saying good-bye?

Delete All, Brigid pressed. She snapped her laptop shut, wishing she *could* delete them all. Lanky Jarvis bounding round London on his Guggenheim-funded lark; buxom sharp-tongued Casey sulking in her new Associate Prof. niche at Syracuse. And those fellow summer-stragglers sipping iced coffees in the grad. lounge, snubbing Brigid. Worse: ignoring her. Except the new Spanish Lit. TA. Brigid smoothed her legs, picturing his mock-macho grin; his trim Rhodes Scholar body. A fittingly risky last fling for her Providence self?

So sensible work-wise, Casey bragged of herself and Brigid; so reckless sex-wise. Brigid halted her hands. If Casey dropped her, would she regress to her more sensible, less sexy self? She forced open the last drawer of Aunt B.'s nightstand, dreading what she might find.

With the folder she pulled out, she swatted a fat mosquito, grinding it onto her last title page. *What Dickens's Women 'Want': Incest, Id, and Infantilism in* OUR MUTUAL FRIEND.

Brigid smeared the bloody mosquito over that tenth draft retro-feminist title. *A telling gesture,* she imagined Casey drawling. One good thing about Casey being in Syracuse, Casey being pissed-off. Brigid hadn't had to show her this too-late-to-change title, to await Casey's thumbs-up or thumbs-down.

From the humidity-softened folder, Brigid lifted—one by one, the stiff cardboard fragile—Great-Aunt Brigid's Providence Catholic Girl's Academy grade cards. Year after year of hand-printed A's preserved in violet-blue ink. But, Brigid knew, no graduation certificate. Aunt B. had quit school in her senior year to tend her ailing father. Forty years of tending.

"A poignant detail," Brigid muttered as if to Casey. She shuffled the cards, remembering her mom's collection of her own old cards. All those fading A's.

Brigid dumped Aunt B.'s grade cards into THROW AWAY. She groped again, the drawer empty but for dust. So she snapped off the light, slipped off her glasses, burrowed into her own silky pillowcase. Brigid breathed deep, wishing she could smell the varied musks of her sexual adventures. Pillow talk always the one big letdown: that sinking sensation as she felt her brain click away faster than her bedmate's. Except, Brigid thought groggily, with Jarvis.

Although despite Casey's girl-talk hype, he hadn't been, sexually, so great. His famous tongue sluggish; his big cock too quick. But wine and guilt had inhibited them both, that night. Brigid rolled over. From the corner, Aunt B.'s cat's-eye glasses watched her. Haunted-house cliché, Brigid thought as she sat up scared. Blindly, she padded across the sticky yet cool painted floorboards.

Was this the spot? she wondered as she stopped. Aunt B. had been found lying in her bedroom but not—the close-mouthed lady next door had reported—on the bed. Brigid crouched, bare-assed in her oversized Brown University T-shirt. The humid air felt cooler from below. Before Casey, she'd never have gone bare-assed to bed. I'll win her back, Brigid vowed in the dark. Gently, she lifted Aunt B.'s cracked—she felt but couldn't see the crack—glasses.

———

Date: Wed., Aug. 13, 1999; 9AM
to: calutz@syracuseu.edu
from: brigfly@brown.edu
subject: hello, co-brain

hey Casey—just had to write you on my D day. wish you could BE here for me & my diss's beer bash; YOU'RE the only one i'd want toasting me/it.

now, this anxious AM, i'm putting off (still!) printing out my FINAL-final pages to type this olive-branch-of-an-e-mail.

but let me start over. i just had to write you—that part's true—because i was hurt when you slipped away to syracuse without even a good-bye. of course i've got my suspicions as to WHY. but can't *all that* wait till we see each other face to face? tonight i begin my drive to my 1-year Replacement Gig (yep; i couldn't talk them higher) in ann arbor, so i could swing by & visit you.

that way, i could avoid scranton, PA. where, needless to say, MOM needs my PhD to feel like a Big Payoff after her years behind the olde craft shoppe cash register. only i'm not *up to* pretending all this is the thrill i expected.

Mom doesn't know the half of it! the funk i'm in here. i mean, Aunt B saved dozens of little restaurant packets: 20 YEAR OLD mustard/ketchup/relish, all rotting in her fridge's cracked-plastic vegetable drawer. & in the bathroom: 50 YEAR OLD pharmaceuticals; *gold cross medicated foot powder* and *irish mist toilet water* & purply red belladonna; *to check secretions & spasms,* the label says; *may cause vision to become darker & brighter.* maybe Aunt B got into hallucinogenics? wish you were here to accompany me to her ATTIC.

i want a look before Jaworski the trash-hauler arrives, in case Aunt B's leather Dickens volumes—&/OR love letters to that neighbor lady you & i have wondered about?—are lying up there in the dust.

30

god, Casey: did you feel so DOWN on your D day? i've got certified closure on the *golden dustman* and martyr-ish Aunt B-ish *liz* and infantilized *bella* cuddling on her daddy's lap. i've got a good shot at landing my First-Choice Beer-Bash Possibility: young Ricardo, that new spanish-lit whiz.

speaking of whizes, have you heard word from *our mutual friend* Jarvis? c'mon, Casey. aren't WE still—*for good,* we bad-girls used to say—friends?

b

———

Brigid stepped briskly into the midmorning dark of the attic stairwell. Halfway up the wood steps, she slowed, steadying herself on the stone wall, her fingers sticky with cobweb. Decontextualized Irish lace, she'd have joked to Casey. In the attic's church silence and high heat, the dust smelled pure. Freed, Brigid reasoned, from day-to-day sweat and food crumbs. Her sandals scraped sawdust. She bumped what she knew by touch was Great-Grandpa Flynn's trunk from Ireland. The rusty buckles, the oily-feeling rust-crusted metal exterior. Brigid edged around the empty trunk. She used to pretend it was her casket.

Hot long-gone afternoons. A thrilling sweat would come over her as she lay in the trunk-casket, her bare knees up and her head aching against the dented metal bottom. *The world is mourning me,* she'd tell herself, trying to decide what it was she was famous for: scientific discoveries, brilliant books.

Brigid the Brain, the world would call her. Unlike her classmates, the world would say it with respect. Lutz the Slut, Casey was called in school. Just the sort of smart sexy tough-girl Brigid had admired from afar. Brigid coughed, her throat dry. She remembered her fear that the propped-open trunk lid would slam down, that she'd pound her fists against its curved inner side, that no one would find her. Steadying herself again, Brigid touched the storm windows the Jaworski brothers had stacked up here, the panes not yet dusty.

As she bent under the slanted roof, something pricked her scalp. Nail-tips driven through for the roof's shingles. Shuddering, crouching, she tore open a lone box. Plastic bags; limp, onionskin thin. Hundreds of bags, years of groceries. She raised two fistfuls. The plastic disintegrated into dingy confetti.

Brigid shoved back that box. Beneath it, a china heart lay like a flattened mushroom. A lid to something lost. Far downstairs, a door thumped. What, who? Grabbing the heart, she rushed to the attic door, reached for its knob, and found none. Hadn't Aunt B. told her not to shut that door? "Hey," Brigid rammed her shoulder against the door. Who would hear her, miss her? "I'm *trapped*—" She pounded the door with one fist, Aunt B.'s diamond ring winking in the dark.

"Miss Flynn?" Footsteps were thumping toward her.

"Ja-*wor*-ski?" Brigid clutched the cool chipped heart-lid.

"Lemme get this for ya—"

She stepped back, panting, bracing herself for Jaworski to bull through the door, break it down. Instead, the knob on the other side turned. Politely slow, as if she might be undressed, Jaworski opened the door. His sweat smell preceded him. Brigid breathed it like oxygen, realizing—as he stepped in, shadowed and stocky—that she liked his frank funk.

"I was so stupid!" She tried to smooth her humidity-frizzed hair, to compose her flushed face. "Locking myself up here, it was just so *stu*-pid—"

Jaworski shrugged. His own wary blunt-featured face held high color; his mass of black hair looked too thick to comb. He darted his eyes cannily around the darkened attic he'd be emptying today.

"But look what I found! A lid to some old jewlery box. And it's *engraved*." Brigid squinted at the grimy china heart. "'You're Witty and You're Pretty.'"

"Gee, thanks."

She raised her eyes to deadpan Jaworski. "Thank *you*," she told him with a Nice Girl smile. "I halfway thought I might die up here."

Jaworski shrugged, his eyes unglinting. He folded his bare sturdy arms over his Pawtucket High Football '95 T-shirt. "Far as I can tell, you're alive."

———

Date: Wed., Aug. 13, 1999; 11:36AM
to: calutz@syracuseu.edu
from: brigfly@brown.edu
subject: brain to co-brain; do you read me?

hey, Casey: just had to write AGAIN (despite the cyber-silence from you @ Syracuse U) because i'm in love with my ex-jock of a trash-hauler named Jaworski, more so w/ each boot-stomp above me. This Jaworski no doubt straight-forwardly dumb; no doubt *straight* too. in THAT way, maybe LESS risky than the effete elite @ Brown, i.e. my/our usual?

anyhow, i felt SPARKS between us this AM when cute but Cro-Mag J rescued me from Aunt B's attic. though we only talked business: Jaworski saying he'll THROW everything in the attic out the window to his PRE-Cro-Mag brother. "a de-fenestration of providence," i quipped. then, stammering like teenage me, i explained the *defenestration of prague.* Jaworski shrugged (i love it when he shrugs) & told me, "prague. i got a dead grandpa in prague."

we'd have NOTHING to talk about. thereby eliminating THE source of my letdowns! too bad for Jaworski i'm setting my last-night sights a bit higher.

speaking of whom: Ricardo, still my #1 hope for my *last-lay* here, has provided me w/ a Borges-quote *last-word* on our—yours & my—Greatness Debate. asked if V. Woolf was *greater than* J. Joyce, Borges replied: *she was an in-teresting writer of her times; that is all that matters.*

so true. so why do i find myself obsessed lately w/ the question of my own mind? is it, Woolf's mr. ramsay asks him-self, a *great* (in my case, read *good*) mind that can run from *a* to *z* or is it only a *good* (read, *mediocre*) mind that gets stuck at *v*—or was it *t*?

YOU know that loop. remember when Our Man Jarvis

revealed to us that the faculty RANKS each lit.-crit.er to determine $ aid? & our secretly DEEPER horror when J further revealed that the TAs had their own ranking system for students' BODIES? even when we co-tickled J's ribs, he wouldn't reveal OUR ranks. which drove you as batty as it did me. face it, co-brain. you & i SHARE the same Obsessive Competitive Disorder. & with whom else can you/can i TALK about its symptoms? aren't we able, still, to talk about anything?

here goes a test of THAT theory. my bottom line:

i know you might've heard/sensed something between me and Jarvis. i also know that Mr. Globe-Trotting *Genius* is off balling Brit.-Chick *Bobbies* now, like he'd be doing whether or not he'd balled yours truly. (i'm NOT saying he did; just that WE need to talk this out, my # 1 and only friend).

don't i deserve that, at least?

b

———

Brigid was dressing to go. She'd hung her sleeveless blue linen top and short linen skirt in the steamy bathroom to unwrinkle. As she dried off from her shower, Brigid heard the Jaworskis march back and forth, a wall away. She hooked on the push-up style bra Casey had convinced her to try ("My boobs are too *long*," Brigid had confidentially complained. "Soon they'll sag down to my waist like poor Aunt B.'s!"). Then she stepped into her high-heeled '70s Candies ("Subtly slutty," Casey had prescribed in the incense-scented Thayer Street shop she'd dragged Brigid to). Casey had taught Brigid how to strut on heels, how to make the most of what they'd dubbed Brigid's all-but-flat butt.

Brigid stood on tiptoe in her Candies and stared over one bare shoulder. In the sink mirror, she admired her thumbprint-sized tattoo. Casey had gasped in shock and glee when Brigid had first shown it off: a blue diamond centered on the small of her back. "I can't be-*lieve* you did that!" Casey shrieked like a sleepover teen. "Matching *my* birthmark! Plus the blue of *your* eyes!"

Brigid slipped on her linen top now, buttoning it, à la Casey, less than halfway. *Ready,* she mouthed like Casey used to do for both of them.

Strutting on her heels into the stripped-down living room, Brigid set her Mac to print her final ten pages. She kept her back to the Jaworskis as they stomped in. Her Mac's printer was clattering away on the spindly legged desk Jaworski would haul off after Brigid had left for the Brown Library.

"You haven't found any old leather *books* round here, have you?"

"Nah." Jaworski was easing Aunt B.'s rotted mushroom couch from the wall. His voice stayed impressively unstrained as he and his always silent brother hoisted the couch. "Y'know, a few years back, before he retired, I think my father built your aunt some kinda special hidden bookshelf—"

"Done!" Brigid exclaimed. Her last thesis page reeled off the printer. "I won't have time tonight to look for secret shelves," she added as the Jaworskis upended the couch. Its puffy gray-white cushions fell off, its springs revealed.

"Come to me," Jaworski grunted to his brother, so breathless he might've been Brigid's one and only professor lover, delivering hoarse position instructions midintercourse. "Not your hands; your legs," Jaworski, measurably more tender than Brigid's prof., instructed his panting brother.

They strained to force the couch out the door. "Nah, nah." Jaworski shook his head. "The feet gotta go. Hand me my hammer, will ya?" Flushing as if at a Scranton High jock, Brigid lifted the hammer. She poked it headfirst at Jaworski. He gripped its handle, his wiry-haired fingers brushing hers.

"*Back*—" Jaworski commanded. And he wielded the hammer like an ax. Four hacks: the wood-carved feet of the couch clopped onto the floor. "*Now.*"

The brothers log-rammed the couch through the door, its mushroom-gray fabric ripping. With a cheer, Brigid shut off her Mac. "Hey, *great!*"

Cradling her dissertation box in one arm, she stepped onto the porch, into the fresh hot air. Like a wife, she stopped beside Jaworski;

she patted his damp upper arm. Stirringly firm muscles; dense skin steamy from the heat he seemed not to feel. "See you later," Brigid told him. "If you're still around."

"Huh?" he muttered, ignoring her touch. He positioned the couch for its bumpy slide down the porch steps. Spurred by Jaworski's snub, by the inclination to keep something in reserve for tonight, Brigid lowered her voice.

"I said, I'll *see* you later on. If I come back, y'know, sooner than I think."

---

date: Wed. Aug. 13, 1999; 3:18PM
to: calutz@syracuseu.edu
from: brigfly@brown.edu
subject: good-bye, co-brain

Casey: just got home, alone, from my final Brown Letdown to find Jaworski loudly & indifferently busy in the attic; to find—on my Mac, in my blue New Messages—your first and (you say) last Syracuse U e-mail to me.

ok, ok; of course it should've been obvious that you knew about Jarvis & me. but i've always had a problem with the *obvious,* with the *simpler* sides of life. you & i SHARE that tendency (surely you remember quoting Yeats to me over beers, first year? "the fascination of what's difficult/ has dried the sap out of my veins & rent/something-something out of my heart").

honest to god, Casey, i was thinking/hoping he didn't mean SO much to you. remember those damn RANKINGS? the night Jarvis & i got together, after getting blasted @ the ratskeller, i made him admit that YOU had ranked *slightly higher* than ME on both the mind and body lists. aren't you, despite everything, happy to hear it? can't you, despite everything, understand why i (as we used to say) *found my-self* leaning close & telling Jarvis that at least i beat you in TATTOOS. That i'd gotten one whereas you'd only TALKED about it. Jarvis didn't believe—at first, till i showed him—my diamond was real.

afterward: i rationalized that, even if he & i had done
NOTHING, you two would never survive his year in london.
(ARE you two surviving? it's the ONLY thing you don't make
clear). i hoped this not because i was plotting to steal Jarvis
(girl-to-girl: he wasn't THAT *great*) but because i (an idiot,
i admit) half-consciously hoped once you'd freed yourself
from his diverting (yes) but ultimately dissatisfying company, WE'd go back to the way we were first year.

remember hooting over raw-lipped postfling coffee in the
grad. lounge? remember the KISS Jarvis orchestrated between us? you and me giggly drunk w/ him in OUR booth at
the rat; Jarvis saying in his intent yet laid-back way he'd always wanted to see two femmes kiss. & me turning brashly
to you, bussing you on your warmer-than-any-man's lips?
maybe it meant NOTHING to you; but after, i wondered if
that KISS would haunt me like mrs. dalloway's one-and-only
girl-kiss. c'mon. don't our Soul-Sister feelings count for
ANYTHING?

i know, i know. i hear you from Syracuse: how can I ask
that to YOU? No doubt you, like everyone else, no longer find
ME worth-the-trouble. or so i sensed this afternoon, pacing
fake-casually up & down the library's marble steps. see,
Casey, NO ONE showed up there to beer-bash me.

i waited/ paced in the sun for almost an hour, empty-
handed. my dissertation turned in, the high windows of the
english dept. glinting at me. were some of them crowded
inside, LAUGHING at me? did they catch the oh-so-
predictable glints in my eyes as i finally—no longer fake-
casual but marching, my back straight—strode away. my
pale face already aching from sun.

ok, i told myself: if my thesis becomes *famous* for nothing else, it'll be famous round Brown for being the ONLY
thesis no one wanted to toast.

all of them (you w/o your usual analytic objectivity now
claim) disgusted with me over my (read, *our*) arrogant
aloofness; over my *breaking up* (so you ARE broken up?)
Jarvis & you; over the profs. (really, as you know, only one)
i allegedly sucked off first year; over my passing my first-try
orals as a result of said-profs. (a variation was whispered
about YOU & Syracuse, though i TOLD everyone Jarvis

pulled NO strings for you). see? part of me knew you & Jarvis were *for real*; which may have been exactly WHY—

but you won't hash this out over beer. you want our friendship finished, like our dissertations: bound and shelved w/ the volumes NO ONE checks out.

what can i do? yes; i had my *sights set higher*—but maybe the Caveman hauling boxes above me w/ his Pre-Cro-Mag bro might consider checking ME out. he might be feeling as lonesome as sunburnt me: old Cro-Mag Jaworski.

i may or may not send you this final missive. like many unwise moves, it'd be temptingly easy: two seconds, two fingertip key-taps. good & bye—

b

Brigid sat on the floor of the Sun Room, watching Great-Aunt Brigid's attic stash fall outside the house's front windows. Floating plastic bags; a slow-whirling hatbox marked *Worth's of Boston*; a single plummeting pointy-toed high heel. She heard but couldn't see Jaworski's brother feed the fallen objects into the brothers' trash truck, its metal jaws grinding and crunching.

The Defenestration of Providence. Brigid studied Aunt B.'s sun-livened diamond on her finger. Aside from the initial boxes of papers, china, and crucifixes that she'd shipped to her mother and the china heart she'd found today, the heirloom ring was all Brigid had kept. Was it the most valuable?

Brigid glanced back through the archway into the living room to see her reply message to Casey poised onscreen, still safely unsent. Jaworski had been trooping in and out of that room. Brigid had barely listened. Now she wished he would find her here, her short skirt awry, her long legs exposed. Maybe then she could stop wondering, for tonight, whether to actually send that e-mail to Casey. She could stop thinking—put off *starting* to think—about this day.

Brigid peered through her glasses at the sunshine Aunt B. used to read by. She'd sit in an armchair stained by her dead father's hair oil.

The porchlike Sun Room had been papered then, Brigid remembered, by the same glitter-sprinkled wallpaper as Aunt B.'s guest room. Brigid straightened, studying the Sun Room's new wood paneling. In her last year, Aunt B. had feared "someone" might steal her Dickens. Brigid fingered the paneling's ridges, tugged them left and right. Creaking sideways, the wall gave way.

The Dickens. Safe in its walled-in shelf; fine-grained red leather spines dusty but intact. The volumes seemed tiny. She opened *Our Mutual Friend*, palm-sized. Inside the cover, in pencil print so old it was part of the page, Aunt B. had recorded each year she'd read this novel. *1937, 1949, 1952, 1966, 1970, 1978.* Ten-year-old Brigid had penciled a bold *1980* in the book she'd inherit.

"Because you're the one," Aunt B. told her. "Who can ap-*pre*-ciate Dickens." Tears had wakened Aunt B.'s watered-down blue eyes, her gaze in her deflated face startlingly young. Slipping *Our Mutual Friend* back in place, Brigid remembered Aunt B.'s girlhood hair, how young and shiny black it had looked in her own hands. Flushed under her sunburn, she stumbled to her feet.

She headed into the living room, meaning to save that hair. The least she could do—wasn't it?—for the aunt who'd *appreciated* her young self more than her mother ever had. And Casey, Brigid thought, appreciated Brigid's Providence self more than any man did. Brigid stopped at her computer. Kneeling before it, its desk gone, she studied the Casey message suspended on the blue-lit screen. Oddly, a capitalized line was printed at the message's end, beneath the "b." Brigid squinted. Had she typed it by accident, in her distress?

UGGA UGGA UGGA OOOH

Brigid backed up on her knees. Was all this tension messing with her mind? She ran to the back of the house. A subconscious message: *Ugly ugly you?* She halted, breathless, in the bedroom doorway. Stripped. The bedstand and dresser and THROW AWAY box hauled off. All that was left was the stained mattress and a white baby's coffin-sized cardboard box. Dust furred its lid.

Brigid swept back her hair, let it fall. Hours before, when she'd peeled her sheets off the mattress, she'd averted her eyes from its stains.

Now, stepping forward, she fixed on those overlapping continent splotches: golden brown like years' old burns, dark brown like freshly spilled iodine. Vomit, piss, blood.

She sat down on Great-Grandpa's mattress. Her bare thighs pressed its gritty nearly rotten cotton top, the buttons popped off. Ugly: inside and out. She sank sideways, resting her face against the darkest brown stain. Brigid inhaled its fusty sickbed smell, remembering the gently expert sponge baths Aunt B. had given her one feverish summer week. The week that bed-bound nine-year-old Brigid first read Dickens: *Tale of Two Cities,* straight through in two days, Aunt B. tiptoeing in and out as if Brigid's reading trance was something important, not to be broken. Brigid sat slowly upright.

What famous writer had said on his deathbed that all the books he'd written seemed so much sawdust? Had Aunt B. fared any better the night she'd heaved herself up from this mattress for the last time? Maybe all the nursing she'd done all her life *had* seemed, in the end, worth it. Brigid lifted the big white box. She pried it open, its cardboard heat-molded together.

A dress. Brigid parted the brittle tissue paper covering it. A faded matronly 1950s-style dress. Lavender blue with pearl buttons. Attached by a pearl-tipped pin to the crepey untied collar-bow was a carefully lettered note:

Burial Dress: Papa's favorite. To knot collar properly: loop up twice and once under; pull and flatten knot; afix pearl pin directly under knot, securing both tie-ends in place; With my thanks—Miss Brigid Flynn; 1996.

Brigid Flynn studied first her own name. Then she reread the note, realizing who Aunt B. had meant to find it. The next of kin who would've emptied her bedroom the week she died, instead of letting it stand for months. Who would've delivered her note and dress to the morticians who'd prepared her body. Stiffly, Brigid fumbled with the crepe ties. Loop up and under *where*? She stuck one end beneath the other. But nothing looked right.

"Miss Flynn?" Jaworski stood in the doorway. Brigid startled like a young Aunt B. Facing, Brigid imagined, the suitor who'd found her witty and pretty.

"Didn't know what to do with that one box. Found it under the bed."

"Oh, it's—my aunt left—" Brigid's throat felt thick; she thrust up the note. Jaworski stepped forward and lifted the note. He scanned it.

"'Burial dress,' huh? Little late for that."

"I know." Brigid widened her eyes behind her glasses, wondering if Jaworski might comfort her. "Aunt B.'s last request. God, I should've been the one to find her." She swallowed. Jaworski watched her impassively. "When I think how *I* felt, locked in that attic, scared no one'd find me—"

"Yeah, well." Jaworski hitched up his pants. Heavily, he sat beside her, not close enough to touch. She inhaled his funkiest-yet sweat. She was half-hoping that he'd sweep this dead woman's dress off her lap, press her onto this sad mattress. That he'd pound her hard, grind her bared back and ass into its stains. The two of them making, maybe, the first-ever love on this deathbed.

Jaworski sent Brigid a sideways glance. Was she a new task to be undertaken or not? "Lemme see here." He lifted the box and set it on his own knees. He glanced again at Aunt B.'s note. Then he reached into the box, his dirty square-tipped fingers deft. He lifted one bow-tie end, looped it around. He pulled a smooth knot, his touch—Brigid noted—light and sure.

He unfastened the pearl stickpin, centered it under the knot. He fingertip-touched the pearl. Like—Brigid thought, aware of her own— a clit. "There," was all Jaworski said, the pin pinned. He shifted the box to her.

"Thanks," she breathed into its tissue, thinking that Jaworski and his father had performed countless tasks for Aunt B. over the years. This last—Brigid studied the neatly tied dress—the last.

Jaworski gave a one-shouldered shrug. Distantly, Brigid heard his truck still crunching. In the dusky sunlight of Aunt B.'s bedroom, Brigid waited for Jaworski to touch her bare shoulder, to say something sweetly predictable like, *Y'know, Miss Flynn* . . . before she'd shut him up with a greedy full-lipped kiss. Sucking the meaty taste of him, squeezing shut her eyes to forget—the best way she knew how—this day, this dress, this house, everything.

Jaworski exhaled loudly. Maybe playfully? He started to pull himself up.

"Y'know, Jaworski—" Brigid turned, clapping her hand on his knee, the gritty oily cloth of his pants. "Y'know," she began again, wanting him to cut her short with a rough fed-up-with-her kiss. As she leaned close, the box clopped off her lap. The neatly folded lavender dress spilled onto the floor.

"Her dress," he started to say. Brigid took hold of him, jarring her glasses, pressing her face into his football T-shirt, his solid sweaty chest. Roughly, Jaworski hooked his chin over her shoulder. Checking out her ass? She gripped him, her blouse inching up. He flattened his hand on her bared back.

"What's that?" Jaworksi pressed her tattoo with one finger like he was pressing the talk button on a mechanical doll. Brigid pulled back, facing him: his face grainy with sweat close-up; his eyes too narrowed to read.

"My tattoo," she answered, wondering if she'd found a man old-fashioned enough to be shocked. "Wanna see?" she added. He didn't blink. Boldly, she bent over Jaworski's lap as if to be spanked, standing on her hands and knees. Her breasts in the push-up bra hung down above his thighs; her upraised ass felt flatteringly curved. This crudest of moves had worked with Jarvis.

"Hmm." As if measuring her, Jaworski passed one slow hand under her breasts. With his other hand, harder than Jarvis had done, he gave her ass a pat. "What, you wanna play rough? Play like we're living in caves?"

"Caves?" Brigid giggled dazedly. Desmond Morris, she found herself thinking. Jaworski as her *Naked Ape*. Staying on her hands and knees, she braced for Jaworski to hike up her skirt, mount her from behind.

"Yeah. Let's play caveman. You know. Ugga ugga ugga oooh."

Brigid jerked her head around; she stared at him over her tensed-up shoulder. Unsmiling, Jaworski winked. Brigid jolted upright, shoving his bent leg sideways for balance. She stood on her knees; she glared down at him.

"You? *You* typed that line? You *read* my message?"

Jaworski shrugged. "Too bad for you I got my sights 'set higher' tonight."

More heavily but more gracefully than her, he pulled himself to his feet. Still kneeling on the mattress, Brigid had to stare up at him.

"Couldn't help but see my name on that computer screen o' yours." Jaworski jerked his chin sideways. "What: did you think I can't read?"

Brigid twitched her shoulders in tense imitation of his shrugs. She was fighting for control of her face as she'd done during the first mini-jabs of the tattooist's needle, quick as a sewing machine, hurting only a bit at first.

"I got a girlfriend in Boston. She got ol' Cro-Mag me online." Jaworski brushed his knees, still unsmiling. "Hate to break it to you, but I'm en-gaged—"

"I am too—" Brigid shot back stupidly, flashing her diamond ring.

"What—to your little girlfriend?"

"You leave her out of this!" Brigid felt both their voices going high-pitched, turning teenaged.

"An' you leave my *brother* outa it." Jaworski drilled his stare into hers. What, Brigid had to think, *had* she called his brother? Pre-Cro-Mag?

Jaworski turned his back on her. I'm sorry, she drew breath to make herself say. But he was striding to the doorway. He hollered: "Joey, ya all set?" And he clomped into the living room, thumped the distant front door. Brigid let out her held breath. It had been years since her face had burned like this.

She slid off the mattress onto her knees; she reached for Aunt B.'s spilled dress. At least she had made Jaworski feel, however briefly, worthless too. Brigid buried her face in the clean yet musty dress. Wasn't it such thoughts that kept her brain from being, in the Mr.

Ramsay/ Virginia Woolf sense, first-rate? This, if nothing else, she regretted. Brigid lifted her head. She gasped, seeing the stain she'd left. Pinkish beige: fresh sweat, hours' old makeup.

Stumbling up, she refolded the dress so her stain wouldn't show. Brigid settled the dress back in its box, her face burning all over again. She lifted the hollow-feeling dress box. Setting the box on the mattress, she fitted its lid. Brigid remembered the Woolf quote Casey had thrown back at her in her final e-mail. *What does the brain matter compared with the heart?*

Numbly, Brigid walked into the living room. She wished she could revive the disconnected phone. Call the old Casey, make Jaworski a wry story. Although famous for her class interruptions, Casey was a good listener with Brigid. Or with—Brigid remembered how raptly Casey used to listen to him—Jarvis.

Outside the windows, Brigid saw Jaworski and his brother pick up trash from the lawn. Glad to duck down low, she knelt again at her computer. She reread her last message to Casey. Stiff-fingered, Brigid deleted *UGGA UGGA UGGA OOOH*. Not giving herself time to think, she added her own rapidly typed PS:

> *i AM sending this, Casey. though it's mainly my way of putting off saying, for what it's worth: sorry. since i won't see you again, i'll add another confession: i made an ALL-OUT play for Jaworski, who turned me down flat. & i could tell from his hands that he would've been—YOU know i don't use this word lightly—great. oh, well. at least i know what i lost.*
> *b*
> *PPS: bottom line, Casey (though i know it's both too little AND too late): Jarvis is the one i screwed but you are the one i loved.*

After she'd sent the e-mail to Casey, after she'd paid Jaworski—she and he averting their eyes as if they *had* had sex—after the Jaworski brothers had roared off in their truck, Brigid carried her shoe-boxed

Dickens volumes and her own dissertation copy to the door. She hefted the two boxes, comparing. They had the same weight. "Ha," she muttered out loud.

It was still light at 6 P.M., cooler now. Brigid's Mac was still plugged in, keeping her company. She planned to pack it last. Shouldering the door, she rattled her car keys as if hurrying up Casey when they dressed for a night out. But where was Brigid headed by herself? She'd been planning on Ann Arbor via Syracuse. Should she go someplace different? Someplace new? She stepped outside into hazy blue-black dusk. Brigid felt as if she'd dipped into Great-Aunt Brigid's belladonna. Everything looked darker and brighter.

In her Honda Civic, in the passenger seat, she set the boxes on Aunt B.'s dress box. As she walked back up the porch steps, empty-handed, she wondered if the laws of gravity—of what things weighed—had been altered for her, here. She stepped into the living room, its creaky hollowed-out silence. She yawned.

Brigid stepped up to her Mac. She crouched in its light to type her last Providence e-mail, suspicious of her own sentimental speculations. Of changes-for-the-better that she'd believe in Dickens but not in life. The screen lit her smudged glasses. She squinted as if still seeing through Aunt B.'s glasses.

---

date: Wed. Aug. 13, 1999; 8:08PM
to: flynn@oldecraftshoppe.com
from: brigfly@brown.edu
subject: change of plans . . .

hi Mom. FINIS: my degree, Aunt B's house, my now ex-friend in Syracuse.

so i'm going to swing by scranton, after all. since we both went AWOL for her funeral, you & i can at least drink a toast to Aunt B. no doubt i threw away too many of her belongings. guess i didn't inherit from you much sense of how to (as you say in the antique biz) *value* things.

anyhow, EXPECT me tomorrow. we can divide up what
i had the sense to save: her diamond, her Dickens, her dress.
now, i've got to make myself move.

first, the easy part.

two fingertip key-taps & my words will be gone.

Celebrities in Disgrace

a novella

The Tonya moment has passed. Newsweek,
Time, *and* People *have moved on to less impor-*
tant cover stories and we are left with an inner
emptiness too deep to be fathomed all at once.

—Matthew Gilbert, *The Boston Globe,*
February 1994

1.

He stapled his face over hers. In the subzero dawn of Skate-Off
Day—7 A.M. in Lowell, 1 P.M. in Lillehammer—the staples shot back
at him, the kiosk's corkboard as ungiving as ice. So Daniel reflattened
his Xeroxed flyer over Kathryn Byrne's professionally printed flyer. All
around Lowell, all winter, he'd stapled up his own name: *Daniel*
Sanders. Today, Daniel was posting new flyers that displayed only his
own face. Starting here, outside Kathryn B.'s pinkly lit window. He
formed a mittened fist. Kathryn Byrne: so sweet-seeming last night on
the local-yokel news. Daniel Sanders hammered his fist onto his
stolen stapler. It bit.

In the beginning, in fragile clippings his mother had saved, there
was Patricia Hearst (my terrorist-heiress, Daniel thought fondly)
whom he'd loved most as *Tanya* (never more lovely and wanton than
in those blurred bank-camera shots: "Tanya" wielding her SLA assault
rifle, her red wig becomingly tousled, her wide formerly blank eyes
wild); then: a valentine-faced murderess for his own times, Pamela

49

Smart (*Pame,* Daniel knew her nickname to be, as in pain plus fame), and now: sweet-seeming dark-haired Nancy Kerrigan. Another ice princess poised, like Patricia Hearst, to *turn Tanya?* Daniel Sanders lowered his staple gun with a jerk. Was it mere coincidence that Nancy Kerrigan's archenemy skating rival bore that same fateful name? Tanya, Tonya.

Something wooden thumped. Daniel pivoted in the crunchy virgin snow. Ghost clouds—shower steam?—curled out from Kathryn Byrne's suddenly cracked-open window. Daniel stuffed his stapler into his backpack and reached for another Hershey's Kiss. Frozen like bullets. Half-accidentally, he pulled out too his foil-wrapped condom. Which he slipped into his jeans' front pocket. For easier access, tonight. Seventeen years old, and this his first condom. For courage, he thumbed another chocolate under his muffler, into his mouth.

Hi, I'm Daniel Sanders and I'm "famous" too. Maybe you've seen my name?

Sucking hard, he retightened his muffler over his new John Lennon goatee. Which made him look eighteen, at least. Her steam spiraled in the cold air. Daniel shivered, picturing Nancy Kerrigan and Tonya Harding aspin in their sparkly Olympic Skater skirts. Did Kathyrn Byrne, who hoped to play Nancy K. in an upcoming TV movie, possess that same superhuman energy?

Daniel intended to find out tonight. What Kathryn B. possessed, inside.

Impulsively, he lurched down her unshoveled sidewalk. Halfway to her window, he stumbled. Like, he remembered as he fell, Kathryn's spastic sister. A Home Movie clip the news had shown with Kathryn's interview. Daniel pulled himself up. Shin-deep in snow, he drew a big breath the way he did before Groups. As he trudged forward again, he listed to himself the Groups he had duped, making those earnest folding-chair circles believe he was one of them.

Teens with ADD; Children of Convicts; Teens with STD; Phone Sex Anonymous.

He slowed his steps, bit his Kiss. Her marbled-pink window only a few feet away now, and open. With a rush of chocolate saliva, Daniel

50

recognized the pink as terry cloth. A mere towel and a pane of steamy (inside) frosty (outside) glass separated him from her. He hugged his numb arms, wide awake for once.

Most mornings he killed sneak-reading *People* in Star Market, seeking out celebrities brought low enough for even him in his unwashed underwear to look down upon. His longtime pastime; his specialty. Claudine Longet, Pete Rose, Michael Jackson, Woody Allen. Celebrities in disgrace.

In cold, all sounds carry. Through the killingly still air, Daniel heard—more clearly than Kathryn in her shower?—Kathryn Byrne's phone ring. One elongated buzz. Daniel swallowed his dwindling Kiss. At the second buzz, he staggered into his last snow-slowed steps. Clumsy and urgent like that sister of Kathryn's who wasn't—what Daniel's mother said about him—all there. *Nobody,* Daniel thought as he halted under Kathryn's iced-up lit-up window, *home.*

Whipping open her plastic curtain on the third buzz, Kathryn Byrne leapt onto wet tile as if onto stage, naked. In her breathless rush, she tugged down the pink towel she'd hung as a window shade. Shocked by her bared reflection in the blue-black glass, Kathryn spun around, dropping the towel. As the fourth buzz sounded, she skidded onto the shock of her bedroom floor. Icy linoleum.

Cutting short the fifth buzz, Kathryn lifted the receiver in a slippery hand. She always answered her phone hopefully. Awaiting, today, news on her chances to play Nancy Kerrigan in a jump-the-gun TV movie already being cast. "Yes?"

"Kath."

"Oh, Mom." Half-relieved it wasn't her agent, Kathryn hugged her body with one arm. Her space heater ticked beside her, toasting her wet skin. "How come you guys didn't call last night? Did you see it or what?"

"Of course we saw it, Kathryn. Of course we wanted to call but Lisa. Well. . ."

"'But Lisa' what?" Kathryn straightened, dripping a puddle.

Remembering how the mike cord had snaked up under her best

wool dress last night. How she'd told the interviewer: *"Special needs," the teachers say my sister Lisa has. But God, when you think of it— I mean look at me; throwing myself onstage since age eight—don't we all?*

"God, Mom, I'm worried Lisa might've gotten weirded out by that whole interview. By seeing her face on TV—they asked at the last minute if, along with the long-distance shots of us skating, they could show those *close-ups* of Lisa and me playing in the snow—and hearing me, you know, talk about her. God, I *never* would've brought up Lisa myself but they were waiting for some update from Lillehammer and that ditzy news lady kept pushing, getting all personal—"

"I understand." Mom sounded, for once, like she might not.

Guiltily, Kathryn glanced at her nightstand photo: twenty-six-year-old Lisa looking like a younger plumper Kathryn, her darker green eyes intent behind glasses. Lisa's witchy trance-stare. Watching over her big sister. "Can I talk to Lisa?"

"Well, I'm not sure she's up. . ."

"Oh, Mom. You know she always wants to talk to me!"

"Let me check." Mom cut Kathryn short with a brisk sigh. Phone static filled Kathryn's ear. She shook back her thick damp ponytail. It spattered the *Boston Globe* she'd spread on the floor. THE BIG CHILL: Nancy in white and Tonya in garishly flowered black passing each other on their practice ice, forming one girl with two determined profiles pointed in opposite directions.

Lowering her phone, Kathryn met the unlit eye of her camcorder on its tripod. C'mon, she thought as if to a casting director. Look me over. Her taut twenty-nine-year-old body poised, her damp skin aglow in the space-heater light, Kathryn inched one wet foot forward. With her toes, she pressed the *on* switch.

The camcorder shuddered into life. Its eye lit. It filmed Kathryn naked now as she lifted the cordless phone receiver like a mike. Her nipples sharpened. Her whole body felt—though it wasn't sexual, exactly—turned on.

"Where do the bubbles go," Kathryn began to sing softly into the phone. "When they bub-bub-bubble a-way?" Baby Lisa had loved that song. Cooing her bubble-beards; tugging at Kathryn's hair. "That's the on-ly thing I'd like to know," Kathryn sang on, since Lisa would squeal with laughter if she answered now. "Where they bub-bub-bubble away. . . ?"

The phone stayed staticky. Videotape whirred forward like the pulse in Kathryn's ears. She'd never been filmed naked before. But this giddy week, anything felt possible. Kathryn pirouetted on imaginary skates, waiting for her sister's halting always-incredulous voice. *Kath. Ryn? Is. You?*

"Kath?" Mother's faraway voice stopped Kathryn's second spin cold.

"Where's Lisa?" Kathryn caught her balance, raising the phone again. "I need to talk to Lisa *now*, Mom. I've gotta leave in fifteen minutes for the rink—"

"I'm sorry, Kath. Your sister. She's. . ."

"What?" Kathryn demanded, trying to remember what all she had said last night about her autistic sister. What self-consciously "sensitive" babble?

"Lisa's curled up in her tightest ball under her covers. With, you know, her head down low." And her toes in her mouth, Mom didn't have to add.

"Oh," Kathryn breathed with a stab of guilt.

Lisa had sucked her toes for twenty-six years now. "Kath's kitten," three-year-old Kathryn had nicknamed Lisa. It felt like she'd cast a spell when Lisa turned so quiet, mewing instead of crying, sleeping in a ball, batting Kathryn's hair yarns.

"—Tired from last night, all the excitement. But: Kath? Try not to worry about anything except tonight. Tell me again who all they're sending out? From L.A.?"

"A camera crew, Mom. No director, no producer. No one big'll see me in person." Kathryn pressed her bare thighs together, picturing Lisa curled up so tight. Chilled now despite the space heater's fierce glow. "The bigwigs are gonna watch the *tape* of my Maddie show and use *that* as my 'audition.' Also Wally's FedExing them my little interview. Hope it wasn't too cheesy of Wally to claim I'm 'the leading contender' for the Kerrigan part. Am I, really? I mean *Wally* says it's a good sign that ABC's flying out their own people, but what does Wally know? He's so Boston, Mom. God, I can't help but wish I was still with—"

"Don't even think about that man," her mother commanded. Both their voices hardened at the mention of the New York agent who had secured Kathryn a tiny role in a TV movie about UFOs, then had unceremoniously dumped her.

"After all, Kath, it's Wally who set up this whole Kerrigan-movie possibility, sending them that tape of you in your ice thing—"

"'Show,' Mom. Ice *show*. Concord Winter Fest, my 'big break,' ha ha. Now Wally's saying he's too nervous to drive up tonight and watch me—"

"Sure you don't want *us* there, Kath, Dad and I?"

"Yes." Kathryn shivered in earnest now. "Just tell me. *Is* Lisa OK?"

"Kathryn." Mom sounded stern again, tired too. "We—Dad and Lisa and I—we all want you to concentrate on tonight. Afterward, you give us a call and we'll talk. About Lisa. And Lisa will talk too. All right, Kath? Kathryn?"

"Aye aye, Mom." Playing for the camcorder that she remembered was still filming, Kathryn hung up. *I, I,* she thought, guilty not to have pressed Mom harder. Could Lisa have gone off? Sighing, Kathryn stepped slowly forward.

Conscious of her breasts and pubic hair, she shut off the video camera. Then blinked into its unlit light, surprised she'd shot herself nude. But success, even the chance of it, made her bold. She took one step back. Hadn't most of the sex in her life begun as impulsive flirtations in the afterglow of a successful audition or the raucous celebration of a postperformance cast party? Kathryn turned from her camera. And now, if she did land "Nancy"? What all might she do then?

She stepped over the *Globe,* imagining her own headline. LOWELL GIRL MAKES GOOD: KATHRYN BYRNE NABS NANCY ROLE IN TV FLICK. But, she wondered, what if Nancy won nothing today? Would the proposed TV movie even be made? Kathryn shut the bathroom door behind her. Determined to focus only on her own show. Her *Maddie Mill Girl* monologue. A jerry-built gig funded by Lowell Public Schools

and Merrimack Repertory Company; a teaching-and-performing con-
tract ending in three weeks. Her future plans, as Mom put it when
people asked, *open.*

Shakily, Kathryn wrapped herself in the worn towel she'd hung on
the bathroom door. She knotted it above her breasts, stepped up to
the cold open window. Dissipating lavender-blue dark. A ghost of a
chance, she thought. She hugged herself through the towel. That's all
I've got tonight, but that can be enough.

So Kathryn Byrne was telling herself when, with a start, she spotted
him.

A tall male in a pinhead ski cap, backing up in high-kneed steps
down the snowy sidewalk. A student? Kathryn squinted without her
contacts. Sometimes, this past drab winter, her boy students eyed her
in a way she shouldn't like. Or—he ducked behind a Kennedy Plaza
kiosk—maybe he'd seen her last night on TV? The prospect of even a
psychotic "fan" gave Kathryn goose bumps. Was she crazy (her mom
demanded) standing in her lit window in only a towel?

You exhibitionist you, Kathryn heard her oldest friend AJ drawl.
Hurriedly, she rehung her pink towel on its curtain rod. Mom was always after her to buy regular shades. But Kathryn never planned to live
long enough in any of her apartments to measure the windows. Or *was*
she an exhibitionist of sorts?

She turned to her sink mirror. Leftover steam blurred her face, as in
her new touched-up Head Shot. Was Lisa still hiding in bed, sucking
her toes?

Cold and sour, Kathryn always imagined, though she'd never tasted
her own.

Fingers shaky, she popped in her tinted contact lenses. Her light
green eyes transformed with a blink into jewel green. Kerrigan green.
Vigorously, Kathryn brushed her reddish brown hair. Its full mass settled on her shoulders. All winter, she'd pulled into a ponytail what AJ
called her "trademark hair," disguising herself against old high-school
friends on the slushy streets of Lowell.

Kathryn Byrne didn't want to be recognized—not because she with her single resume-page of acting credits was famous, but because she wasn't, yet.

She rolled on underarm deodorant. How she hated running into former Thespians hauling their babies down Market Street. Yes, she was back at Lowell High as a temporary teacher; yes, she'd been performing at the Merrimack Rep. ("a 'little theater' company," she'd explain, "but they do, but barely, pay!"). And, she'd always end by saying, she was spending lots of time with her sister Lisa. *Oh,* they'd breathe, respectful at last. Years before, Kathryn had told all her drama friends about her "special" sister, how close they were. Wasn't that why she'd let the newscastress talk her into talking about Lisa? Kathryn unscrewed her Oil of Olay. To make herself look good.

With smooth circular motions, she rubbed in the ointment. The best skin ages the fastest, AJ warned back when he was Thespian makeup whiz. Kathryn squinted to check her crow's feet. They were barely visible on film, she had noted this week as she'd played and replayed her monologue videos. Thank God, she thought, she photographed better than she looked in person. Younger.

And my body? Kathryn wondered, stepping back. Curious to see— but there was no time now—if it, like her face, was transformed by the camera. She pulled on a black leotard that outlined her small well-shaped breasts. Small breasts age best, AJ had decreed. Kathryn's ideals of beauty ran toward Audrey or Katharine Hepburn or, body-wise, slender Nancy Kerrigan. Silicon implants were for sex, really. And Kathryn didn't care all that much about sex, really. Or cared only in bursts. She tugged baggy jeans over her leotard, hiding her long legs. Her pride.

Then she hid her torso, too, under a bulky olive sweater. She didn't want any men approaching her. She chapsticked but did not lipstick her lips. It'd been half a year since that last time with her oldest most fatherly MRC costar. Didn't AJ always tell her she channeled her libido into her work like a super-straight all-American male? Like a nun. She turned from the mirror at last, her hair bouncing on her shoulders. *But,* AJ added, *you need to put it first, your talent. Don't know about you-as-you sometimes, sweet Kath. But as an actress*—Kathryn Byrne thumped shut her bathroom window—*you're for real.*

He was tall, was the one good thing. Tall for seventeen; tall for any age. Easily, he had seen over her windowsill. Half an hour later now, he reached far above another of her *Maddie Mill Girl* flyers in dumpy grandly named Kennedy Plaza. Daniel Sanders aimed at the taped label on the stapler: *Kinko's.* His latest so-called employer. He pounded his fist extra hard. Charged up from his one electrifying glimpse. Kathryn B.'s pink breasts—round and pert like a teenage girl's, not floppy like his mom's—then her Nancy-esque hair as she turned. Daniel jolted down from tiptoe. He faced her face on the *Mill Girl* flyer.

Too angular for Nancy Kerrigan, he decided. Maybe, he thought as he stepped back, a thinner-lipped less sexy Julia Roberts? Or a much classier much smarter Pamela Smart? He glanced at his flyer above hers. Was *she* seeing now, outside her door, his face on this flyer? Maybe that was why he'd been stapling up these crazy flyers all along. So she'd recognize his name and face, tonight.

A crunch of steps approached. Daniel peeked around the kiosk— his timing today heaven-sent—just as she passed.

Her hair was loose, electric in the early sun; her face was pale, distracted, tight-lipped. A ghost of her TV face. Oblivious to him, Kathryn Byrne crossed the street, ice skates slung over her shoulder. Two-hour practice sessions at the local rink, the news lady had stated. So Daniel had time for his usual black coffee at the Sundance Café, historic hangout of Jack Kerouac. Would it surprise Kathryn B. to know that Daniel Sanders had read a smattering of Kerouac, read the whole of Ginsberg's *Howl*? That he'd aced all his IQ tests while flunking all his classes.

Daniel stepped from behind the kiosk, swinging his unhinged stapler. Had she gotten a look at him before, outside her window? So tall she might report "some man," not "some boy," was following her. Stalking her, some might say.

Would she be scared, he wondered, when she discovered tonight what he intended to give—no, "lose to"—her?

Daniel stowed his stapler like a rifle as he approached the '50s neon sign outside Sundance, #1 stop on the Kerouac Bar Tour of Lowell. Would she put up a fight? And if so, what would he do? He cleared his throat to deepen his voice for whichever waitress he drew. A man-sized voice, when he wanted.

His mother had taught him how. So: when her twangy Kenny Rogers–voiced man phoned, Daniel would answer in the neutral tone of the brother Mother claimed to live with. And if his mom's lover worried about this "brother," that was OK. Anything, Daniel had come to understand, was better than the seventeen-year-old son he really was. You sound kinda sexy, his mother would murmur from the folded-out sofa, lifting the receiver from him. Shifting to her own Southern-flavored phone voice. Daniel shouldered through the Sundance door.

In her youth, his mother had looked like a poor-girl Patricia Hearst. She'd followed the whole Hearst saga raptly because, she claimed, her Born Again father was a distant relation to *the* Colonel Sanders of fried chicken fame. Supposedly—not that Daniel believed a word of hers—her dad was in line to inherit big money. To become Greenville, South Carolina's own William R. Hearst. After she'd fled north to give birth to Daniel in disgrace, his mother had fancied herself a sort of kidnapped heiress. She was, if nothing else, a born performer. Like him.

"'Icy Showdown,'" Daniel read to the whole room, taking his seat. A *Boston Globe* lay on his table. A ponytailed man reading a Loam Press poetry book gave a companionable grunt. Brings people together, Daniel thought. A good scandal like this. He studied Nancy Kerrigan's born-winner smile; he tore out the ICY SHOWDOWN headline. Folding it, he slid it into his pocket behind his condom.

Tonya and Nancy headlines decked the wall above Daniel's TV/VCR at home.

ON THIN ICE: TONYA TIED TO NANCY KNEE ATTACK and IS SHE HEADED FOR THE OLYMPICS, OR FOR JAIL? and NANCY DRAWS STRENGTH FROM FAMILY, PRAYERS, and GILOOLY COLLUDED and, Daniel's personal favorite: EX-HUBBY GILOOLY APPEALS TO SCANDAL SKATER: "FESS UP, TONYA."

"Today's the big day, huh?" Daniel commented to his waitress, giving the words a mocking edge. After all, the Sundance piled poetry books on its jukebox.

"Yeah, we're listening on the kitchen radio. 'Live from Lillehammer.' Tonya's supposed to be out soon but she's making 'em wait." The waitress—the Joan Rivers-esque one—rolled her eyes. Daniel unwrapped his muffler.

"Ooh. Like that new beard. Ice in it, though, hon."

Daniel brushed his crystallized sweat from his goatee. Older women loved him. Tall polite black-haired kid. Maybe half Greek or Italian (who knew what his dad had been?). Anyhow: he could grow a decent beard; that was the other good thing.

"Skippin' school again?" the waitress asked, a note of admiration in her scold.

"You know me." Daniel shrugged. Man on the run, always in hiding: from the Lowell High officials who knew him as a star truant and from Mom's as-yet-unseen lover, who didn't know Daniel existed at all.

"Black?" The waitress started pouring before Daniel nodded.

The '50s jukebox kicked on: "Love Me Tender." Beside it stood the '60s photo booth in which Daniel had snapped the flyer shot he'd enlarged at Kinko's. He scanned the café for witnesses to his past and present activities. But the place was nearly empty. Everyone gathered round the radio at home, as in days of old?

"Tell ya what I think." When the waitress raised the coffeepot, Daniel leaned over his full cup to expound. "I think they're going after the wrong girl."

Like drunks discussing the Red Sox with bartenders, Daniel had bonded with various waitresses here—the one who wisecracked like Rhea Perlman, the Slavic-accented one who resembled a bedraggled Raisa Gorbachev—by trading opinions on various disgraced celebrities. Woody Allen (whom Daniel secretly related to though he feigned shared outrage); and, more recently, Michael Jackson (about whom Daniel planned to write a tragicomic Rap/Rock Opera: Jackson's bleached and distorted face the perfect symbol, Daniel told his waitresses, for the all-American obsession with making yourself into someone you aren't).

59

"Kerrigan colluded." Daniel tapped his spoon on his cup. In the grand tradition of real mothers, the waitress leaned on one leg to listen. "Think about it." Daniel spread his long fingers, imitating Donald Sutherland in the climactic revelation scene in *JFK*. "As with a political assassination, the first question we ask oughta be: who benefits? Was it mere coincidence that Nancy's knee was injured *just enough* so she didn't have to compete in the Nationals but *not enough* so she's not back in tip-top shape today, for this gold medal Skate-Off? Now, sure enough, Kerrigan's aced Round One. And if she even limps onto the ice tonight, she skates away a million-dollar martyr. . ."

Joan Rivers hedged a pink-lipsticked smile. A you're-kidding-aren't-you-kid? smile. Daniel slurped his coffee. He'd drunk it black since he was little, jacking up his heartbeat. One sure way to feel half-alive.

"And don't you—think about it—*want* Nancy to turn out bad?" Daniel met her wry tired gaze. "Don't you *want* Nancy to be, y'know, disgraced?"

"Huh?" The waitress took a step back as "Love Me Tender" ended.

"Don't we all?" Daniel half-rose from his seat. "Sure we do! Everyone in America does, but *I* admit I do. I *admit* I'm addicted to it."

"To what?" The waitress asked, side-glancing at the ponytailed man.

"Celebrities in disgrace," Daniel told them both, loudly. "And, see, *I've* distilled this—this addiction to its essence. Its purest form. Celebrities born of their own disgrace. The ones famous because of, not in spite of, it. Patricia Hearst, Pamela Smart. And soon, if my theory proves right, little Miss Nancy Kerrigan."

Daniel sank back into his seat. He jiggled his foot furiously.

"Jeez, kid," Joan Rivers replied. "You gotta lighten up. Y'know?"

Daniel slumped, sullen now, as she turned. *I'm not a nut,* he thought toward her retreating pink-striped back. *But I play one on TV.*

Her blade cut the ice. A shaved-ice circle shaped itself around her. She tightened her thigh muscles, dipped down her hip. She was spinning as fast as her hyper sister spun on skates. But she wouldn't think of

Lisa now. Tree your troubles, Tonya Harding had told an interviewer. Hang your troubles on an imaginary tree when you step into the rink. Ice in all its shades of white spun beneath Kathryn. Under her feet, it felt solid yet not. Like a stage.

The empty rink seats and the huddle of Nancy-struck girls by the Coke machine and the radio she didn't want to hear all rushed by Kathryn Byrne as blurry background, only her own body in focus. She cut down the middle of the rink, legs scissoring and blades flashing. She felt the way she rarely felt offstage but always felt on. Like the bold center in a childhood finger painting of Lisa's. Mom had said it was of fireworks but Kathryn had known it was of her. Her to Lisa: a vivid burst of orange against murky no-color dark.

One: she tensed her upper body. *Two*: she stepped hard on her right blade. *Three*: she leapt up and twisted into a half-spin, landing off-balance, but with her left leg straight behind her. Half-right. Gasping, Kathryn pumped her legs to regain her speed, try again. Hurl herself into the jump like tough Tonya Harding in her hometown mall rink. Spins like Lisa's quick quiet fits of rage.

But no. Kathryn's ankles wobbled as she slowed. Nancy; think Nancy. Her perfect posture, her careful tentative leaps. *Spirals and stars,* Kathryn told herself, remembering a recent *Boston Globe* article. *A fragile psyche,* Nancy the Nice was rumored to have after skating *in a seeming daze* in the 1992 World Championships in Prague, Nancy finishing a disgraceful sixth, Nancy on camera sobbing that she wanted to die. Fragile psyche, Kathryn Byrne repeated to herself. God knows *I* can play that. She stepped hard again on her right blade. But she twisted her torso too soon, her feet too low. Her left blade caught, spitting chips. Then the ice, the whole rink tilted, dumping her.

Damn. She landed hard on her ass. Like one time on the backyard seesaw when she was up and Lisa down and Lisa stared from under her bangs then swung her leg over the seesaw. Kathryn winced now, pulling herself back up. She aimed a determined smile at the imaginary audience sitting forward in their seats.

An attentive hush: the audience halfway rooting for you to fall again—fall apart in front of them!—yet cheering all the louder if you pull yourself together. Kathryn skated forward, her ponytail flying be-hind her. Her blades sliced and sliced. Hadn't she always felt herself—at least onstage—to be sharper and brighter than everyone else? Yes: a sharp bright figure dancing above the dull gray stretch of everyday life.

Zigzagging across that gray now, marking it. White scars like light-ning bolts. Kathryn glided with easy strides. *Just thought you'd like to know,* she'd tell her ex-agent in New York by phone should she nail Nancy. Her true message being: ha ha, you dumb fuck. She lifted her knees, her blades chipping ice sparks. You were dead wrong about me. All of you who've tried to keep me down: wrong, wrong! I sprang right back up in your fucking smug faces!

She crouched into a furious Tonya-spin, her ponytail whipping her cheeks. Death-drop spin, this was called. Then Kathryn Byrne was ris-ing again, gliding again in quiet triumph. She sent Nancy's *trademark stars* out to the empty seats. *Kerrigan's arms extended and her hands opened to the heavens.* Her skates felt as natural as a horse's hooves, her ankles strong as a thoroughbred's. Neat shavings of ice shot from under her heels.

As she wound into her easiest spins, dodging wobbly kids, Kathryn fired off in her mind the Four Essential Character Questions she'd learned in Acting 101.

Who am I?
Nancy Kerrigan, skating star!
Where do I come from?
Stoneham, dull as Lowell.
What do I want?
To beat Tonya and win the gold!
Where am I going?
All the way to fame, fame, fame.

In the slush-streaked lobby, Lowell High girls grinned at him. Daniel Sanders fancied himself a celebrity among the local truants. Most of them knew his name, anyway, thanks to those *Daniel Sanders* flyers he'd stapled up for fun, at first. Although it was becoming clear to him that his old name and new face flyers really could help him tonight.

That he *could,* maybe, plausibly introduce himself to Kathryn Byrne as a local-yokel celebrity, too. A "poet" perhaps, he mused now. Spiritual descendant of Jack Kerouac. Yeah, man.

Daniel leaned in the wide archway to the rink, hidden by skaters sipping Cokes. He was tall enough to see inside: the never-filled rows of seats; the ice crisscrossed with scars like folds in wax paper. A few little kids were fooling around out there today, clumsy on their double blades. And, yes: weaving her way between them was Kathryn Byrne in a black leotard and serious skates.

Daniel Sanders watched her spin into mild loops and T-stops. Not a real athlete, but she'd play one on TV. His nervous leg began jiggling. Under his muffler, he smirked over how much he knew that she didn't know he knew.

For starters: that even before he'd chanced upon her Late News interview last night, he and she had met. Daniel ducked his head as Kathryn spiraled in his direction. Back in December, he had hovered in the doorway of the Lowell High Auditorium at the so-called Open Auditions for Kathryn Byrne's Winter Theater Workshop. The first time he'd entered Lowell High in weeks, and in fact he didn't enter. He stood in the doorway watching other kids jump up onstage and deliver their stiff amateurish readings. Daniel Sanders had stayed silent. No fool, he.

Finally near the end, Kathryn Byrne stood up and called out from the front row a question Daniel found himself unable to answer: *Excuse me, who are you?* Her hair, backlit by the stage lights, seemed on fire around her face. Her hair had lit up more subtly in intermittent streetlights as silent Daniel had followed her through the December dusk to her apartment building. Noting her address.

"Wanna listen on our radio, Daniel?" a plump frizzy-haired girl asked him. She motioned inside with her pimply chin. Her friends huddled around a radio by the makeshift NANCY KERRIGAN SKATED HERE banner.

"No thanks," Daniel answered in his patented polite yet distant manner. "I'm with her." He aimed his own brief nod toward Kathryn Byrne, alone on the ice. Just like Nancy in Lillehammer, who alone had finished her practice routine after two other skaters collided. A cold-blooded display of discipline that the *Globe* sportswriter had just as cold-bloodedly admired. THE LADY IS A CHAMP.

"Whatevuh." The truant girl shrugged him off, ambling back to her clique. Her broad butt swayed in rebuff. Daniel smirked again under his muffler. It had become easy to snub the females, who—frequently, actually—approached him. But *he* had never approached one of them, was the one bad thing.

He hovered in the rink's archway, watching Kathryn Byrne glide by, her gloriously careless ponytail streaming behind her like a horse's tail. She staggered, recovered. The truant girl group giggled, shooting backward glances at Daniel. Disbelieving his lie? he wondered, keeping his gaze deadpan.

Funny, really, that Daniel Sanders couldn't act onstage, when he was such a great actor offstage. Especially for—he mentally captialized the word—Groups.

His favorite hobby, of late. He'd choose a Group from the Star Market bulletin board. He'd settle into another folding-chair circle, pseudo-shy. Families of Addicts. Tearfully, he told that Group a made-up story: how his mother locked him out while she shot up. Or: at OAFA, Orphans Against Foster Abuse, Daniel described in a stoic choked-up voice how he'd hidden from an imaginary pervert of a Foster Father at the Star Market magazine racks. Trolling for stars, day after dull day.

But he hated the idea of joining a Fan Club, he had explained to the one Group he'd attended as his real self. Living With Your Obsessive Compulsions. Fan Clubs were for wimps too meek to imagine approaching their idols.

Look at Tonya Harding's Fan Club president, Daniel thought contemptuously now. Hospitalized last week because it was *all too much for him.*

"Not for me," Daniel muttered as Kathryn Byrne skated another lopsided figure eight, not thirty feet away. Not that he ever *had* approached any celebrity; not that Lowell, MA, ever had provided him with a celebrity *to* approach. And then—though he was a seventeen-year-old virgin; that was the other bad thing—to seduce.

"'Scuse me?" a whispery-voiced teenage girl asked, materializing at Daniel's elbow. "D'ya know if Nancy Kerrigan's skated yet?"

Daniel knew Nancy Kerrigan wasn't slated to skate till 3 P.M. or so, U.S. time. But he answered, keeping his eyes on Kathryn, "She's skating now."

As the mousy girl scurried over to the radio, as Kathryn Byrne circled the ice faster, maybe gaining speed for a Big Finish, Daniel stepped back farther into the archway shadows. He breathed the snow-scented lobby air.

You're on thin ice, Scandal Skater, Daniel thought, pretending to be Shane Stant. Tonya H.'s (or Nancy K.'s own?) hired hit man: lurking in a bigger rink's wings, waiting to smash Nancy's kneecaps. Hadn't Stant hidden his face in black just as Daniel was hiding his own overheated face behind his muffler? Daniel narrowed his gaze. Before the attack, had Shane Stant watched Nancy K. skate the way Daniel Sanders now watched Kathryn B.? Loving yet hating her grace.

That, Daniel decided in the analytic mode he liked best, was the primal appeal of figure skating. How you both wanted and didn't want the girl to take a fall.

"Miss Byrne? It is 'Kathryn Byrne,' isn't it?"

Kathryn could barely nod, leaning against the plastic-padded barrier she'd crashed into, panting from her workout. Her skin was flushed and damp, her heart was suddenly throbbing. God. Skating felt the way sex was supposed to feel; the way acting always did feel. A rush so intense that only afterward could your body return: a flesh-and-blood mass all over again. Grounded.

"I recognized you from your interview last night, dear." A stout Betty White-type woman stood before her, closer than a normal stranger would dare.

"Oh, right." Kathryn pulled on her skate guards. "That was me. . ."
She glanced back at the ice. A frozen ocean she'd crossed: her own

zigzag marks tracking her mood. Up so high only moments before; now plunging.

"Would you like to listen on my radio, Miss Byrne? 'Live from Lillehaumer'?"

"No, no. I'll *watch* the TV show tonight, instead." Kathryn stood, shakily.

"With your family, dear? And your *sister*? I just wanted to say that I think you're very—brave. To show her off like that—or not 'show off,' but you know what I mean—and to say how we *all* have our 'special needs'—"

"Excuse me, please. I've gotta go." Kathryn hobbled on the sheathed points of her skates to a bench. Then she sat, trembling all over. She smoothed the springy tendrils of her hair, guilty to have brushed off an actual fan.

Sighing, Kathryn unlaced her skates. She remembered how she had "treed" her troubles, her sister. Now, as she tugged off her first skate, she pictured Lisa hanging on their old backyard dogwood tree. From her branch, from behind her strapped-on glasses, Lisa watched Kathryn star in Chinese Jump-Rope games. Kathryn hopped high inside the rubbery rope, feeling she was holding Lisa in air.

Kathryn pulled her baggy jeans over her tights. Her stocking feet felt weightless; the rest of her body felt heavy. She thrust on her boots. And she strode toward the phone booth, passing the cubbyhole shelves. Each block-lettered skate size: 14 (Boy) down to 4 (Girl).

"Dad?" Kathryn gasped into the receiver when he answered, curtly. "What're you doing home? Is something—wrong?"

"Where are you, Kathryn?" Her father sounded far away. When famously revitalized Lowell had declined again in the late '80s, Dad had moved the family to Lexington. So all winter, Kathryn's calls had been—had felt—long-distance.

"At the rink. Oh, Dad, I'm sorry about last night. I thought they were just going to show me *skating* with Lisa—both of us looking alike, looking 'normal'—so I gave them the video you made of our Home Movies. But then the newscastress wanted to show that close-up clip, too. And I'm worried Lisa got upset—"

"So your mother told you?" Dad gave his why-didn't-she-listen-to-me sigh. His voice stayed level. "Try to put it out of your mind, Kathryn. We don't—we never—know for sure. What sets Lisa off."

"'Off'?" Kathryn leaned on the phone's metal shelf. "Lisa went off?"

"Yes." Another deeper sigh. "We think it was seeing herself onscreen up-close, so—so awkward next to you and the other TV people. Seeing how she looked and moved differently, relatively speaking. . ."

"Oh, God," Kathryn burst out. "God, Dad, I didn't think it through at all! I *never* should've let them run that damn clip, ask those damn questions. I was so insensitive to Lisa, to all of you—" She paused so he could cut in; but he wasn't one to dole out false reassurance. "What *exactly* happened?"

"Look, Kathryn." Dad's lowest let's-not-fly-off-the-handle voice. "Lisa started clapping in the middle of your interview, right after they showed the Home Movie clip. 'Inappropriate clapping,' her school would've deemed it. A 'ploy' to 'get attention' they'd have informed us." Another sigh. "And she wouldn't stop, Kathryn. She clapped harder and louder and then it became. . ." Dad coughed. "Lisa raised her arms and kept clapping, only now she was slapping her face. Slapping both sides at once. Bruising herself, I'm afraid."

Kathryn rested her forehead against the phone. Icy dirty metal.

"—But we know, of course, you didn't mean to cause any such reaction. Your *mother* feels it might have been the word 'special,' but Lisa's heard that word all her life. Her 'Special Classes,' 'Special Needs Counselor'—"

"Not from me." Kathryn faced the ice: its blue-gray depths submerged yet visible, like bruises. "Lisa hadn't heard those words from *me*. . ."

"No. Perhaps not."

Kathryn felt her eyes tear up at her father's disappointed-in-you tone. "Oh, Dad, please just let me *talk* to Lisa now—"

"Tonight," Dad answered decisively, a manager closing a Digital company meeting. "After your performance we'll talk. As your mother told you. But Kathryn. Listen to me. From now until then, we—all of us, Lisa, too, in her own way—want you to focus on this, this opportunity you've been given. This big chance."

Shadow of a ghost of a chance, she wanted to tell him. Instead she mumbled a graceless good-bye and hung up. She slung her skates over her shoulder. She brushed by a black-haired teenage boy in the rink archway, wishing she'd worn a wool muffler like his. Half his face hidden.

Bitter gritty wind woke her. She leaned her full weight against it. True cold: stunning after the tame refrigerated cold of the rink. Ice needles bit her face. She trudged forward in a whirl of snow, her shins aching. Maybe this, Kathryn found herself thinking, was how everything felt to Lisa. A gigantic effort, leaning your whole self against a relentless frozen wind.

Would it blizzard again? Would the theater cancel her show? And how—Kathryn bowed her head lower—how could she wonder such things, having just learned Lisa had gone off over her? That she'd slapped her face harder than this wind was whipping Kathryn's? The wind tilted her sideways but Kathryn kept walking, determined despite her guilty thoughts to get home in time for a quick restorative nap. Although no doubt it was all in vain. Her skates blew sideways, too, tipping her more off-balance. The higher her zigs, the lower her zags. Pathetic, she decided, to have imagined phoning New York, bragging to her ex-agent.

Kathryn clenched her jaw, her ponytail blindfolding her. No matter how far she toned herself down tonight, she'd come across as too intense for "Nancy." They'd cast someone prettier and blander, someone like Tara Kelly, a costar of Kathryn's from Cape Cod Summer Stock. Twice Kathryn's bra size and half her talent. An embittered thought Kathryn usually tried to squelch. But she couldn't stop it now anymore than she could stop the mini-blizzard sweeping over deserted Kennedy Plaza. Tara Kelly; God. Wish I could give *her* kneecaps a good whack.

Too bad, Kathryn reflected as she turned onto her street, I'm all wrong for Tonya. Blond stocky Tonya Harding, hiring a hit man to cripple her rival. All wrong outside, Kathryn ammended silently, but maybe not inside. She paused to breathe. The wind had lost its force for her. Sheltered from it by her brick building, Kathryn glimpsed her own snow-blurred face in the first window she passed. Looking twenty-nine at least; thirty even, today. If she didn't land the part of twenty-four-year-old "Nancy," would she wind up teaching high-school drama for real, for good? Hell no, Kathryn told herself. Dad was right; she had to seize this chance.

She glanced at the wood kiosk by her walk, seeing the black and white blur of a new flyer. Was it covering her own *Maddie Mill Girl* flyer? A Xeroxed photo of a striking face: a pale young man with a black goatee and black bangs as dense as Lisa's. Black eyes framed by rectangular glasses. Another would-be star.

Knee-deep in snow, Kathryn bulled toward her door, her nose running. Tea with honey and an hour hunched over her vaporizer, but what if her voice still cracked? Or came out hoarse and weak? She blinked, her eyes too cold to tear up. Automatically, Kathryn told herself to remember this hopeless feeling. To use it tonight when poor Maddie faced the black cloth that represented her bleak future.

Where am I going?

Nowhere.

Kathryn fumbled for her keys, her gloved hands shaking. The keys jangled wildly. Feeling so low now might be good later. After her hot tea and hot shower, she'd swing back up. Tree her troubles and kick ass. But first she needed her nap. She couldn't afford to look or feel— she stabbed her key into the lock, deciding she'd best wait till tomorrow to view her nude video—too old.

2.

*Kathryn Byrne, a graduate of Lowell High and Boston University's
drama department, has most recently appeared with the Merrimack
Repertory Company. Her roles at MRC have included the lead in*
Prelude to a Kiss, *Emily in* Our Town *and Marianne in* Tartuffe.
Other favorite roles include: Dorothy in The Wizard of Oz *(Boston
Children's Theater), Tracy Lord in a* Philadelphia Story *revival (Cape
Cod Summer Theater), and Miranda in* The Tempest *(Bennington
Shakespeare Festival).*

Classy but small-time, Daniel Sanders decided as he skimmed his
program and jiggled his foot, guarding his front-row seat. This latest
venue was a distinct step down. So playing Nancy K. in the first-ever
TV Movie of her saga would be a coup for Kathryn B. A huge coup.
Daniel straightened his faux glasses.

. . .*Her film credits include regional TV ads for Nantucket
Nectars and Bennington College and an appearance in the 1990
TV Movie* LIGHTS IN THE SKY.

Wait; hadn't he seen that? Something about UFOs, about sexually
repressed coeds in a fancy dancy women's college, all but the semi-
famous lead killed in the first half-hour? Daniel chewed his half-
sucked Hershey's Kiss. A sizable crowd was gathering around him, he
realized as he raised his head from the program. Nervously, he fingered
the foil condom in his jeans' front pocket. (One of Kenny Rogers's
condoms, wedged amidst cracker crumbs in the cushions of the fold-
out couch Daniel slept in by night and his mother by day). Daniel
rested his hands on the wood handle of the preppy umbrella he'd
stolen from the Harvard Coop.

A tweed shoulder pressed his. Despite the blizzard this afternoon, the 100-seat theater was full, some people standing in the back near the ostentatiously tanned camera crew of two. As if toward a sun, the pale winter faces of Lowell kept turning toward that pair of boyish-looking middle-aged Californians.

"—Flown out from L.A. especially to tape her performance," the tweedy man wedged beside Daniel murmured to his fellow Lowell University professor-type.

"—So unfair, how it turned out today," a woman behind Daniel was telling her seatmate in a louder surer voice. "In Lillehammer, I mean. That tarty Ukrainian girl taking the gold. You wonder if they'll even go ahead with the TV movie when all Nancy won was a silver. Maybe we oughta ask that to *this* Nancy-girl; they said in the lobby she's gonna do a Q & A after the show. . ."

Daniel Sanders raised his brows. Disappointed to hear the results of the Skate-Off, which he was videotaping, but pleased to hear of the Q & A. *May I lose my virginity to you tonight, Miss Byrne?* The house lights blinked their warning. No; of course, he had to stay subtle, stay cool. Daniel readjusted the glasses he'd lifted from an eye doctor's display, samples with nonprescription lenses. Woody Allen but less goofy: dark, rectangular frames. The glasses made Daniel feel old as he studied the program's black-and-white soft-focus head shot of Kathryn Byrne.

He touched her face with his fingertip. But he didn't dig in with his nail as he'd done on an old snapshot of his mother looking like an un-kidnapped Patricia Hearst. A sweet-seeming girl posing on her daddy's sunny lawn beside a black-haired boy whose own face had been scratched out by Mother's sharper nails. Gently now, Daniel wiped his fingerprint smudge off Kathryn Byrne's vibrant face. Her cheekbones worthy of K. or A. Hepburn. Classy to the max.

C'mon, Daniel urged, willing the house lights to go down. Shows or movies could never start soon enough for him. He shut his program like a menu. I know what I want, he thought. As the lights began to dim, he leaned back in his seat, savoring the rightness of the black turtleneck he'd filched from his mother's drawer (tight on him, but that in a different way felt right) and (because Kathryn Byrne might well

71

see these, too) his newest cotton briefs: freshly laundered at Scrub-a-Dub. Behind the round glass window, his clothes had churned like his stomach. As the theater went black, Daniel felt safely hidden in this crowd, its smell of damp wool and cough drops and muffled sweat and fresh snow.

Then, with the light, came Kathryn. Entering strong: her loose hair aflame, red-brown-gold; her eyes pale yet fierce. All the stage light seemed to emanate from inside Kathryn. Her ghostly day-face came to life: burningly white above her black high-necked 1800s dress. She held up her hands, fingers spread. They alone looked old, the raw hands of a Mill Girl. Her voice entered strong, too: clear but husky as if she'd been breathing Mill dust and flax all day. *Maddie Malloy,* she told them. She delivered her new name with a force that made Daniel sit up straight and a warmth that made him unafraid to lean closer.

—*Must seem most strange to all of you,* she was telling them, raking her gaze over the whole house and catching—Daniel felt sure—his eye. Then she was sweeping to the far side of the stage, describing with her words and open-country strides her farm-girl childhood. Back and forth she strode like something wild displayed in a cage with no bars. Nothing between you and it.

Kathryn let loose a rowdy laugh and everyone was laughing together, Daniel too. Then Kathryn snipped it short like a thread she'd spun (suddenly she was seated at a giant mock loom). There she froze her pose for the first brief blackout.

Onstage, Daniel was thinking, Kathryn Byrne's blank street-face had turned into the face of a potential Tanya, terrorist-heiress. Or a Tonya, killer-skater. The lights blinked on. Yes: Daniel saw that same untamed flash in Kathryn's gaze and that same animal tension in Kathryn's stance.

A flashback: a youthfully light-footed Kathryn was dancing with her invisible sister. She circled the stage gaily in light that was suddenly sunlight. *Thinking of her real-life mental-case sister?* came the motherly murmur behind Daniel. The rest of the crowd stayed hushed; Kathryn spun in place. Slower and slower, her skirts hooping out.

Deeper than Nancy's, Daniel decided in the whirl of pause between words. An artist's, not an athlete's grace.

Goddamn girl-grace. Kathryn Byrne stood poised above him at the stage edge as if about to leap into the crowd. She was declaring her love for a farm boy straight to the camera in back. And Daniel was staring up into her flared nostrils. (How he loved it when Nancy Kerrigan flared hers; when the fierceness only he saw in Nancy showed through—showed even more vividly in this Kathryn Byrne, this actress born to play *his* Nancy).

With another black wheeling whoosh of skirts, Kathryn swept back to center stage, where she belonged. She knelt at her sister's grave. Daniel imagined her kneeling before him, sucking his now gradually hardening cock. She clasped her raw-looking hands in prayer, her fingers splayed and knuckles standing out.

Mill Girl hands, Daniel reminded himself, trying to deflate his erection.

Flushed now in his turtleneck, he leaned farther forward to hide it. As Kathryn strode to her loom, as his cock inexorably hardened, Daniel lost the thread of the cornball plot. He simply listened as if to music to her bell-like voice. Simply watched her face change: each emotion clearer and more intense than any he'd ever experienced himself. Love now, as she rose from her loom. The next blackout startled Daniel. He blinked, his eyes dry from staying open so wide.

Lights up, and Kathryn was laughing again, this time flirtatiously, passionately. *Teach me,* Daniel found himself thinking, his eyes half-closed. He shifted in his seat, arranging his coat to shelter his hard-on. (A historic hard-on; before tonight he'd only gotten hard for actresses on TV, never for anyone live).

Center stage again, Kathryn spun around fast, in terror. Had he—Daniel—ever felt real terror or real joy? Anything real? *No,* Kathryn Byrne protested. But it was true: her boyfriend was gone or dead. So she was back in the Mill, for good. Gaunt-looking all at once, she entered into a final sad dance with a bolt of cloth. As she struggled to contain it, it enveloped her. She turned, half-staggering. Daniel tensed, ready despite his hard-on to leap up and catch her. Kathryn's arms

73

stretched wide, her expressive back frozen in a Y (a bit much, Daniel thought even as his eyes brimmed with foolish tears; a bit Jesus Christ-esque). She jolted one elbow low to break the shape.

A real-looking jolt. Was she really losing control? She staggered around again so the cloth hid her. The lights went black, then white. Kathryn had vanished: the mountainous black cloth left limp behind her, the stage barren. Just as the crowd around Daniel breathed in, be-lieving she might not return, Kathryn reappeared, striding back on. She bowed before them.

Her mile-wide smile snapped everyone back to life. Daniel Sanders began clapping a second before everyone else, leading them. Applause burst forth like—he thought, barely keeping himself in control under his coat—an ejaculation.

Kathryn Byrne stood straight: an Olympic winner on the highest platform. A Nancy who *had* won the gold.

Daniel was clapping so hard his hands hurt. The woolly sweaty audience rose on the wave of their own applause: everyone standing except Daniel, scared his still-hard cock might show. He stayed hidden by the thighs and hips on either side of him, by the arms pumping above him like his heart.

One elbow bumped the glasses Daniel had forgotten he was wear-ing. But his own hands clapped on, in time with everyone else's. A gangly Don Knotts man in a red tie and a classy-for-Lowell suit rose from the front row to present Kathryn with a bouquet. The applause passed its peak, steadied. Daniel, still clapping madly, imagined ris-ing, too, and unzipping his pants and handing Kathryn his hard-on. She bowed more deeply. The roses matched the auburn of her hair and the lipsticked but real-seeming red of her lips. One final gold-medal smile.

Although the ovation around him was dying down, Daniel pounded his palms all the harder. He pleaded with his eyes for Kathryn Byrne to keep standing onstage, keep charging up this pale-faced crowd with the fake-yet-real feelings that had swept them all to their feet. The realer-than-real feelings that woke his virgin cock and speeded his vir-gin heart, still.

Teach me. Daniel formed with each clap the clasped hands of a beggar. *Teach me, teach me.*

Kathryn had already switched herself off. That, she'd decide later, was the problem. She was stepping toward her curtained corner, ready to drop her roses and rip into her Hershey's bar (she'd only forced down oatmeal before the show and now she felt famished) when Mr. Ron Whitman, codirector of the Lowell Arts Council and member of the MRC board, gripped her elbow.

Wait, he told her, breathless from sprinting across the stage. Hadn't she received his note? Hadn't Mr. Olaf (the surly stagehand known as Old Olaf) given her that note? Chinless Mr. Whitman's eyes bulged like Gene Wilder's as he rushed to explain: the Arts Council had scheduled a Q & A for Kathryn with the audience; Mr. Whitman had brought along a videotape of her interview from the night before; hadn't she seen Old Olaf setting up the monitor?

Kathryn nodded at Mr. Whitman's rapid words, hearing the audience: so weirdly wrongly still in their seats. Gathered, now, in a murmurous and expectant hush. So Kathryn in her scratchy Maddie dress let Mr. Whitman in his funereal suit and jazzy tomato tie lead her back out. As in her worst dreams, she found herself stepping onstage without knowing her lines.

While Mr. Whitman had been talking, Old Olaf had set up a giant-sized TV and a stool. Now Kathryn perched on that stool, stiff-spined, watching in the sudden darkness as the screen lit up: Kathryn Byrne last night, poised yet tense.

So how could *I* ever be a film actress? she wondered. Then, springing to her own defense, she remembered that she wasn't acting last night. She was trying to be herself; one art she couldn't master. But as always she *looked*—in the monitor—several degrees better on film than in life.

Frozen atop her dunce-cap stool, Kathryn watched her prettier self tell the newscastress how much she wanted to play "Nancy"; how she'd skated for years and could do the easier jumps; how she and Lisa had loved to skate together.

Then she was stammering to explain Lisa: how we all had our "Special Needs," didn't we? (This remark drew scattered polite laughs from the crowd in the Lowell Visitors' Center Auditorium, laughs that made Kathryn shift on her stool).

The video rolled on relentlessly: the newscastress explaining that they had a Home Movie clip of Kathryn's *skating debut,* of Kathryn Byrne and her *very special sister.* . . a jolt of white. The picture quality shifted to the fuzzier grainier texture of film shot on a Home Movie camera.

First: Kathryn and Lisa as distant skaters on Walden Pond, holding hands, making jittery swoops between other skaters. Both so quick they look, at first, like twins. Plump red-skirted Lisa is almost as tall as Kathryn; almost as graceful, on skates. Her glasses flash when she spins. A panning shot of mottled ice. The scene switches to Kathryn and Lisa on the snowy banks, close-up.

The part that—Kathryn fidgeted, her stool squeaky—she shouldn't have let them show. But you're so sweet together, the newscastress had insisted.

Thirteen-year-old Kathryn models her skating skirt with jerky flourishes: hands on her hips, head tossed back, red-brown ponytail swinging and shining. On the tendrils that frame her sharp pretty face, starlets of snow glitter.

Another blur of sunstruck white. Ten-year-old Lisa lurches into the light, her ponytail half-undone. Camera-shy and clumsy, off the ice. She stomps the snow; she chews her red-mittened hand. A string of drool glints as Lisa jerks her hand from her mouth. Her eyes glint, too, behind her strapped-on glasses.

Angry eyes, Kathryn thought now, watching. If, she added to herself, you didn't know Lisa. Eagerly, Lisa onscreen turns and runs toward her big sister.

But she stumbles in the snow and—the film skips so she seems teleported—falls on her knees at Kathryn's feet. Gazing up from under her mussed bangs, Lisa chokes out urgent silent words. Begging her big sister to skate some more? Electric scratches flicker around Kathryn. In slow-motion, she nods. Lisa—released from a spell—scrambles to her feet, spinning and laughing. Her ponytail comes undone, her thick springy hair bursting loose. Not to be upstaged, Kathryn hurls a sparkling handful of snow. The camera tracks it. White-out.

Kathryn Byrne winced. She felt the audience in the Lowell Auditorium stir in their seats. A few tittered. Then twenty-nine-year-old Kathryn was back onscreen with the newscastress, the film quality clear again. A return to real life from a dream. The newscastress thanked Kathryn for *sharing* her memories of her sister and wished Kathryn luck in her performance tomorrow night. Her "audition" for the role of Nancy Kerrigan. Kathryn Byrne flashed her Nancy smile. Alone of all her interview expressions, it appeared genuine.

Lights up. Kathryn stood so fast her stool wobbled. Was it her imagination or was there a sense, in this crowded overly warm auditorium, that something shameful had just been witnessed? Bracing her knees, she blinked out into the quiet crowd. How cruel it seemed to her now, given her sister: the Princess game Lisa used to love. Lisa kneeling to make her breathlessly jumbled requests; play-Princess Kathryn hesitating before, almost inevitably, granting them.

"Questions?" Eager-beaver Mr. Whitman asked in his Amateur Actor voice. He stood at the stage edge, one foot planted on the steps leading off. From the murky dark, several prompt pale hands shot up.

"How do you feel, Ms. Byrne, about what happened in Lillehammer today—?"

"Oh stop—" Kathryn halted the question with a shaky hand. "Please don't *tell* me what happened in the final skate round because I don't *know* yet. I asked the guys backstage—" (actually there was only Old Olaf, who'd barely grunted at her) "—Not to tell me either so I can watch it later tonight like it's happening live!"

A warm communal laugh. Now that she'd dispelled the tension she'd sensed, why couldn't she relax? Her pulse was thumping, her empty stomach fizzing.

"What?" Kathryn had to ask, realizing she'd missed the next question. She strained her smile. Guided by no blocking, she stepped forward. The timid question was being launched again by a teenage girl too far back to see.

"—An actress myself someday—wondering if you had any, any tips or—?"

"Tips?" Kathryn echoed. "Well, your. Your school must have a drama program? I see—a few of my own Workshop students here tonight. . ." She scanned the crowd and spotted student faces alternately smirking at her and averting eager-to-be-seen gazes. "So that's— a good first experience. . ."

God, she was sounding idiotically bland. Kathryn could see the front-row faces now, some of them Lowell celebrities: a local TV sportscaster; Terri Antonelli, an MRC costar who'd left a Break-a-Leg message this afternoon on Kathryn's machine. Plus the goateed face from the flyer Kathryn had noticed today.

That young man watched her intently as, from the middle of the crowd, another question rumbled forth, something about her sister.

"What?" Kathryn took another step toward the edge, sweating in this heavy dress. In two sets of lights. The California camera crew was still filming her. Their camera's twin red lights beamed like distant fiendish eyes.

". . .And so." The grandfatherly voice held an accusatory edge. "So I was wondering, Miss Byrne, how your *sister's* been affected by your career, by seeing herself on television last night, how *she's* handling all this. . ."

Kathryn swallowed, her throat dry. The old man was so hunched she couldn't see him. As she squinted in the white vibration of the lights, she remembered a cartoon show Lisa loved. Luminous clay animals that Lisa watched so hard she believed *she* was causing them to change shape.

"My sister Lisa—" Kathryn tried to lick her lipsticked lips, her tongue sticking. She swallowed again, her mouth so dry her head felt like it was made of clay, glazed clay. "My sister Lisa is—"

Very special to me. These absurd words hung in her mind, unsaid. Kathryn blinked into the stage lights. Beyond them, she felt the all-important red camera lights burning like Lisa's deepest trance-stare. Kathryn's pause enlarged around her. The polite quiet was shifting into an uneasy all-the-more rapt silence.

"Lisa. . ." Kathryn swallowed again. *Lisa needs some water,* she wanted to say. She blinked and pictured twenty-six-year-old Lisa clap-slapping her face, her clay head shattering between her hands. "Wha— what was the question—?"

"—Simply wanted to know, Miss Byrne, did your sister see herself on television last night, in that rather odd film excerpt? And how did she—I'm curious about her side here—react?"

My sister Lisa. Kathryn tried to turn, her feet welded to the stage. *Rather odd.* Her shoes heavy as melted-down skates. Her body swaying. Control yourself, she told herself sternly the way Mom often told Lisa. Kathryn staggered back one step. The audience drew a collective Oh-My-God-Is-She-Losing-It? breath.

Maybe she swayed again. *No,* she shouted to Lisa, tottering atop the seesaw. But Lisa hopped free. *No,* Kathryn shouted again as Lisa's end flew up.

Then the drop. The stage—like the rink—tilted sideways, tipping, dumping her. A jolt to her shoulder first. She blinked and found the world sideways. Her stickily made-up face pressed floorboards that were dusty and scuffed and mapped with masking tape marks. Why was she lying here in front of all these people? Beyond the lights, they were rising, head after head.

Kathryn pressed her palms to the wood. A mighty push-up. She shoved the floor: setting her world upright, scrambling to her feet. Skirts in her fists.

"I—I'm OK—" she called out, everything still askew. The audience, which should have been seated, was standing; Mr. Whitman in his flaming-tomato tie was leading a charge toward her, followed by Terri Antonelli.

"Water, I'll get her some water," Terri called out in a stagey elated voice.

"I'm OK, I'm OK," Kathryn felt herself protesting. The person who reached her first came up on her blind side. He gripped her elbow like a proper escort and pressed into her palm a Hershey's Kiss—that pointy hardened-nipple shape—which she popped onto her tongue. A rush of saliva and bracing bittersweetness. Dazedly grateful, Kathryn

Byrne stumbled with her new escort into the musty unlit wings. Then she turned to see, first, her own white wide-eyed face reflected in this tall young man's rectangular glasses.

"Th-thanks," she told the face from the flyers: eyes pupil-filled; hair and goatee lushly black; plum lips parted to speak.

"Kathryn—?" Mr. Whitman called onstage. She pawed open the dust-furred curtains blocking her quickest path to escape.

"Gotta go," she mumbled through melting chocolate. She ducked into Old Olaf's passageway between a rack of lights and a scrim. She shouldered through like a mole, blind but sure of its frantic steps. At the end, she gasped for air. How utterly unprofessional to run off like this. To faint in the first place.

Beneath the EXIT sign, Kathryn grabbed her coat and purse. The voices behind her were many. But only one body seemed to be pushing through her passageway, making the scrim shudder. Kathryn swallowed her Hershey's Kiss. Pressing with her sore shoulder, she bucked open the rear door.

Blew it, she thought as she faced the bitter cold. I blew it.

She braced herself in the doorway. The first wave of what she knew would be an ocean of humiliation hit her. She bowed her bared head and stepped forward, letting the EXIT door swing behind her. Kathryn's stage shoes barely dented the crusted-over snow. Just before the door shut, she heard another shoulder buck against it. Only one person— she realized with an irrational pang of disappointment—had followed her. Half-annoyed and half-glad, Kathryn Byrne turned her head to see who on earth it could be.

3.

Afterward, it would be difficult for Daniel Sanders to reconstruct exactly how he wound up alone with Kathryn Byrne in her apartment (though he would try to relive each step, over and over). It would be even more difficult for Kathryn Byrne to reconstruct (not that she wanted to, but she would be forced to, over and over) exactly how she wound up alone with him.

"Thanks, but I'm all right now," Kathryn shouted when she saw who had followed her. The frozen clouds of her shout dissipated between them in the Staff Parking Lot. Turning from him, Kathryn lifted her broadcloth skirts and crunched in the leaky stage-shoes over to her Toyota. Still shaky from shock, she fumbled with her ice scraper, her hands aching without gloves.

"Oh, thank you," she found herself saying as the young man in black crunched forward to help. (Kathryn was used to men of various ages materializing to push her out of snowdrifts). Shoving her hands in her skirt pockets and shooting glances over her shoulder, she watched him scrape her frozen windows. She ducked behind the Dumpster—he bowed his head, too, behind her car, its engine still off—as the EXIT door thumped open.

"Miss Byrne?" Ron Whitman called out the opening. "Are you there?"

After the door thudded shut, Kathryn edged closer to her car. Despite her light head, she managed to thank her helper and rally some small talk.

"S-seen your face on a flyer. Are you some kind of—performer or—?"

"Poet," Daniel Sanders found himself filling in with an assurance not his own. He chipped a big ice chunk from her windshield. Tone,

81

he knew, was crucial here. "I—I give Readings sometimes at the Sundance Café. And I—well, I just graduated from Lowell University and I'm about to have my first book published by—" (the name came to him from the Sundance stacks) "—Loam Press."

He watched Kathryn Byrne nod, buying it. "I think I've heard of them. . ."

He nodded back as if this were to be expected. (*How* did he get so brilliant?)

Then Kathryn was gathering up her Mill Girl skirts and sinking into her front seat. Yet she kept her car door open as her engine revved. She stared up at him, lit by her inner car light. Her green eyes in their stage makeup looked huge. Not fierce now, but anxiously glazed as she thanked him yet again. Daniel nodded and stepped back. After her door slammed and her engine rumbled and her wheels spun against the icy snow, he wound up pushing her Toyota.

Rocking it first: his shoulders braced and his feet dug into the snowbank. He grunted when the car finally rocked free, rolling onto crusted snow. Kathryn halted it, risking a loss of momentum. Did he need a lift? she called through her window. Kennedy Plaza would be great, Daniel Sanders answered. He feigned surprise when she told him that was just where she was heading.

So: incredibly, Daniel sealed himself and Kathryn Byrne together in her Toyota's freezing front seat. She sat inches away, her legs lost in her mass of skirts. Daniel's own knees stuck up high. He coughed; she jolted into Drive.

"So those cameras," Daniel began as she turned onto well-plowed Market Street. Instinctively, he was using the softer breathier voice he'd concocted for the AIDS Bereavement Group he'd visited only one night, leaving halfway through, ashamed of himself for once. "They really were there to tape your show as an audition for this Nancy Kerrigan movie?"

She gave a stage-sized sigh: a glamorous cloud of frozen breath like cigarette smoke. Daniel could smell her Hershey's Kiss.

"Yeah, yeah, my 'big break.' I guess I blew it pretty bad at the end there. Their camera caught it all. God. I can't believe I fucking fainted in front of all those people. Sorry," she added, touching her still-lipsticked lips as if to slip the "fucking" back inside. "Sorry to unload on you. I mean, I don't know you at all. But, but—" (Daniel was nodding encouragingly; go on, go on). "But you *do* remind me of an old friend, AJ Schwartz. My best friend in Lowell High, see. These days he's always telling me how I should move to L.A. with him. God, he's waiting right now for me to call and say that tonight went great, say I'm gonna fly out there, break into film. But instead all I'll be telling him is—I blew it."

She braked the car to a sullen stop. A red light glowed through the cold dark like melted cherry candy. "You didn't blow it," Daniel told Kathryn.

"Really?" she asked, reminding him of Diane Keaton as Annie Hall. *Really, do-you-think-so, really?*

"The *show* is what matters, not what happened after," he assured her. Straining not to jiggle his damn teenaged knee. "And in that show, you were—" (Gay; sound safely gay.) "Fan-*tas*-tic."

"Oh, no no. I felt I was way 'off' tonight, really, I—"

"Listen, no, you *are* going to be 'Nancy,'" Daniel Sanders insisted. Her car plowed forward onto what he remembered not to act like he knew was her street. "So you'd better get yourself home fast to watch the big Skate-Off. . ."

"Oh my God, the *Skate-Off!*" Kathryn halted her car at the curb. Her eyes fixed on her car's clock: quarter past nine.

"Don't worry." Daniel started to touch her arm but stopped himself. "You *know* they'll save Tonya and Nancy for the very end."

"Oh, and I *do* want to see that. Just in case." She shifted into Park, turning to him. Her lined eyes and lipsticked mouth stood out, dark in her made-up face. "Well, anyhow. You said Kennedy Plaza? It's right down the sidewalk. Thanks again for helping me so much; that Hershey's Kiss saved my life." Daniel dared a sheepish smile. "Hey, what's your name, anyhow? I want to look for your book. . ."

My book? he stopped himself from asking. He drew a deep breath for his largest leap yet. (Tone most especially crucial here.) "Daniel Sanders."

"What?" Predictably, Kathryn Byrne's eyes widened further, her face a mix of real and stylized shock. "You? You're the one whose name I've seen—?"

Daniel waved his hands—wrists a bit loose—and answered self-mockingly, as if he'd said it many times: "Oh, I know, I know: those *flyers.*" He rolled his eyes. Then he launched into the monologue he'd planned today at Scrub-a-Dub Laundromat. "—This crazy promo stunt. See, the Sundance Café posted these flyers that had only my *name* on them; then this week only my *face*. And next week: the whole thing together with my Poetry Reading dates. A gimmick, I know, but—" Another shamelessly limp-wristed wave of his hands. "What can you do when you're a—" He shot her a companionable glance. "Lowell 'celebrity'?"

She bit. "Yeah, what can you do?" She shook her head with him, returning his wry fellow-Lowell-celebrity grin. "It *works* in a way. Because I've seen your name and face so much, I feel like I already sort of 'know' you. . ." She fiddled with her key, maybe not wanting to shut off her engine, not wanting to climb out of this half-warmed car, into the frozen dark.

"I don't suppose," Daniel further dared to suggest in his great new Daniel-the-gay-poet voice, "you'd care for some company at the Skate-Off? I didn't listen today either. And *I'm* rooting for Tonya to triumph, myself."

Kathryn Byrne felt herself laugh loudly, as if at a cast party. Drunk on failure tonight the way she used to get drunk on success? "Not Tonya," she gasped. "That'd be bad for 'my' movie. Though Nancy *is*— God—so damn bland. Maybe I don't *want* to play her; maybe it's *good* that I blew it tonight. . ."

Daniel Sanders rushed to protest again. As he reeled off earnest-sounding reassurances, Kathryn stared out at her unshoveled walk and unlit windows. She couldn't stand the thought of going in there alone. Sinking onto her couch; slumping down low enough to feel the full force of her humiliation, its weight.

And this young man, as she turned to invite him in, seemed so pleased. So harmless and sweet. Like a high-school boy, almost, trying to act casual. Waving his long-fingered hands. *Was* he gay, like AJ? They climbed out together into the cold. No doubt, Kathryn knew, she was half-crazy to let him come in. But, God, she'd go all-the-way crazy if she had to spend this night alone. If she had to phone Mom or AJ, anyone whose genuine sympathy would make her feel pitiable.

Her keys chattered in her hand. Leftover fits of snow swirled around her. Daniel Sanders raised an expensive-looking wood-handled umbrella above her head, leaving his own hatless head exposed. Kathryn's stage skirts tripped her up in the walkway snow. Briefly, polite Daniel took her elbow.

"Maybe I've got a touch of flu." Kathryn auditioned that explanation as she unlocked her door. But she knew it wasn't anything physical that had made her—in front of so many strangers!—faint. She swung her door.

She hit the lights lest this stranger get the wrong idea. Adopting a brisk manner, Kathryn bustled inside and shook snow off her skirts. "I *am* recovering from a bad cold—" (actually, that had been weeks ago, at Christmas) "—and I was so nervous I didn't *eat* much before the show, which was so *dumb* of me, a violation of basic Professional Performer Procedure, Acting 101..."

Kathryn faced Daniel Sanders in the light, startled by how young he seemed behind his rectangular aging-beatnick glasses. Just out of college, he'd said, but he seemed maybe eighteen, nineteen. He turned from her gaze and studied her living room. It looked embarrassingly spare to her own eyes.

"Got to get the heat on here." She wondered as her numb cold fingers adjusted the heating dial if she *were* having some sort of breakdown. Acting like a nineteen-year-old herself: inviting in this perfect stranger, this boy.

"Is that your sister Lisa?"

"Yes, oh yes." Kathryn spun back around, her skirts flaring. Suddenly she was hungry to see Lisa's plump sweetly dazed teenage-girl face, framed beside the door along with a childhood shot of the two of them dressed as Halloween witches.

"Lisa's stare—" Daniel Sanders focused on the photo of teenage

Lisa without her glasses. Then on an old newspaper photo of the Beatles Kathryn had framed and hung beneath it. "So soulful, like young George Harrison's."

"*Yes—*" Kathryn burst out, genuinely incredulous. "*I* think that too! Lisa's eyes—see?—mystical, like his. And Lisa's always had her hair cut in those Beatles-like *bangs*. To hide, to tell you the truth, the bruises she sometimes makes on her own forehead. Anyhow, that newspaper clipping's one my mom saved. I framed it under Lisa because it's just so 'her.' To me. It shows the day the Beatles arrived in America. See? Standing in the windy JFK airport, surrounded by thousands of screaming fans. There's something in poor George's expression—so puzzled and lost and bemused. The quiet Beatle. The photo caption *quotes* him." Kathryn drew herself up in her stage dress, mimicking a British accent: "'So these are Americans. Why, they all seem out of their minds.'"

Daniel Sanders gave her a crooked-toothed grin. Wry, appreciative. He alone of anyone she'd told seemed to get the joke. "And, see," she rushed on, "maybe that's what Lisa—my quiet sister Lisa—*feels* every day watching me and everyone else run around so busy and anxious and ambitious while she. What Lisa wants—seems to want—is to sit and rock and—watch us. Watch so damn *hard*."

"Yeah," Daniel Sanders answered, his voice lower-pitched than before. "In grade school here in Lowell, I'd watch everyone like that, like TV. My mother used to tape the knob of our TV 'on' when she was out, back when I was so little I'd sometimes turn it 'off' accidentally then she'd come home and find me bawling. No wonder I still see real people as looking like, y'know, celebrities. Tonight for instance, that guy who gave you the roses? Did he remind you of Don Knotts?"

"Gene Wilder." Kathryn unbuttoned her coat, beginning to feel at home. "Yeah, I do that, too." She stepped away from their gray puddle of snow. "See people as celebrities, I mean. See all faces as imperfect versions of famous faces. Hey, maybe later tonight we can tell each other who *we* look like."

They laughed together almost comfortably. Or at least, Kathryn felt, not uncomfortably. *Is* this guy gay? she wondered. As she hung up their coats, she sensed that she might be alone with a straight male for the first time in six months. Fifty-five-year-old Peter Wynn, with his "New England's Richard Burton" voice, had been her last. He had played her father in *Our Town*, tenderly. He had escorted her home from the cast party, tenderly, too. He'd told her he was her Designated Driver because he hadn't drunk all night because (this was a secret, he thought, though she knew everyone knew) he was a recovering alcoholic. She'd told Peter Wynn she'd had so much wine because, frankly, she *didn't* have any future gigs lined up, except this High School Workshop stint. Peter Wynn had said she shouldn't worry; she was (only relative to you, she'd added silently) so young.

"So." Kathryn shut her closet. How did young Daniel Sanders see her, relatively speaking? As a predatory older woman? "I'm gonna get changed. Turn on Lillehammer if you want." She whisked her skirts over to her bedroom.

As she cold-creamed off her stage makeup and pulled on her Cape Cod Playhouse sweatshirt over her leotard, Kathryn listened to her phone machine. First, for comfort: AJ in L.A. two hours before, *phoning from my—soon to be "our"—apartment just forty-six minutes from Sunset Boulevard. Hey: break a Kneecap tonight, Nancy-to-be.* Then two new messages, both recorded in the last half-hour: first Terri Antonelli's rounded comedienne's voice sounding ominously sympathetic: *What the Hell happened, kid?* Then, worse: Mr. Whitman, his own less expert comic delivery all dried up now. He was *concerned*, he proclaimed—and embarrassed, Kathryn gathered—by her *collapse* and her *abrupt departure*.

Christ, Kathryn Byrne thought as the tape halted with a squeal. "Departure" is right. Maybe I'll have to kiss MRC good-bye. No more Rep. Theater; no Nancy. Hello again, Lowell High. Pulling extra hard, Kathryn twisted her hair into a rubber-banded ponytail. God: how was she going to tell Mom?

"Excedrin PM—" Kathryn burst out of her bedroom, raising a desperately cheery voice above the Lillehammer sportscasters'. "After a show I always pop a couple Excedrin PMs to wind down; everyone does; but then a friend of mine from Cape Cod Rep., Tara Kelly? She's got the lead in the Midwest touring company of *Phantom of the Opera*—Tara's great, I'm really happy for her—she phoned me from Chicago the other night to tell me she'd read the Excedrin PM bottle label at, like, 1 A.M. in her hotel room? And it said in teeny print that regular doses could cause 'chronic bronchitis,' which Tara thinks explains why everyone in every road company has chronic bronchitis. Which is the last thing *I* need now. So, God, if I can't have my Excedrin PM, I'm gonna have a glass of Gallo. How 'bout you?"

Daniel Sanders raised his head. He blinked at this wired-up Kathryn Byrne from behind his glasses. Shaking himself out of a tentative TV trance. Here he was alone with a live actress; what the Hell was wrong with him?

"Sure." He revived his wry-poet tone. "We'll need it since Tonya's about to 'take the ice.'" Daniel looked back at the screen, trying not to seem disappointed by Kathryn's bared face and unbrushed hair or by the sloppy sweatshirt and jeans she'd pulled on as if he was—of course he was—no one she cared to impress.

Kathryn's kitchenette door swung behind her. Daniel peeled his eyes again from the hypnotic Chinese skater twirling on TV. He scanned this empty motel-like room. The walls stood bare but for a Bennington Shakespeare Festival poster for *The Tempest* with Kathryn Byrne's name printed below the title, first because of the "B," and the framed photos by the door. In the second photo, chubby young Lisa and slender young Kathryn stood face-to-face in pointy witch hats. They both raised claw-fingered hands, casting spells on each other.

From behind a wall, her phone buzzed. "Oh, that's probably my mom, my family—" Kathryn shoved out of the kitchen and slipped back into the bedroom, leaving her bedroom door half-open. Daniel lowered the TV sound.

"Mom?" Kathryn's stagey voice rang out so plainly Daniel felt somehow sorry for her. "Fine, fine, except for. Oh, never mind, Mom: I'll tell you all about the show later. OK? But listen, *Dad* told me today what happened last night with Lisa. And right now I just really want to talk to my sister. Please?"

Daniel felt his own shoulders tense up. Tonya Harding approached the Olympic ice in a tragically unflattering purple-sequined skirt. She clasped her hands in corny "prayer." Her rouge too heavy, her lipsticked mouth too tight.

"Well, OK, Mom." Kathryn's voice went shrill. "OK, then just *hand* her the phone. See if she'll talk once she hears it's me." A long pause; Daniel watched Tonya bobble her first jump. And—incredibly, as Kathryn's voice rang out again—halt her entire routine. "Lisa? Lisa? It's me, Kath. Hey now, sis, c'mon. Come outa dreamland now. *Talk* to me, OK? How's Starlight? She still coughing up hairballs like Mom says? We'll brush her good, the two of us, when I'm home next. OK? Lisa? Oh Lisa, I'm *sorry* the TV showed that silly Home Movie scene. . ."

Then, after a sigh-sized pause—Tonya onscreen was weeping soundlessly, limp-skating toward the judge's stand—Kathryn tried a smaller voice. "Lisa, I *know* you're upset about last night. About the Home Movie thing? Or about something I *said* on TV?" A short pause. Her voice rose in eagerness. "Wha'd you say, Lisa? 'Shull?' *'Shell?'* Can you say it again?"

Daniel waited with Kathryn. Tonya pointed to her skate, gesturing wildly. Daniel's own shoulders sagged when Kathryn's voice gave in. "OK, I can tell you don't want to—or you just plain won't—talk to me right now. So please give the phone back to Mom, OK, Lisa? We'll talk later when *you* want to, OK?"

Another long pause. The Olympic judges pondered Tonya Harding's complaints. Kathryn singsonged in her bright voice: "Oh no, Mom, don't *make* her do anything. Lisa's just—spacing out on me. What's this 'shell' business? That's all she'd say when I asked what she was mad about. 'Shull' or 'shell.' What? 'Spe-cial'? God, you're right; that *is* how she'd say 'Special.' So, God, maybe that *is* it; Lisa's mad that I used that word and I bet she doesn't even know what it *means,* what it's *supposed* to mean. No; no Mom, really, don't make her talk. Really, really; it's fine, everything's fine and look." Daniel felt rather than heard her drawing a deep breath. Onscreen, Tonya was pleading again, weeping again.

". . . Look, Mom, I really can't talk now anyway because there're some *people* here. Yeah, some from MRC and a poet from U. Lowell and, yeah, we're going to watch it together. Now. So: I'll tell you all about tonight—tomorrow."

At her phone click, Daniel inched up the TV volume, leaving it low enough so it could seem to have been on all along. So he could plausibly pretend to have been engrossed in Tonya's public disgrace. The kind of psychodrama he usually relished. Tonya Harding, the TV commentator informed him, had broken a lace on the ice. Or so she was claiming. After rattling cupboards in the kitchenette, Kathryn Byrne reentered the front room as if stepping offstage after a performance that hadn't gone well. Daniel turned from the screen and blinked as if surprised. Kathryn hoisted a jug of red Gallo. A good sign, he knew.

"Sorry I'm such a wreck," she told him flatly, setting two glasses on the TV.

"No, no. You're 'Nancy' and *she's* not the one who's a wreck tonight." Daniel gestured toward the screen, impressed by his own steady hand. Could it be he was calmer right now than Kathryn Byrne herself? "Tonya Harding fell on her first jump and now she's trying to explain to the judges that it was because her skates aren't tied right. . ." Daniel turned the sound up further.

"Tonya *fell*?" Kathryn settled next to him. Together, they watched Tonya Harding's face stretch into a Lucille Ball grimace. She begged the judges to examine the skate she raised so gracelessly fast she almost sliced their noses. Muffled mikes caught Tonya's insistent: *They won't hold me.* The skates, Daniel realized she meant. Her garish gold-bladed skates.

"Oh, please," Kathryn muttered, taking a swig from her glass.

"Still, ya can't help but root for her." Daniel dared one sour sip of wine. "Y'know that kids' magazine, *Highlights,* the one they have in doctors' offices?" Kathryn nodded. Daniel hesitated, worried she'd somehow sense how often he'd visited doctors' offices as a fake patient. Hanging out in waiting rooms, sucking free hard candy and rifling *Highlights* and basking in motherly glances. "See how poor ol' Tonya's still playing 'Goofus' to Nancy's 'Gallant'. . ."

Onscreen, in a backstage hallway at the Olympic rink, shot by a skewed camera—weird, Daniel thought, to remember this wasn't truly "live"—Tonya Harding pressed her palms against a cinder-block wall as if braced for a police frisk. Kneeling, her hapless blond coach fussed with her skate laces.

"You ever notice," Daniel Sanders went on, sinking into a TV trance that was, for once, shared, "how 'beating' is, like, this huge *theme* in Tonya Harding's life? How her Monster Mom 'beat' her with a hairbrush if she'd lose at skate meets; how Tonya always talks about wanting to 'beat' Nancy?"

"'Whip her butt,'" Kathryn added, quoting Tonya. Looking almost as pale and grim as Tonya herself, who was at last taking the ice again. Tonya Harding with her aggressive red slashes of rouge and her skimpy clenched mouth.

Tonya is the only one in gold skates, the nasal sports commentator pointed out. The soundtrack music from *Jurassic Park* thundered forth. Daniel felt Kathryn Byrne beside him hold her breath, rooting for Tonya the Loser now, too.

Steps out of her triple loop, the commentator noted with snippy satisfaction.

"Ol' Tonya skates best back in Clackamas. Practicing for tabloid cameras in that cheapo shopping-mall rink." Daniel faked a wine sip. "Our Scandal Skater."

"Those spins like fits of rage," Kathryn added as Tonya onscreen began to pick up velocity, nailing her next Lutz. A heavy shower of ice chips.

"Now *there's* a part to play," Daniel told Kathryn Byrne as Tonya flashed her feral grin. Her strong pony legs propelled her around the rink, faster and harder than Nancy. Kathryn nodded; Tonya hurtled into her final leap. "What a mix, that Tonya. Tough yet helpless, dumb yet sly. . ."

Nice position on her death-drop spin, the commentator conceded.

The Lillehammer crowd burst into sympathetically heightened applause. Making the most of *their* moment. Tonya Harding threw kisses at the crowd; they threw limp bouquets at her. Daniel formed a bemused smile but cut it short when he side-glanced at Kathryn Byrne, her own face unsmiling.

91

Un. Believable.

At the commentator's bitchy endnote, Kathryn's mouth twitched on one side.

I skated great, Tonya Harding boasted to a huddle of reporters as she gulped into her asthma inhaler. It sounded to Daniel like a line delivered by a bad actress.

"'America is full of Tonyas who want to be Nancys,'" he murmured, quoting the *Boston Globe.* Jiggling his giveaway teenage knee.

"You said it." Kathryn leaned toward him, confiding in a wine-scented rush: "And *I* used to feel like a 'Nancy.' But lately. . ." She took another swallow of wine as Tonya Harding's distinctly mediocre scores flashed onscreen.

5.5, 5.3, 5.4, 5.5, 5.5, 5.6, 5.5, 5.4, 5.4

"Oh God, I can't believe I blew tonight so bad." Kathryn covered her eyes. "Can't believe I said all that stuff on TV last night, hurting my sister so bad. By accident, by carelessness. God, I hope *Lisa* doesn't, deep down, feel that Tonya-Nancy thing about me; 'Course, Lisa's so sweet, so *spiritual,* she'd never be like crude old Tonya. But you never know what's going on inside anyone, in-*side.* . ."

"You said it." Boldly, Daniel inched closer to her, ready to position a comforting arm around her shoulders like a sensitive Tom Hanks type. Her phone buzzed again. Daniel jumped in his skin; Kathryn jumped to her feet.

"Shit, I don't want to talk to anyone. What if it's one of the L.A. guys?"

At the fifth buzz, her machine clicked on. Daniel heard an eager-to-please Jay Leno voice swell out from the live tape.

"Kathryn, great guns! You there? You there? Kathryn, listen up now." (Kathryn Byrne turned to Daniel with wide scared eyes and mouthed: *my agent.*) "—I just spoke to one of the two they sent out tonight. Turns out this one *was* someone, an 'assistant casting director' and—this could be big—he *loved* the show, *loved* you in it, even loved whatever the Hell happened during the Q & A. You collapsed or something when they asked you about your sister or something? Whatever it was, Kathryn, it worked. Forgive me but: the whole sister story could *work* for you the way Nancy Kerrigan's 'legally blind' mother works for her. Not that I'm saying you're faking any faints. But whatever it was—and of course, Kathryn, I pray you're OK—it seems to have fed into this image they want of sweetness and light. Because this *will* be the pro-Nancy version of the saga, the *Disney*-backed version. 'The Kerrigan Courage' is their working title. Anyhow, Kathryn, we'll talk more tomorrow. Get some sleep, Ms. Byrne; we're on a roll!"

As her machine clicked off, Daniel kept his eyes riveted on Kathryn Byrne. While her agent had babbled, her face had transformed itself into her stage face. No makeup now, but the same extra-alive gleam sparked her green eyes. The same charge lit her incredulous, slowly widening smile.

"Did you *hear* that?" Kathryn burst out, giddy with a hopeful lightening inside her chest. Relief, disbelief.

Daniel Sanders, her witness, was nodding at her as if she were suddenly—she could feel it herself, could always feel it—beautiful.

"Congratulations," he told her, his voice so grave she began to believe it might actually happen. She shifted her weight like a surfer. A new wave of excitement was welling up under the other rising waves that hadn't yet crested: her humiliation over her faint and her guilt over Lisa.

"God, I can't *think*, I'm so overwrought. And I can't believe that crap Wally spun out about my sister. I wish everyone would leave my little sister alone. I'm gonna *make* 'em leave her alone! But, God, I gotta say: Wally's really come through for me as an agent. And what if I do get it? I mean, how the Hell am *I* gonna play *her*? Look how crazy-calm that Nancy is!"

Onscreen, on the prerecorded film, Nancy Kerrigan skated onto the ice in gold, her face intent, her hair knotted in a severe bun.

"Nancy loses her oomph with her hair schoolmarmed up that way," Kathryn told Daniel, sitting beside him, intent, too. Grateful to refocus on her TV.

"But it does show off her long neck," he answered as Nancy Kerrigan arched back her head, circling the Olympic rink in her final warm up.

Kathryn Byrne knew that feeling: one last tense round of pacing backstage. She raised her own head high.

"You've sure got the neck to play Nancy," Daniel Sanders murmured. Then, shyly, as if he feared he'd gone too far, he coughed.

"Thanks," Kathryn answered, keeping her tone neutral but feeling pleased inside. Flushed outside. So he was attracted to her, this tall young Daniel. Not handsome, but "attractive," too, in a bony tormented-poet way.

"The swan of Stoneham, that Nancy. Long as she doesn't talk. How're you gonna make your voice as grating as hers? A swan with a goose's honk. . ."

"Ya think I can't do Stoneham-speak?" Kathryn demanded playfully in a Nancy whine. She and Daniel Sanders laughed together, then stopped together. Nancy Kerrigan halted in the center of the ice. She stood poised on her skates as if on a high dive. Her slim arms stiffened, her long legs braced.

This is the moment she's been waiting for, the commentator intoned.

Nancy's music began. Kathryn drew her breath. Nancy glided forward with tentative grace, tensing her upper body for her first jump. *The world is watching,* the commentator reminded everyone in a near-whisper. Kathryn couldn't help but nod. She savored such moments: the first step onto stage, first big line. You know that instant if you're going to spin true. Nancy took off, her gold skirt whirling. Ice sprayed up behind her as she landed hard. *Doubled it,* the commentator informed them, sounding nervous for her. Then elated a few beats later as she spun, touched down, and spun again: a triple-toe combo.

Nailed 'em! the commentator crowed.

"Ha!" Kathryn Byrne shouted, sure that she'd nailed her Nancy role tonight. The Olympics scene shifted to Nancy Kerrigan's rapt adoring parents. Nancy's squinting mother bent so close to her special TV monitor her nose touched its screen. Kathryn felt another stab of guilt over Wally's words about Lisa "working" for her. But she sipped more wine, determined to enjoy this moment she'd been waiting for. Her big break, landed at last. Nancy's ice spritzed up, up, up.

Nailed her Triple Lutz!

Kathryn and Daniel cheered together from their separate sides of the couch. With her big jumps safely behind her, Nancy Kerrigan relaxed into the spirals and loops even Kathryn could do. Close-ups now. Kathryn studied Nancy's strong Irish jawbone. Her own eyes narrowed like Nancy's. Alive, Kathryn thought, setting down her wineglass. How intensely alive Nancy must feel now as she glided toward her finale, throwing back her head and drawing deep breaths.

"Those Nancy nostrils," Daniel Sanders commented. "Her most interesting feature. When she flares them like now, like a racehorse? Her nose more expressive than her mouth—full lips but not, y'know, sensual lips—or even her eyes, which even now seem a bit—how're *you* going to mimic this?—blank."

"*My* Nancy *won't* be 'blank,'" Kathryn answered grandly. "Anyhow, I won't play her by face. I'll play her by body. 'Cause that's where *her* soul resides. . ."

"Yeah!" This Daniel Boy sounded a bit drunk, too, to Kathryn. "Yeah, but it's an athlete's not a—not an artist's soul. . ."

"Mine'll have *both*," Kathryn insisted. As Nancy Kerrigan hurtled into her final leap, Kathryn Byrne held her breath again, imagining herself to be Nancy: this Irish girl from Stoneham, kicking ass when it mattered most. Silly tears sparked Kathryn's eyes as Nancy landed solidly, as she smiled wide in triumph.

Can a smile GET *any bigger?* asked the commentator, choked up himself.

Nancy Kerrigan glided into her final spiral, flinging out her arms and opening her hands to the heavens. Yes, Kathryn Byrne was thinking, her eyes brimful. Must feel like heaven to win so big. She flung out her own arms, almost smacking Daniel Boy, knocking his glasses askew. But he laughed.

"Nancy's 'trademark stars,'" she told him apologetically, opening her hands.

Nancy Kerrigan stood triumphant again in the center of the ice, pelted by flowers. Daniel and Kathryn clapped, Kathryn clapping so hard her palms hurt. She stopped, thinking again of Lisa, her reddened palms when she used to applaud Kathryn's songs. Lisa couldn't stop clapping sometimes: clap-slapping her face last night because Kathryn had called her "special" and Lisa thought that was—a mocking word? Behind the mini-blizzard of TV fuzz, Nancy Kerrigan's blind mother was crying. Kathryn turned to Daniel, who was still clapping.

"*My* Nancy'll have soul," she repeated, making her words slur. Making herself sound higher than she was on a mere glass of wine.

"*Yours* will, oh yes," Daniel answered, his voice above the TV cheers unexpectedly reverent. Cold sober. Kathryn met again her own face reflected in his glasses, vivid and bright-eyed. Wasn't he her first real fan, this soulful poet?

5.9, 5.8, 5.9, 5.9, 5.9, 5.9, 5.8, 5.8, 5.9.

"To Nancy!" Kathryn kicked back the rest of her wine. She grinned, her lips stained. Her face flushed from more than wine. From success-to-be.

And she IS a Fair Lady, the skate commentator was declaring, but not about Nancy. To strains of *My Fair Lady,* Oksana Baiul took the ice. The "orphan girl" from the Ukraine, Kathryn remembered vaguely. Oksana flew into her first spin, light as a hummingbird. So light, Kathryn decided, she made you realize how earthbound and effortful had been Nancy's technically correct spins.

"God," Kathryn pronounced as Oksana flitted across the ice, vamping for the judges. "That girl. Is a star. Betcha she wins it. . ."

"Hey—" Daniel Boy elbowed her ribs. "You *said* you didn't *know* who won!"

"You said *you* didn't," Kathryn protested, shoving his shoulder lightly in turn. "So this orphan kid *did* win the Gold? Not my Nancy?"

Daniel nodded as if he could not tell a lie. "Kerrigan took the Silver. I overheard people in your audience talking before the show. . ."

"Well, shit." Kathryn reached for the TV, snapping off Oksana Baiul midtwirl. "I don't wanna watch *that,* then. Nancy *losing!*" As the TV sucked in its sound, Kathryn turned to Daniel in mock anger. "Why'd you go and tell me?"

Harder than she intended, she slapped Daniel's bony shoulder. He grinned again, endearingly shy. And he stood. Awfully tall: this Daniel

Boy in his tight black turtleneck and loose black jeans. His dark eyes framed by his glasses and his boyish face fringed by his goatee. She blinked. A not-unattractive young man stood above her in her dim apartment. Who did he look like? Maybe a darkly intense Charlie Sheen mixed with a gentle goateed Julian (son of John) Lennon.

"Hey." Daniel Sanders rubbed his shoulder in mock pain, thrilled by Kathryn Byrne's tipsy abandon. *"Nancy* shouldn't go around *hitting* people!"

"Oh yeah?" Kathryn pulled herself up, too. She raised her fists in a boxer pose. "Betcha she—whachamacallit—masterminded the whole attack! So she'd get good and famous even for winning just the second-best Silver!"

"I've known that all along," Daniel told Kathryn, suddenly serious though she laughed as if he were joking. Of course, he reminded himself, forcing a smile in return, she was probably joking herself. Laughing harder now, so he laughed, too. But maybe they were *sharing* the joke of Nancy's hidden black heart? He and Kathryn alone knew, Daniel decided. He felt his own flesh-and-blood heart pump faster. Though his voice remained as relaxed and teasing as hers.

"So you've gotta *play* it that way. *Reveal* the dark side of Nancy!" He waved his hands like a director. "Try it now. Practice Nancy for me; please, Kathryn?"

"Oh no, no," she protested so extravagantly that Daniel knew she liked the request, really. "You just *saw* my whole Maddie show. Besides, I'm outa steam. I've been practicing and practicing all week for that damn camera—"

She pointed toward her half-open bedroom door. Daniel spun round to see a camcorder mounted on the spindly metal legs of a RadioShack tripod.

"What camera?" he asked, already bounding into that doorway. A glimpse of her unmade bed; an hours' old whiff of hair spray. Deftly, Daniel unplugged the wire connecting her bedroom TV to her unlit camcorder.

"No, don't move that," she called from the couch, but languidly.

"I'll be careful." He carried the light tripod and heavy camera out the doorway, the wires stretching. "I'd *love* to film a sample of your Nancy, a private preview? I got some videotaping experience in high— in college." He fussed with the wires, lowering his eyes to hide his half-lie. (The only club he'd joined at Lowell High was Speech and Debate, where A-students videotaped their speeches and sometimes Daniel set up the video machines, goofing around afterward, fascinated like everyone else by the heady sight of his own face onscreen.)

Hurriedly, before she could pretend to protest anymore, Daniel positioned the tripod and camera, which already held a videotape. Then he set the AUTO-START foot-switch device on the floor, midway between her couch and her TV.

"What am I *thinking*? I'm a mess here." Kathryn stood with a lurch.

"Please? Just for fun? I'd love to see what you look like onscreen, please?" Stepping over the video cords, Daniel Sanders knelt in front of Kathryn Byrne.

"Oh, no, don't *kneel!* I'm such a sucker for that." She shook her head but didn't step away. Daniel's eyes were almost level with her breasts, softly outlined under her sweatshirt. "God, seeing my sister kneel in that crazy Home Movie scene made me feel so guilty. But Lisa used to like to! It was a game. She'd beg me to keep singing or keep seesawing with her but I was always so busy—off to play practices; even in Junior High I was doing Children's Theater—and now I wish. . ."

Daniel tensed his arms, ready to embrace her, comfort her. "Then at BU, my first real boyfriend there, God, we got together at a cast party for *The Glass Menagerie,* me as Laura, and the stereo blasting *Rocky Horror Picture Show* songs and he fell on his *knees* in front of me singing, 'Let's Do the Time Warp Again'. . ."

"Let's!" Daniel staggered up from his knees. "Let's jump ahead to when you *are* playing Nancy. Please?"

"Welll. . ." Kathryn turned her back on him and the camera. He watched her matter-of-factly pull off her sweatshirt and jeans, a black leotard underneath. Nancy the athlete changing in a locker room, no trace of striptease. Then—surprise—Kathryn unknotted her ponytail. Tossing back her lavish hair, turning, she posed before him in her leotard, one long leg extended.

"Perfect!" Daniel scrambled behind the video camera. A relief to his speeding pulse to view Kathryn through a lens: miniaturized, colored blue-black and gray-white. Her body floated in his own private TV screen. The date blinked in the lower right corner. *2/26/94.*

"Flare those nostrils," Daniel commanded, fumbling for the zoom button.

Laughing, Kathryn arched her neck dramatically. She met the camera's eye with a stare fiercer and brighter than Nancy Kerrigan could ever muster.

"Beautiful, dahling!" Daniel called out. "Now spin for me, Nancy!"

Still laughing, she spun in his viewfinder, her arms over her head, her face blurred, her hair a grainy dark cloud. Daniel gripped the camera's snout, adjusting the focus like a real director. Never before had he felt so in control. Kathryn transformed by his camera—à la Patricia Hearst and the bank cameras—into a wilder, more alive version of herself.

"Whoa," Kathryn gasped, staggering. "Lisa can spin like this for *hours*—"

"No no; stay in character," Daniel the Director commanded. "You're Nancy, *Nancy* coming outa her final spin!"

Obediently, Kathryn Byrne caught her balance. She raised both arms above her head like Nancy Kerrigan at the end of her performance.

"Yes, yes; let's freeze that and pan here—" Carefully, Daniel tilted the adjustable camcorder, aiming it at her feet then inching up. "Let's capture those Vanessa Williams legs, that Peggy Fleming figure—"

Kathryn was giggling, visibly struggling to keep a straight face.

"—That Audrey Hepburn neck, that Julia Roberts hair, those Katharine Hepburn eyes and cheekbones, that Nancy Kerrigan *smile*—"

Kathryn Byrne let her brightest smile burst forth.

"You're Nancy Kerrigan, only you've *won* the *Gold!*"

As if she believed him absolutely, Kathryn in his close-up widened her tremulous smile. She blinked an extra teary brightness into her eyes.

"Does a smile *get* any bigger?" Daniel asked, light-headed with his own power. With the steady swelling of his cock. Luckily, he was bent over anyway. "Then suddenly," he went on, inspired, watching Kathryn's smiling face go attentively blank. "In her moment of triumph—" (His voice felt strained with the pressure of his erection.) "Nancy Kerrigan 'flashes back' to her attack. And then—then—"

Kathryn's face slipped out of focus in Daniel's viewfinder. She swayed on her feet—deliberately this time?—and finished his sentence in her own inspired-sounding rush. "She up and fucking *faints!*"

Down she went, Kathryn Byrne. Her fake faint indistinguishable to Daniel from her real: her knees going loose, her head tilting like a sleepy child's. Her whole body tipped. She fell sideways again, landing on her shoulder. Which must be, Daniel thought as he AUTO-FOCUSed the camera, doubly bruised.

"F-flashback!" Daniel's voice came out high-pitched, high-schoolish, strangled by his definite hard-on and his tentative alarm. In absolute stillness, in his lens-eye viewfinder, Kathryn's small blue-black body lay curled like a floating fetus. "I- I mean flashback *to* the attack!"

Despite his hard-on straining his jeans, Daniel straightened up behind the camera. He blinked at Kathryn's body, so startlingly solid and near. He breathed the scent of her sweat. Letting the AUTO-FOCUSed camera whir on, hunching to hide his cock, Daniel staggered to her front door as if fleeing a murder scene.

"Wait there—" Impulsively, he seized his wood-handled umbrella. He shook it out, droplets dotting her linoleum. When he turned back around, Kathryn was sitting on the floor. She blinked into the red camera light as if wondering what it was. As if she had, in fact, fainted, blacked out. Or was this an act, too?

"*Shane Stant* approaches with his *collapsible baton!*" Exaggerating his villainous hunch—but couldn't she see the bulge in his jeans anyway?—Daniel crept forward, raising the umbrella in his fist. So heavy it tilted as he approached her, as she turned her convincingly dazed face to him.

She was sitting up straight, her shapely black-clad knees raised. Her eyes were lit with real-seeming fear. How Daniel's cock ached at that. He halted above her. As he lifted the umbrella over his head, he saw Kathryn shift to stylized fear. Her eyes rounded; her mouth formed a Perils-of-Pauline "O."

"And he gives her—" Daniel's cock was so hard he struggled to deliver Nancy Kerrigan's famous description. "—a '*good whack*'!"

Kathryn Byrne screamed—would her neighbors hear?—though Daniel swung the umbrella in super-slow motion. Suddenly aware of the video camera whirring away behind him, suddenly stiff in his own performance, he maneuvered the umbrella so it tapped her upraised knees.

With a gasp, she flinched at the touch, then doubled over.

"S-sorry—" Daniel backed away fast, the metal umbrella tip scraping the floor. He watched Kathryn stare up at the camcorder, her mouth stretched like Nancy Kerrigan's in the news shot taken moments after her attack.

"Why *me?*" Kathryn Byrne wailed. Daniel wondered if she was going crazy on him. She seemed to sob. His umbrella dropped with an ignominious thud.

"Why *me?*" she wailed on, insistently. Daniel remembered these had been Kerrigan's actual words. He inched forward so he stood over Kathryn again, hunched even lower to hide his even-bigger hard-on. He squinted from behind his now-tilted glasses at Kathryn's contorted face. He saw no tears.

"Why *me*, why *me?*" she demanded, turning from the camera's eye to his.

In a flash, Kathryn switched expressions. She shut her eyes like a kid making a wish. Then she opened her green eyes, her face flushed from her mock-sobs, her hair wild around her shoulders. She grinned.

Freshly incredulous, Daniel stared down at this live actress sitting before him in her professional black leotard. This can't be real, he was thinking, breathing like he might start hyperventilating, a stale chocolate taste in his mouth. That crazy camcorder still hummed away. His crazy erection still strained his zipped jeans. About to burst through, like Superman. Now was the moment to show her, the moment he'd been waiting for.

Painfully, Daniel Sanders straightened to his full height, proud of his five foot eleven inch body and of the as-yet-unmeasured bulge at his crotch. *I am tall is the one good thing.* He touched his sweaty goatee, making sure it was still there. Would she love him in return, fly him to L.A.? All he managed to say in his so-hard-I-can-hardly-speak voice was: "You're. Beaut. Iful."

Like Lisa, Kathryn thought as Daniel Boy spoke. Breaking up his words like Lisa broke hers. Baby syllables. Daniel's face had gone all sweet and blank. From behind his crooked glasses, he trained on her the worshipful gaze Lisa and only Lisa had ever given her. My fan, Kathryn reminded herself, holding herself motionless. The camcorder whirred above her; it was still, she knew, aimed at her on the floor. Daniel kept staring down at her, too, unblinking like those red lights. Kathryn hugged herself, chilled in her flimsy leotard.

"Thank you," she told the tall young man who found her beautiful.

She knew she should feel afraid of this stranger. But as she noticed the erection under his jeans, what she felt most clearly was her power over him.

"And you." Lightly, she licked her wine-sweetened lips. She saw him draw a shuddery breath. None of the vain handsome actors she'd slept with, not even kindly old Peter Wynn, had faced her in such thunderstruck awe. None had made her feel—as she did with her best audiences—that she could control them with a wink, a mini-flash of tongue. She leaned on her hands, her hair swaying.

"You," she repeated softly, lying back on the floor. Under her leotard, her nipples felt hard as ice chips. The flush in her skin was deepening. Had it really been six months? "Aren't you going to give me. A good whack?"

Daniel Sanders dove into her. Young: oh Christ, this Daniel Boy was stunningly young. So Kathryn was thinking in the central part of her mind that stayed detached even as his body crashed hers. The two of them grappled. He inexpertly kissed her clothed shoulder, her bare neck; he bussed her ear and sucked at her mouth, his tongue tasting of chocolate more than wine.

A boy. The word hung in her mind with tornado's-eye clarity. But like the words she'd tried to say just before she'd fainted, it did and did not register. This time, instead of feeling weak and dazed, Kathryn was feeling strong and dazed. Strong and sexy—in her real life, she seldom felt sexy—as she blinked at her bright distorted face in Daniel's glasses. The lenses twin movie screens.

"See me?" she whispered. He nodded; she unhooked the stems from his ears. She tossed his glasses aside, aiming for the couch but hearing them crack, delicately, on the floor. "Sorry," she breathed. "I'll—I'll pay for them. . ."

Without the glasses, she saw, his face was a boy's face: smooth oily skin, plum swollen-looking lips, wet eyes brimful with pupil.

"No, wait," Kathryn made herself say above the mechanical whir and Daniel's harsh pleading chocolate breaths. His body rubbed hers with a pure urgency she hadn't felt in years. Fumblingly, Daniel unzipped his own jeans. She felt his penis poke her crotch, hot through the cloth of his briefs and her leotard. Its touch was like that Hershey's Kiss: one taste and, God, she went wet.

"No, no; wait, we gotta wait," she gasped, but she couldn't make her words at all urgent compared to his, thunderous in her ear.

"Please, please—" He pawed at her leotard, tugging it down past her shoulders. He struggled with the hooks of her bra. Then he gave up on that and thrust his hand into his bunched-up jeans' pocket. He slipped out a condom, dangling it between them. His hand trembled so badly Kathryn took hold of the gold packet herself. She closed it in her fist.

Decisively, she shifted her weight, shifted their positions. Now Daniel was on his back. She was straddling him on her knees. She was feeling—a half-panicked half-thrilled pulse thumped her throat—the video's red eye on her bare back.

"Is that thing still on?" she murmured, bracing her hands on his shoulders.

"No, no," Daniel Sanders mumbled. He's lost his mind, she told herself; she'd forgotten how college boys lost their minds, all their energy gathering into their strong young bodies. Her own half-bared body felt cold. For warmth, she sucked at his mouth the way he'd sucked at hers, drawing fresh chocolate-flavored energy from him. She rose back up on her knees, still straddling his bony hips.

"You—" he gasped below her. "Look. Like. Pam-ela. Smart—"

"Pamela? Smart?" Kathryn swayed at that name from the blue.

Distantly, she connected it with murder, with a garish tabloid photo in the *Boston Herald*. A fuzzy blown-up snapshot: a dark-haired woman in a bra and panties posing on her knees with her fists on her hips and her head flung back.

Intoxicated by the video hum behind her, Kathryn pursed her lips into Pamela Smart's taunting dare-you sneer. She tossed back her head to further muss her own dark hair. Murderess; a murderess's come-on. Daniel Boy groaned.

Kathryn arched her back, holding Daniel's body between her knees like a surfboard she'd mounted. A wave beneath them about to crash. He panted, starting to pull down his briefs, his hands so shaky he couldn't grasp the elastic.

"Teach me—" he seemed to be saying.

"You mean—this is—I am—your first?" she gasped back from above him. Still clenching the condom in her right hand, she gripped Daniel's shoulder with her left. She no longer felt at all drunk. He jerked his goateed chin—a nod—and she nodded back, slowly. Pleased, flattered. She had never been anyone's first.

As she smoothed her hand over his black wool chest, she thought: And you're my first fan. Tremulous too, Kathryn tugged down Daniel's briefs, freeing his penis so it sprang upright like (this was Kathryn Byrne's final clear thought) the steeple of a church erected to worship her.

4.

When hours later she began to wake, Kathryn Byrne was dreaming of Lisa. Lisa melting Kathryn with her laser-stare. *It's only fair,* Kathryn was shouting. Then as she stirred, she was remembering how the night before Lisa had only managed to say, like a curse, "shell." Special, Mom had guessed. Kathryn yawned. A sour taste of wine. A word Lisa must have hated for years and now her own sister had gone on TV telling the world Lisa had "special needs."

Fresh regret hit Kathryn like the ache between her still-shut eyes. Fresh pride too since she remembered too how she'd nailed—almost for sure—Nancy. She stretched. She was lying alone on her couch. Only as she rolled over and felt sunshine—too strong for morning sun—pierce her eyelids, lighting them with scarlet veins, did she remember Daniel Sanders.

She sat up blinking in the light. Remembering first what had happened last.

After the sex—anticlimactic, as sex most often was for Kathryn; Daniel came with a jolt the instant he entered her, his hips bucking her up and his head jerking back as if in a seizure and he didn't know enough to be apologetic; only, in a puppy-like way, grateful—then after she lay beside him holding his hand as his breaths regulated; after he rose to piss in her bathroom and to shut off the soothing whir she groggily recognized as her video camera, she stared up at Daniel Sanders from the floor, his face without his glasses stunningly young again, and at last she asked: Hey, how old are you?

To which—Kathryn remembered now, opening her dry eyes—Daniel answered, groggy, too; therefore, no doubt, accidentally truthful: Seventeen.

God, Kathryn told herself the way she'd told him out loud. Hours before, maybe midnight. Her memory of the struggle that followed made her wince shut her eyes. Her eyelid veins pulsed, electrified by the unshaded noon sun.

Seventeen?

She had sat upright; Daniel had knelt beside her with his needy stare and his stale-chocolate breath. As she'd struggled to pull away, he had planted clumsy kisses on her neck and shoulders. Then she was standing and he was staring up at her: a boy; a student imploring a teacher. *Teach me, teach me.* Those words of his echoed inside her as she told him she was sorry, this had been a big mistake. She'd had no idea he was so young. She was very sorry but he had to leave now, OK?

"But I love you," the boy Daniel blurted out, standing up on his knees.

"'Love' me?" She startled as he hugged her bare thighs. "Who *are* you?" she demanded, stiffening up all over. Finally frightened.

"Daniel Sanders." Then, in a nervous rush: "Just because I'm seventeen doesn't mean everything else I've told you isn't true. I *did* graduate Lowell University—I, I got in years early, see; I tested as a prodigy in high school, see—and I *am* a writer; I'm writing a Rap/Rock Opera based on Michael Jackson and I *do* have a poetry book coming out this spring from, from, from—"

In his confusion, Daniel loosened his hold on her legs. She stepped back. She watched him grope for the name she finally, flatly supplied. "Loam Press."

Still on his knees, Daniel turned sheepish, pleading.

"I *am* Daniel Sanders," he insisted. Above him, she began shaking her head, clearing her foggy funky mind.

"No, no. I know who you are. Oh, God. God; I've been so *stupid.*" She shivered in her bare skin. "Y-you're the boy in a ski cap who was hanging around outside my window this morning. Who followed me to the rink, who must've put up all those crazy damn 'Daniel Sanders' signs—"

"'Cra-zy'?" he interrupted, breaking up his words again like Lisa.

Only not like Lisa, because Lisa never spoke angrily. Lisa never hit anyone but herself.

"You think I'm just some—some *nut?*" Daniel staggered forward on his knees, a mad cripple. Kathryn backed up a step, picturing Lisa spinning herself into one of her clench-fisted fits; Lisa wanting, then, to hit someone, hit her?

"Please just go." Bending, feeling her bare breasts jiggle, Kathryn tied her Cape Cod Playhouse sweatshirt around her waist. Her pulse thumped her throat; she fumbled to hook her bra. "I'm sorry, OK? I just didn't—*see* you. You were right here in front of me but I was so wrapped up in—in my own—God, I just couldn't *see* you're just a boy, so will you please-please just get dressed and get out?"

She planted her hands on her hips: not a Pamela Smart temptress now but a fed-up Mom in a sweatshirt apron. Her ass was bared to the cold room.

Sullenly, his limp cock flopping, Daniel Sanders sat back on his heels. His chest looked bony, his ribs showing through. The triangle of sparse hairs between his nipples seemed as misplaced as the goatee on his splotchily flushed face. That naked boy's face. How could she not have seen what he was?

His eyes downcast, Daniel groped on her floor, too, pushing aside his own black turtleneck and putting on, first, only his glasses. One lens was cracked. Kathryn bent to apologize again for that, for everything. She met in the glass lenses both Daniel's dead-eyed stare and her own fractured face. Pale, drawn, scared. A would-be never-was actress bedding down a boy for a thrill.

"Look, look, I'm really really sorry this happened at all and I'll mail you some money for your glasses—"

"Mail me some money," he muttered as if not comprehending the words.

"But obviously I can't—see you again. I thought—you *know* you led me to think—you were someone else, someone older, and so look. Look: it was all a big mistake. And I need to ask you now, please. Please just keep this to yourself, OK?"

She swallowed, hating the hollow self-serving ring of those words.

107

"You *can't*. See *me*," Daniel repeated with odd emphasis. "*You* can't see *me*."

"Please go," Kathryn whispered hoarsely, straightening.

"But *you* never did tell *me*. Who I look like. What, you know, celebrity."

"*No*-body!" Kathryn backed up, bumping the tripod. She faced her wobbling camcorder. Its eye. Then—because her bare ass was exposed to Daniel—she rushed to the bathroom and slammed the door. She hovered by that door, hugging herself. She listened to Daniel's shuffly steps, to a faint metallic clanking—God, was he loading a gun out there?—then, at last, to the loud thud of her front door.

Alone in her apartment—she checked each room to make sure—Kathryn splashed warm water on her face. Not cold; she wanted to sleep, not to wake up. She popped out her contacts, unhooked her bra, and lay in only her robe on the couch. So she could hear the door should its lock rattle. She shut her eyes, exhausted. Although it was too late, she longed to call home again, talk to Lisa again, apologize somehow. For everything, for Lisa's whole life. Then Kathryn fell into a deep but increasingly fitful sleep, the last hours broken by sounds half-heard: the muffled phone buzz in her bedroom, voices on her machine—her mother? Wally? A strange, strangely fast-talking man? Each time, Kathryn buried her head under her couch cushions and willed herself back to sleep, even as—had she imagined this last, she wondered now, her aching eyes narrowed in the window sun—knocks had sounded on her front door.

Kathryn made herself stand up. Maybe the knocks had been imaginary but the messages on her machine were real. As she steadied herself—not all that shaky, really; it hadn't been wine she'd been so drunk on last night—she focused on her unshaded front window. On the rear bumper of a van, white against new white snow, parked across the street by the Kennedy Plaza kiosks.

Without her contacts, Kathryn had to squint. What seemed a slash of blood shaped itself into a red number painted on the van. Kathryn shuffled closer to her horribly bright window. Your number is up, said a Crazy Daniel voice inside her head. She stood still, piecing together the scene outside: a Channel 7 News van; a knot of a dozen or so people, bundled up unrecognizably, half-hidden by the van and by the sun-brightened icy snow. Sun glared, too, off the miniature satellite dish mounted on the van, off the cameras and high-necked lights two men seemed to be aiming toward her own building.

The camera, said the new Cool Daniel voice inside her. Smile; you're on *Candid Camera*. Kathryn spun around and rushed to her camcorder. She scanned the buttons—PLAY, FSTFWD, RWND, STP/EJCT.

Trembling violently, she pressed STP/EJCT. The side panel popped open with a clank like a shot, its skeletal videotape cage empty. Kathryn gaped, remembering. That muffled clank she'd heard hours before in the bathroom and thought might've been a gun, loading. Would that it *had* been. She touched the empty metal holder, the camera unhinged, hanging open like her jaw.

Her whole two-hour MONOLOGUE tape stolen. Kathryn spun again. Tripping on her terry-cloth robe, stumbling to her knees in front of her TV. The TV she and Daniel Sanders had watched the Winter Olympics on only the night before. Already everything before this moment, this cold linoleum against her knees, was sucking away from her, spiraling away like the world when she had fainted.

Rewind, Erase; would that she could! Kathryn flipped on her TV, gripping the switch as if to yank it free. Sensing that last night's humiliation, her faint, was only the first phase of some huge humiliation yet to come. Only child's play.

God, oh God, she was praying as the electric blizzard of gray-white and blue-black TV dots filled her eyes. Can't be real, can't be real, she was repeating like a mantra as her stiff fingers fought the dial. The channel numbers jumped in front of her, none right till she halted her own hand on 7.

News at Noon. First the newscasters' familiar blurry faces and voices, droning on about Nancy Kerrigan's family, the homecoming parade being planned. *And finally,* the anchor added, *yet another bizarre footnote in the Nancy Kerrigan saga.* Then Kathryn's own beige brick apartment building filled the screen, so surreal to see she couldn't process it at first. It was all dots. Dancing electric dots; surely this was some drunken dream. But Kathryn ducked lower in case the cameras outside could peer into her window. Her forehead bumped the chilled electrified screen, its force field broken.

—*Twenty-nine-year-old Lowell High schoolteacher and aspiring actress Kathryn Byrne faces allegations of sexual harassment by a seventeen-year-old Lowell High senior. In an impromptu news conference, taking place in front of Byrne's Harper Street apartment building, the student has claimed that last night—following her unexplained collapse after the performance that served as her audition for the role of Nancy Kerrigan in an upcoming TV movie—Byrne lured him to her home. There, the student alleges, she promised to grant him late admission into her Winter Theater workshop in exchange for sexual favors.*

The student claims that Byrne, who had been drinking, showed him a nude video of herself then persuaded him to engage in sexual intercourse with her in front of the video camera. Pictured here live: our reporter on the scene displays the box from the videotape that the accusing student says he turned in to Lowell Police officers early today. Lowell Police have viewed the video but will not confirm whether it depicts the activities the student has alleged.

An investigation of the allegations is pending. . .

Kathryn raised her head from her TV screen, leaving behind a cloudy smudge of sweat. The Channel 7 camera shifted from long-shot to close-up of the newsman, his face ruddy in the cold. He held up, as if it were a singularly distasteful object, a black videotape box. Even in the dotted distortion of her too-close view, Kathryn Byrne could see the familiar orange label she'd chosen for her MONOLOGUE video. Orange was always her favorite color, she remembered as if from long ago. Because it best set off her hair.

. . . The boy himself still here on the scene, the reporter was explaining, *making, let me tell you, a very emotional statement to the press. . .*

Daniel, Kathryn thought. Is here on the scene. She shut her eyes against the jittery TV light, picturing his black eyes. Alive last night with a determined sharp-edged gleam that the old Kathryn knew from the inside. That the new numb Kathryn Byrne saw to be the flip side of the meltingly worshipful gaze Daniel had also displayed, hours before. His eyes all pupil; his oily smooth face so young without his glasses. How could she not have known he was a boy? Hadn't she known, really, deep inside?

—*Police have not yet reached Ms. Byrne,* the *News at Noon* anchor was wrapping up, the TV's picture having shifted back to the Channel 7 studio, *who they confirm may be charged today with sexual harassment and one count of sexual molestation of a minor. . .*

Kathryn started to sit on her heels but somehow missed. Her ass thumped the floor like it had thumped the backyard ground when little Lisa had jumped off their seesaw. When she'd crashed down so hard—Kathryn groaned now, sitting on the linoleum—her whole head, whole body was ringing.

. . .More details at five. We'll read excerpts from Byrne's accuser's news conference and update you on new developments in the disturbing allegations that have erupted around Kathryn Byrne, whose hopes of portraying Nancy Kerrigan may be shattered, and whose alleged seduction of a student has already led some to invoke the name of New Hampshire murderess Pamela Smart. . .

As Kathryn watched dumbly, the TV picture shifted to an ad for an Olympics Ice Special, "Relive the Magic." Beginning to sob without tears, she watched flashes of Nancy and Tonya and Oksana and superimposed over them all the reflection of her own stunned face, her mouth stretched out. *Why me, why me?*

But Kathryn couldn't cry, her throat all choked like the night before onstage. Only now no faint came to rescue her. Now, she barked out a name like an animal sound. "Pam-ela Smart? Pam-ela *Smart?*"

The "Smart" hit the pitch of a shriek. "Pam-el-a *Smart?!*"

Kathryn rocked back and forth. How could she have been so drunk—on much more than wine; on a fleeting fucking ghost of a chance of success—that she didn't clearly connect the name to the woman who'd seduced a high-school boy and talked him into killing her husband, the woman who'd given her teenage lover the sexy snapshot that Kathryn had imitated last night.

111

All of it (Incredible but True, gloated the Daniel voice) captured on film.

Was she actually—her diaphragm contracted with another waiting scream—going to be arrested? She, Kathryn Byrne? From somewhere deep in her mind she remembered the last headline of the last Pamela Smart article she'd seen, Smart's celebrity star already fading, this article positioned well below the *Boston Globe* front fold: PAMELA SMART'S LIFE SHRINKS TO THE SIZE OF A PRISON CELL.

"Pamela," Kathryn repeated, the name still as awkward as a foreign word in her mouth. "Pamela. Fucking. Smart."

Suddenly Kathryn was up on her bare feet, her robe flying open. She faced the window again. Squinting, she made out two blurry dark figures crossing the white street. Had they heard her shrieks? Were they reporters, police? Daniel? Her phone buzzed. She spun again. Rushing forward, she brushed by the empty video camera. The open side panel vibrated, sticking out like a robotic tongue.

Knocks sounded on her door, quiet and polite, ordinary knocks.

Kathryn ran into her bedroom. She shut and locked its door. Leaning back on the door, she sank one hand into her loose hair. Her fingers caught in a snarl. Her robe hung open, her body exposed to the windowless room's chill musty air. Somehow, above the muffled *News at Noon* weatherman and the even-more-muffled live voice of the strange man—not Daniel, not yet—calling her name from outside her front door, her agent Wally's phone voice harangued her, unwinding live from her machine.

"—Disney, didn't you hear me say *Disney* was backing *this* Nancy and have you gone *mad*? Do you realize this may carry beyond *Lowell*? Ruining everything we've *worked* for? Goddamn it, Kathryn Byrne: *answer me.*"

In the long pause that followed—tape rolling smoothly beneath Wally's agitated breaths, the TV singing a hymn to diapers and the door-knocker giving up for now—Kathryn drifted from the bedroom door past her vaporizer and space heater to the spot where the camcorder used to reign. She faced the full-length mirror on her closet. In the dark room without her contact lenses, she saw only the narrow white blur of her exposed body, framed by a softer blur of robe. And a pale oval blank surrounded by her hair. Her face felt flat like putty. A sensation so strong, so physical, Kathryn was afraid to touch it, her flattened face.

It's worse when they hit your face, she remembered a Special Ed. teacher saying once when she'd visited Lisa. Another girl had gone off, slapping Kathryn's forehead only hard enough to sting but Kathryn had cried anyway. I mean, the teacher had told her sympathetically, fetching Kleenex. It's your *face*.

"The thing is, Kathryn Byrne is. She's—nuts."

Daniel Sanders, his newly shaven face tingling and glowing in the cold, glanced over the reporter's shoulder at the cameramen's backs, their cameras turned off now but still aimed at Kathryn Byrne's apartment building and not at—his brand-new identity—Kathryn Byrne's accuser. No one filming Daniel yet despite his insistence that he wanted to waive his minors' right to anonymity. Still, though: this real-live TV reporter with his preppy horn-rim glasses and his wool overcoat and his sleek handheld tape player was recording Daniel's every word. No one had ever listened to Daniel talk so long before. No nobody, he.

"I mean 'crazy,' 'not-sane'. . ." Daniel's exuberant breaths plumed the air. Sunlight shimmered on the dazzling cameras, the white TV van, its satellite dish. Surely Daniel would find some cable station willing to show his face, make his face known. No nobody no more; no face scratched into a red-streaked blur so only the hoodlum-sized shoulders and mussed black terrorist-hair remained to hint who it'd been. No: Daniel inhaled another big cold breath to stay focused, his own hair hidden by his ski cap and his chin frozen without his goatee. He had to keep talking or his reporter—more importantly, his TV audience—might get bored.

"'Insane.' That's what I mean. See: she asked me to *hit* her, even, to give her a 'good whack' like Nancy Kerrigan said; remember?"

Daniel half-laughed so his breaths clouded his face. Even the name of Nancy didn't bestir those bored-looking cameramen, packing up now. Where was that thickly lipsticked lady reporter, the one who'd originally interviewed Kathryn? The one who'd nabbed Daniel at the police station along with the lady lawyer and given him a form to sign? A form he'd rushed home to his mom, who at promise of a possible "lawsuit" cosigned instantly then stared at Daniel with more interest than she'd shown for years. Maybe forever.

Daniel narrowed his eyes in the sun, scanning his suddenly smaller semi-circle of local-yokel media people. So he refixed his attention on the short preppy guy still standing closest. Amazing how fast it felt natural to have a reporter at his elbow. But would anything he was saying now make the five o'clock news? Daniel's feet were dead, his mittened hand so numb he glanced down to see that he still held the video box he'd let the news guy show. Hollow, of course, since the Lowell police had the actual videotape. Daniel was feeling hollow, too; fresh out of half-facts; needing now some even wilder outright lies.

"—But listen: before we had—had sex and all, she said something *else*. I mean *besides* that she'd let me in her workshop and all, she said—" He drew another cloudy breath, losing his listeners; yes, another man was crossing over to the growing cluster around Kathryn Byrne's still-closed door; damn her; why didn't she come out and try to stop him? Wasn't she listening at all? "—She said something that the camcorder mike might not've picked up. Something that might im-*ply* something about her and her 'autistic'-or-whatever sister, but. Outa respect for her family and all, I don't know if I should even say this. But."

Daniel blinked into the reporter's horn-rims, his own eyes naked in the cold and he wished he *had* worn his glasses even though they *did* make him look older. But the cracked lens would've been dramatic. It had made the whole world as he'd rushed from Kathryn's apartment look like it was being struck by a flash-crack of lightning. Which had been exactly how *he'd* felt. Hunched by his own VCR, watching Kathryn's video, loving and hating her naked grace. But the thing about lightning: it passes, and fast. Before his flash faded Daniel had to say one more thing to Kathryn Byrne. If she wasn't even now ignoring him. At that thought, Daniel felt tears sting his eyes. He knew those tears would keep the reporter's attention long enough for him to invent the right final lie.

"Kathryn Byrne told me. . . I don't want to say it, but. Just before we had sex, she whispered: 'Pretend you've gotta do what I say. Pretend that—'" Daniel's voice shook because this lie felt somehow true. "'—I'm your big sister.'"

———

Her phone buzzed again. As she turned from the mirror, Kathryn pictured again Daniel Sanders's face last night, pink-flushed under his goatee. Daniel Boy, she'd called him in her mind. Yes: the part of her that hadn't been drunk on her now-vanished chance of success had known exactly how young he was and had rushed ahead anyway. For the thrill, the heady high. The worshipful love, Kathryn thought as her phone finished buzzing, that you get only from children. Or from people who feel as small as children.

The machine clicked on. Kathryn's bedroom filled with Lisa's soft painstakingly clear phone-voice. "Kath. Ryn?"

"Lisa, oh Lisa!" She lunged for the receiver, then pressed it to her terry-cloth chest. Not wanting to scare her already spooked-sounding sister. "Lisa?"

"I die," Lisa said, dream slow. "I die. My. *Self*—"

"You die?" Kathryn was used to repeating in a patient neutral tone the almost inaudible things Lisa said. A Lisa-pause as she sucked in her spit and swallowed, game to try again. Sinking onto the bed, Kathryn pressed the receiver so close that Lisa's moist-lipped whisper-words exploded into her ear.

"Th' foe, Kath. I die the foe."

"Dial?" Kathryn half-relaxed into her oldest role. Lisa's big-sister translator to the world. "You dialed the phone? You knew my number?"

"Uh huh, 'cause I. Watch-Mom."

"Mom's been dialing my number?" Kathryn asked cautiously, her eyes flickering to the lit-up red number on her machine: *9*.

"She see. Pay. Purr."

"The paper? The *Lowell Sun*? Or the—the *Globe*?"

"You. Fall dow, Kath. Fall-dow."

Kathryn drew a shaky breath but kept her voice steady. "I. Fall down? Oh: y'mean *fainted*. When I *fainted* last night, it was in the morning paper?"

Kathryn could feel Lisa nodding her auburn-haired head miles away in Lexington, her eyes hidden by her bangs and glasses, the receiver—the kitchen phone?—pressed too close to her mouth. "Mom. Ree-that. Then she. Die and die."

"She die and die," Kathryn repeated, rocking now on her bed, picturing the newest glossiest Head Shot of Kathryn Byrne dissolving, gone wherever the bubbles go. "W-where is Mom now?"

Lisa drew her own shuddery breath, a woman-sized breath. She pronounced gravely what was usually one of her favorite words. "Tee. Vee."

She sucked in her spit and probably swallowed. She didn't add anything as if she knew she'd just told Kathryn something serious, something sad.

"Oh." Kathryn closed her eyes. Mom frozen before the TV in the den (Channel 4's 12:30 Report no doubt covering it, too) while Lisa huddled in the kitchen clutching the phone Mom would demand she hand over any minute now.

"Oh, Lisa," Kathryn began in a rush as if she'd never get to speak to her sister again. Hot tears filled her parched bloodshot eyes at last, a relief. "That TV interview the other night—when I let them show our skating movie?"

"Um." Lisa's worst sound. Her answer to the questions that most confused her, that most made her feel—Kathryn always sensed when she felt this—stupid.

"I shouldn't've let them show that! It was *my* fault, not the TV's. Because that movie wasn't mine, our Home Movie. It was yours, too, and I shouldn't've let them. I—I shouldn't've talked about you at all, Lisa. I was just, just trying to—" She hesitated to use the words Lisa's teachers always used to explain away Lisa's stranger actions. But in her own case, Kathryn felt they fit. They explained practically everything Kathryn had ever done. "Get attention. I was just trying to get attention. God, Lisa, I'm sorry."

"Um."

As she blinked, her tears lukewarm against her cold face, as she registered the hurt in Lisa's voice, Kathryn pictured what she'd tried to stop picturing all yesterday: Lisa's claps for her turning to slaps. Slap slap, hard against Lisa's smoothly plump face. Those bruises still, maybe, showing. Kathryn rocked faster on the mattress.

"And Lisa, I'm sorry you—hurt your hands and your head that night."

"Kath," Lisa cut in as Kathryn began to silently cry. "'S OK, Kath."

What she used to say when Kathryn would lose at Chinese Jump Rope and come stomping under Lisa's tree. Lisa lying on her branch and reaching down to pat the top of Kathryn's head. Unlike Lisa's usual fumbling touches, Lisa's touch when Kathryn had lost a game felt sure and gentle, companionable.

"I. Sorry. You—fall."

Clenching her teeth so as not to audibly sob, Kathryn slid off the bed. The icy floor made her knees ache, but it felt right to kneel like this. To feel, at the floor's hardness, sorry that she had ever made Lisa kneel. The sharpest stab of regret Kathryn had felt yet in this school of shame she'd entered today.

"Lisa, I," Kathryn managed. "Just wish I could *see* you now." A jumble of sounds was pressing in around her dark bedroom: more live voices calling her name under the TV voices; Mom's faint voice somewhere behind Lisa. In a last-moment rush, Kathryn confided to her sister the one wish she had left.

"I want to get to where I can see you."

—THE END—

117

The Young and the Rest of Us

On the Pennsylvania Turnpike, on the first of our many moving days, my mother jolted up from her supposedly pain-free sleep and told my father, "Stop."

"What?" Dad at the wheel didn't recognize that word. Behind him, I slid my foot off my hidden tape player and pressed the vibrating floor like a brake. Someone had to obey Mom's command, her first since insisting that we go ahead with our planned move as if her accident had never happened.

"Wha'd she say, dear?" Beside me, Grandma strained her quavery voice.

"'Stop,'" I murmured, squinting into the vivid windy mass of Mom's hair, its orange and brown shimmer. Bright as the roadside dandelions. I kept my shoulder still, so not to jar my sister from her own Darvon-deep sleep.

"You OK, LeeAnn?" Dad glanced at Mom, his glasses glinting, his noble nose slicing my view. "Need a bathroom stop?" A blurred curtain of cars closed around us. Cleo meowed weakly from her cage, stacked with our bags in the way-back.

"*No,*" Mom told Dad, clearly despite her swollen lip. "Stop f'r the *day!*"

I tensed; Lee's head bumped my arm. Her hair was limp, silky with grease. Unwashed in the week since the crash. The last week of summer, 1978.

"We in Kentucky yet?" Lee asked groggily, leaning on me harder at the slowing of our overloaded Impala. Mom's black Valiant had been—an offhandedly apocalyptic word—totaled. And what, I'd wondered but felt somehow scared to ask, had happened to the other car, the VW bug Mom had ploughed into?

"No." Mom gripped the dash. "We're stopping at th' next mo-*tel*."

"Already?" I blurted out, nicking my lip on my braces. It wasn't even noon.

"Yes!" Mom sucked in her spit. Dad glanced over again, as if to check who it was sitting next to him. "We need a r-room." Boldly, she added: "'S *time—*"

I dared to twist my wrist, flashing my sister my watch just as I'd done every weekday at 11 A.M. during our all-girl summer.

Together, forgetting our dreaded move to Kentucky, Lee and I would settle on the floor by Mom's ironing board to see: what next? To see, in August of 1978: would Phillip Chancellor II die? Before he could marry poor Jill? We'd written CBS to beg for his life. On our own pretend soap opera, which we recorded on our tape player and which Mom dubbed The Young and the Rest of Us, we killed off characters left and right. Anyone we decided deserved it.

"She mean Soap Time?" Lee whispered hotly into my ear. I nodded once, fast, lowering my watch face before Grandma noticed. Lee muffled her giggle with both hands like a little kid. She was ten, two years behind me.

Dad glanced at us in his rearview. He'd been living alone in Kentucky all summer, while we sold the Penn Wynn house. He knew nothing of our soap opera.

As we swung into the exit lane, Grandma leaned forward, aiming for Dad's ear. "We aren't stopping already?" Propping her, my hand cupped the base of her dowager's hump: intricately bumpy like a hundred-year-old tortoiseshell.

"Lee*Ann* needs to *rest—*" Dad's shout knocked Grandma back into her seat.

"Does she want a Tums?" Grandma quavered, her voice extra weak in rebuke. Solicitous, too—toward Dad, not Mom. For Grandma had picked up Dad's underlying message: Look what they're doing to me now, Ma! "Or some Chiclets gum?" At Dad's mighty silence, Grandma gave what Mom called One of Her Sighs.

A horn blared. A Mack truck barreled by, headlights glaring crazily against the sun. I eased my foot back onto the tape player I'd wedged under Dad's seat.

"There—" Mom straightened up. Briefly, she held her head high like the jaunty Mom who'd once modeled '50s lipstick so dark it photographed black; who'd starred through the '60s and '70s in Lower Marion Little Theater productions; who'd named both her daughters, Lee and Ann, after herself.

"*That* motel—" Imperiously, Mom pointed through the thundering rush of another truck. Her finger wavered. As in her Little Theater performances when we watched close-up, backstage. Of all the actors, only Mom trembled over what was supposed to be fun. Our car veered sideways. The sign loomed above a roof shining with orange as garish and comforting as McDonald's-arch yellow.

"Look," I told Lee in whisper. "Ho Jo's!"

Under the grim crisscross of her forehead bandages, Lee's green eyes brightened. She whispered back incredulously, "Just for our *soap* opera?"

"Wha—?" Peering through her sharp-edged glasses, Grandma took hold of my ticking wrist. Ten till eleven. "Not that, that—program?"

Dad bumped down the exit ramp; Grandma's gray-green Irish eyes sparked.

"Shh—" I shot glances at Dad's stiffly attentive neck, at Lee's "have-I-blown-it?" face. Honest Lee: who played good-but-doomed characters on our show while I hogged the villainesses. In honor of Lee, I faced Grandma and nodded.

We shared secrets, sometimes. Each month, I fetched Grandma's tweezers and plucked—tugged—a recurring gray hair from her puckeringly braced chin.

Our Impala shuddered to a stop under the Howard Johnson's sign.

Grandma knit her thick eyebrows together. But she kept her thin magenta mouth sealed.

"Coming, Ann?" Dad asked me, curt yet shy in his way. Apologetic, maybe.

Following Dad to the lobby, I lagged behind: not so far that I'd seem to be sulking about our fight hours before, but far enough that we wouldn't have to talk. Single file, we passed Ho Jo's restaurant section. I felt suddenly hungry for frankfurters and brown-sugared baked beans. Maybe we'd eat an early room-service lunch, watching our show. In the hypnotic TV light we'd missed for the past week, Mother might be transformed into her old self, real self.

"Dad." I fell into step beside him. "Can we eat lunch here?"

"We'll see," he muttered, sounding almost normal. I half-skipped in the sun, released from the shadows of the last seven days, of our whole past summer. Dad and I faced the shiny lobby doors. Maybe, I thought half-seriously, Mom's command that we stop would somehow halt our whole move to Kentucky.

What, I wonder now, if it had? Would we have stayed rooted in PA, stayed a family, instead of bouncing with Dad's ever-more-demanding promotions across the U.S.A.—KY to IL to CO—only to crash in CA, never to be glued together again?

Dad pushed open the lobby door. As if I'd made them myself, I noticed Cleo's fresh scratches on his knuckles. I followed Dad inside just as, hours before, I'd followed him away from our brick home on Robinhood Road.

"The Young and the Rest of Us will *no longer* be broadcast in your *listening area*." Loudly, as if I still believed in the listeners Lee and I imagined picking up our feeble signal—CB truckers, Ham Radio housewives—I had repeated my announcement into our walkie-talkie all morning, pacing our vast empty rooms. Grandma stood huddled in the tableless kitchen with Mom and Lee, measuring out Darvon. Dad carried our last boxes and suitcases to the car.

122

"The *Young* and the *Rest* of Us—" I stalked past the kitchen archway, hoping the joke name she'd invented would trigger Mom's throaty laugh. The only answer I received was the static crackle of our walkie-talkie. Its plastic body felt hollow as I shoved down its antenna. A toy.

Our tape player felt heavy. A weapon. At quarter till nine (our Estimated Time of Departure, Dad had proclaimed) Lee and Mom walked out to the Impala; Grandma lingered in her rose garden. I crouched by the kitchen archway, the tape player balanced on my knee. I held the mike outstretched. Tape hummed.

"—Stay still," Dad coaxed from the kitchen. But Cleo yowled, twisting as Dad struggled to hold her on the counter. A flash of orange and black fur.

"Ann—" Dad called to me, comically loud since really I was so close. I was gaping through the archway, tape-recording the frantic scratch of Cleo's claws on the Formica countertop. "Ann! Come *help* me with this an-imal—"

An old joke between Dad and me, that Cleo and I were two Ann-imals. Cleo made a hairball-gagging sound. Stop, I wanted to shout, my heart thumping up inside my own tightened throat. I kept firm hold of the mike.

Intent and efficient as her veterinarian, Dad pinned down Cleo. I glimpsed his big thumb jammed between her sharp teeth, prying open her mouth. His other thumb shoved the yellow tranquilizer pill down her throat.

"Don't swallow," I blurted out to my cat. To my mike, too. Dad's back stiffened. Still, he didn't turn. Not even when I pulled myself to my feet. Hugging the tape player and walkie-talkie, I darted out the back door.

I thumped past Grandma, stoic amidst her roses. I threw myself onto the wooden porch swing Dad had hung between metal poles. Its chains gave a mournful creak. There I'd sat for hours with Cleo spread on my lap, a hot fur blanket. Now, balancing the tape player on my knees, I swung back and forth. Through the dogwoods, I faced the ranch house of Mim and Mindy Feldstein. Our companions in games of jacks and walks to school. Built-in friends, even for buck-toothed, pigeon-toed me. We'd said our self-conscious good-byes the night before. From here in, I sensed, we'd be on our own: Lee and me.

"Ann?"

I halted the oversized swing. The chains protested as Dad settled beside me, the walkie-talkie sliding between us. His knees stuck up high.

"We'll get a swing like this in Kentucky. A real porch swing for our real porch there, Ann. For you and—that animal."

I shrugged, though it had been nice of Dad to mention Cleo. His enemy. She liked to sneak into his car, the Impala, and piss in the driver's seat.

"At any rate." Dad cleared his dry smoker's throat. A we're-going-to-have-a-serious-talk sound. Nervously, I steadied the tape player on my knees.

"Why are you carrying around that thing, Ann?"

I shifted, wondering if Dad knew I'd taped Cleo yowling, taped many snatches of Real-Life Drama. Mom singing *Kiss Me Kate* tunes in the shower, Dad cursing as he searched for his mechanical pencil, Mom and Dad quarreling at cocktail time. "It's just a game, something we use for the soap opera we pretend to broadcast, me and Lee." I pulled myself up, my walkie-talkie thumping the dirt. "Mom plays parts on our show sometimes, too."

Dad stood. "Your mother," he began, ominously solemn, "won't be—herself. Not for a long while to come. . ."

"I *know*," I whined, feeling Grandma creep by in the grass behind us.

Dad shook his bald head. His glasses flashed early sun into my eyes, making me squint against his words.

"There's a selfish streak in you, Ann. You need," he told me as I'd once tape-recorded him telling Mom, "to start acting your age."

He strode off toward the driveway, his spine unforgivingly straight. Behind him, I crossed the grass with small steps, hugging my clunky tape player, trailing the cord. My hair hid my face. Ugly: an ugly animal crawling into its backseat cave. I settled between Grandma and sleepy Lee. Up front, Mom leaned against her headrest. Dad began backing the packed station wagon down our driveway.

"Wait; I *forgot* something," I cried, realizing I'd left the walkie-talkie under the swing. Dad kept his rearview eyes fixed on the road. His answer resounded so sternly no one else spoke till we were well out of Penn Wynn.

"Don't start with me again, Ann."

In the lobby, Dad asked if he could rent a room for the afternoon. The clerk shot a quick half-lidded look from me to Dad then recomposed his bland Ho Jo's smile. "We rent by the night, sir."

Not knowing why, I giggled. Dad clapped one hand on my shoulder, hard.

"My wife," he announced with the prim defensive dignity of then-President Jimmy Carter, "—isn't well. She needs to rest."

The clerk beamed his apologetic fake-friendly smile and bustled for keys; Dad lit up one of his quickie cigarettes, smoked out of range of his mother.

Breathing his smoke, I paced the same small circles I'd paced the week before at my orthodontist's. Mom strangely late. As the waiting room had darkened around me, emptying out, all my Novocain numbness had worn off.

"All right, Ann." Dad smashed his cigarette into a brass urn of sand. "Let's go." Side-by-side this time, we walked back toward the car.

"You know," Dad told me mysteriously. "This accident; it's much harder on your mom—than you can know."

I nodded. Then I ducked fast into the car. As I climbed over her, Lee stirred, reaching to her forehead bandages. Lee's head had banged Mom's front seat, knocking Lee out. Her seat belt had bruised her belly, maybe saving her life.

Dad murmured to Mom; Mom nodded. Despite Grandma, I hummed into Lee's ear, her dirty hair. The opening notes of the *Young and Restless* theme. What had Dad meant: more than I can know? Under the engine rev, Lee began to hum along. As Dad drove us to our rooms, I squeezed Lee's clammy hand, my pulse pumping with our favorite soap-opera question. *What next?*

In the chillingly air-conditioned Ho Jo's room—Dad had rented two but we all crowded first into one—Mom lay on the queen-sized bed. Lee and I flanked her. Since I couldn't see her blistered lip, I felt I was snuggling against the same old Mom: her firmly rounded body, her orange-striped blouse and shorts, her warm ashy smoker's-wife smell. Her arms rested around our shoulders, her usually smooth underarms prickly. Cleo, uncaged, lay limp across my bare legs.

TV light bloomed at the foot of our bed. As the theme song swelled, Dad shook his bald head, no doubt wondering if this could be why Mom had made him stop. He didn't ask. He stood near the room door, watching us watch. The soap-opera theme climaxed. I half-wanted Dad mad, instead of so blank.

"Disgusting," Grandma pronounced from her own queen-sized bed.

Scene one: Laurie and Lance entwined in their shower, lathering each other. Lee and I refrained from giggles. My hand stroked Cleo, coaxing her into a fitful purr. Laurie's hand ran up and down Lance's sculpted back; his muscular arms hiding her breasts. But weren't they both truly nude, from the waist up?

Oh, Laurie Brookes's mouth shaped. A sound that usually made Mom stop ironing, steam rising around her, and me stop chewing my peanut-butter sandwich. Though Lee would chomp hers louder, flaunting her indifference.

"Where's Phillip Two?" Lee muttered as the camera pulled back discreetly from Laurie and Lance's drenched kiss. "He better not be already dead!"

"Oh, boy—" I exaggerated my own rowdy voice, wanting stiff-limbed Mom to relax like Lee. "Ol' Victor, Mister Control Freak!"

Onscreen, mustached millionaire Victor Newman hunched over his own screen: a video monitor trained on the bare-chested perm-haired man Victor had imprisoned in his basement. Punishment for having dallied with Victor's prized wife. Julia, forbidden even to shop, was imprisoned, too, inside Victor's mansion.

Pointedly, I glanced at Dad standing like a guard by our door. Didn't Mom remember joking all summer that Victor's deep voice reminded her of Dad's? Mom had even murmured aloud when bored Julia paced her lavish living room: I know how ya feel, honey. Summer nights, Lee and I had speculated that Mom of the 1958 toothpaste ad—her lips black, teeth white, hair even in black-and-white richly auburn—might be a real actress by now if Dad hadn't tied her down. Dad always scolding her about her speeding tickets, about the afternoon wine spritzers she'd sneak before what he called, with emphasis on the final *r*, "cocktail hour."

"Mom, look: Victor's still got that guy trapped!" I dared to face her face, close-up. Her lower lip, bumped on the Valiant's steering wheel, seemed ready to burst, the puffy pink blister rimmed with dried yellow pus. As a strained joke, she'd mumbled to me: Watch out, 'f someone tells you they gonna gi' you a Fat Lip.

"Mom," I repeated, focusing on her nose. "You watching?"

Her nostrils were tinged pink. Had she been—a shocking idea—secretly crying? My eyes met hers: their blue fractured.

"I never wanted these *girls* watching this program." Although she'd been watching it herself all summer, Grandma raised a righteously indignant voice to Dad. "And Ann." Bedsprings squeaking, she heaved herself up. "As long as you're just lying there, you ought to at least wear your shoes."

"Oh, c'mon." Sighing, I faced an Irish Spring soap ad. Grandma clicked her tongue loudly, as if she and I were onstage, performing for Dad in his soldier stance; for stiff Mom and half-dozing Lee and purrlessly sleeping Cleo.

"Don't quarrel, Ann; not now." Grandma turned her hunched back on me.

Mom and Lee kept watching the televised soap bar, sliced to reveal green stripes. Grandma unpacked my shoe brace from its duffle bag. Briskly, loose skin on her arms vibrating, she extended the metal bar.

The shoes were bolted onto either end, tilted so their toes turned out. So my pigeon toes would be forced to turn out, at night. Panting, Grandma hauled the whole contraption—wide as a kite—up onto her bed. The metal bar clanked.

"No—" Mom jerked her head upright. Lee sat up, too. Mom pointed dramatically, as if wearing the blood red gloves she'd worn as the Call Girl in *Death of a Salesman.* "No, Moth'r Healy: Ann doesn't need that *now!*"

Grandma Healy's green eyes sparked. A fight! I thought with a foolish heartbeat of hope. Mom and Grandma often sparred when Mom came home too late to make us what Grandma called a proper supper; when Mom left for rehearsals too early, dressed in jeans as if she were, Grandma'd tell us, you girls' age.

"All right, then." With a defeated sigh, Grandma stepped back, leaving my shoes on her bed. "Whatever you want, LeeAnn. . . " She crept across the yellow carpet. She halted at the curtained sliding doors that led to the motel pool.

"Mother, where are you going?" Dad asked. Grandma fumbled with the drapes. Sun disrupted our TV light, making the picture faint, fragmented.

"Just out for some fresh air." She inched open the glass door, her mint-green dress rippling. "Someone's been *smoking* in this room. . . "

"Wait." Dad lifted her metal three-pronged cane. But Grandma hobbled outside. "You keep an eye on Lee," Dad muttered to me as he passed our bed. As if, I thought, Mom weren't here. He disappeared behind the flapping drapes.

Simultaneously, Phillip Chancellor II's hospital bed materialized onscreen, empty. No, no! Pregnant Jill Foster sobbed, kneeling by the bed. Dear God, no!

What happened next seemed to happen all at once.

"He *is* already dead!" I wailed to Lee above Jill's tinny sobs. "We *missed* it!"

But Lee, her eyes frozen green under her bandages, was gaping at Mom. I leaned forward in the confusing sun-and-TV light to see Mom, too. Cleo sprang off my lap and disappeared under the bed. Wishing I could follow, I jumped to my feet.

I stared at Lee, still hearing Mom's choked hiccupy sobs. Mom's face all distorted, slimy with tears.

"Hey, c'mon, it's no big deal," I found myself saying. "OK, OK, so Phillip Two already died!" Mom's sobs seemed to shift to hoarse laughter. I echoed a phrase we'd mocked our soap opera for overusing: "But that's—'ancient history'!"

Lee gave a scared eager-to-please giggle. Mom offered another hiccup. As she pushed back her hair, I glimpsed the dark stubble under her arms.

Absurdly quickly, our soap-opera characters always shed their skins of boring mourning. A husband would vanish; two episodes later a new man would admonish the wife: Your marriage is behind you now, ancient history!

"An-cien' hist'ry," Mom repeated. Her shoulders began shaking again. A laugh or a now dry-eyed cry? Lee and I giggled along convulsively.

"See? *They're* feeling no pain—" I gestured toward Laurie and Lance, writhing against the shower wall. "Let's play *their* scene! In the shower here!"

"Y-yes!" Mom nodded hard, her fractured-blue eyes confused like Lee's. She shooed us toward the bathroom. "Off with you now," she commanded, waving one hand. Imitating Mrs. Chancellor, soap-opera matriarch. But Mom's next words weakened, as if she were suddenly tired. "Go be Laurie an' Lance. . ."

"*You* play, too!" Lee cried out, bouncing on her heels. "You be our Guest Star! Like that time you *did* play Mrs. Chancellor on our *tape*—"

Mother shook her head of uncombed curls. "No, I—I gotta—" She swung her legs off the bed, standing unsteadily. "Gotta put th's awful thing a- *way*. . ."

She bent over the other bed. Arms spread wide, she lifted my shoe contraption, one hand gripping each high-laced brown shoe.

"Awful thing?" I echoed. Usually Mom defended my shoe brace, its purpose.

"Aw-ful." She sucked in her spit. Abruptly, seeming to lose all interest in her task, she sank back onto her mattress. The shoe brace rested across her lap. I stared. Ugly metal bar, ugly leather shoes, designed to trap.

"I can't," Mom muttered, her arms deflating. "Jus' can't—move."

"That's OK, Mom." Uneasily, I backed away from her, stepping over her purse, its straps torn in the crash. "We'll *tape* the scene for you!" I bent by Cleo's empty carry-cage, hefting our tape player. Relieved to turn my back on Mom, I marched across the room. I spun around at the bathroom. "C'mon, Lee!"

She shuffled forward as if in one of her sleepwalks. Her eyes, like her chlorine-tinged Bicentennial T-shirt, were red, white, and green. About-to-cry.

"Here." I thrust the tape player into her arms. "Towels, towels," I told her like a temperamental director. I stomped up to the yellow-tiled shower, not waiting for Lee to wrap the tape player in towels as we'd done for our last episode. We'd packed our least favorite characters on a cruise ship, recording our real shower's whoosh as our characters screamed, their ship foundering.

I gripped the strange spotless faucets. "Action!" For steam, I cranked on H. "Oh, ooh. Oh, *Lance*—"

Through the shower, I heard Lee giggle. So it seemed safe to turn. She giggled louder, her hands covering her mouth. Beside her on the sink, our unprotected tape player gleamed, already slick with spray. Instead of scolding Lee, I let out another Laurie moan. I opened my arms.

"Oh, Lance, *hold* me!" I wrapped my arms around my sister—her warm body, her gamey hair—both of us giggling, bumping the sink. My palms pressed Lee's spine. Her elbows fought my clenched arms. I gave a throatier moan.

"Mom?" Lee twisted free, her shoulder knocking my chin. "You hear Ann?"

We both crowded the doorway. I poked my head out of the steam, sure Mom must be laughing. But my stare locked with Dad's shiny glasses. He stood by Grandma between the sliding doors. Orange drapes flapped behind him like a cape. I held onto the tile doorway. Dad was staring at me like I was the only other grown-up in this room. And look what I'd let happen.

On the edge of our bed, blurred by steam, Mom sat hunched over my shoe contraption, one knee poking up. One bare foot was half-shoved inside my too-small leather shoe. Slumping further, Mom rested her forehead on her knee. Her legs, I noticed, were unshaven, speckled by dark hairs I didn't want to see.

"What're you doing, Mom?" Before anyone could answer me, I looked down at Cleo's still-empty carry-cage. My insides jumped in fresh panic. She might've slipped out the open door. Where's Cleo? I drew breath to demand.

What stopped me: Dad's unbroken stare. His glasses and bald head no longer shone because he'd taken a step into this darkened room. Suddenly my mouth felt full of metal, welded shut. Grandma on her cane hobbled to Mom's bedside. Mom eased her foot out of my unyielding shoe.

"Ann, turn that off," Dad ordered in a loud level voice.

The TV? Stepping up to its staticky glow, I felt my wet hands tremble. Whose giant Soap face did those electric dots form? I clicked the switch. Live dots were sucked into a dead center star, vanishing. I turned, confused to hear a staticky roar, still. Grandma rested her hand on Mom's shoulder. Mom had set her feet on the floor and shut her eyes. Her hair was crackling with its orange lights. The rest of her seemed dead. My shoe brace rested over her lap like a rigid seat belt.

"No, Ann—" Dad shouted above the crazy wet static. "The goddamn *shower!*"

As if I wasn't worth another glance, he stepped up beside his mother and my mother. Like a brusque doctor, he muttered into Grandma's ear words I half-heard through the now plainly pounding shower.

"—Doctor said—maybe—antidepressants. . . ?"

I turned on my heel. I pushed past Lee in the bathroom doorway. And I plunged into the swirl of fog I'd made.

"I *can't!*" I groped for the knobs. "It's too hot!" Squinting so hard I couldn't tell C from H, I dared a shocking touch. "Ahh!" I snatched my burnt hand back.

Startled into life by this welcome new crisis, Lee shrieked, too. "Dad-ee!"

131

Our father shoved into the bathroom. I huddled with Lee in the doorway. Through the steam, Dad cranked off the all-surrounding roar. The faucets' high screeches mocked our own. A drip. A steamy silence; Dad's heavy breaths.

"We're sorry," Lee piped up—or was it me or both of us? We backed together into the yellow room. Our mother still sat on the bed, still held in place by the metal bar. The tilted shoes stuck out on either side of her hips, soles facing us. Unscuffed. Mom's eyes looked bright but dry.

Dad filled the bathroom doorway. His glasses were steamed-up. His hands, pink as hams, held our Sony tape player, so shiny-wet I knew it was broken. It dripped. Dad cleared his throat mightily. "The Young and the Rest of Us," he anounced. "Will no longer be broadcast. Period."

Bending, he wedged the dripping machine into the motel trash basket. Then he straightened fast, as if from an actor's bow.

Lee and I laughed. Even Mom managed a wan blister-lipped smile. I piped up—a fellow adult, gamely buttressing the fragile cheer—a promise. I tried to make it sound real, for Lee. "We'll start a whole new show in Kentucky!"

Hearing me, Cleo slunk out from under the bed, wobbly as a kitten.

"Look, Lee!" I cried. We both rushed to our cat. But I let slow Lee be the one to scoop her up, Lee the one to bury her face in Cleo's funky mussed fur.

"—Down to our own room," Dad was muttering. Grandma was setting my shoe brace back on the empty bed. His glasses still fogged, Dad helped Mom up. Her legs wobbled like Cleo's. Her orange-striped blouse and shorts looked so intricately wrinkled I couldn't imagine the cloth ironed crisp and smooth again.

"We'll all get some rest, then decide what to do," Dad mumbled to me. I nodded.

My parents crossed our room, Mom leaning on Dad. Like a grown-up seeing off children, I stood in the doorway. I watched them head down the orange-carpeted hall. Barefoot Mom weaved back and forth.

And I remembered Mom stagger-drunk at the cast party for the play she'd called, with casual actressy flair, "Death." Chatting between the teenage boys who'd played the salesman's sons, Mom had twirled her red stage gloves and—Gotta keep up with you two, she'd insisted—downed so many plastic glasses of champagne Dad had led her home by her arm, early. How Victor Newman-like he had seemed to Lee and me as we'd followed them out, protesting.

That first day of September 1978, I felt relieved to see Dad's firm grip on Mom's arm. Steadying her as he'd often do in the years ahead, in the lengthening cocktail hours he tried till the end of their marriage to ration. But as we moved west, the sun set later. In California, it was warm enough almost year round for Mom to sit by the pool, sipping. Lee and I learned to tell Mom school news as soon as we got home, saving nothing for supper. Nothing for after four.

Later, in high school, when we'd phone Mom's apartment from the house we shared with Dad in San Diego, we'd never call after two. Nowadays, in that same ranch house (Dad at sixty, with high blood pressure, needs watching; I at twenty-eight with a B.A. in Theater Performance need a rent-free home) I phone my mother before noon. Mornings, her voice is the most hoarse but her mind most nearly clear.

Although our Howard Johnson's room was full of dusty sun, Lee, doped up on another dose of Darvon, fell asleep right away. We all need, Grandma decreed, a nap. She drew the orange drapes. On the bed we'd shared with Mom, I curled up in front of Grandma, feeling her faint Chiclet-gum breath on my neck, feeling protected from behind by her tortoiseshell back.

Before I could slip into sleep, Grandma whispered, "You know your mother will never get over it. . . "

"What?" I was almost too scared to ask. My tongue toyed with my braces, the tiny rubber bands hinging my upper and lower jaws.

"A boy," Grandma whispered. "A little boy, four and a half." I stiffened my own back, listening without wanting to. Grandma's whisper softened so that doped-up bandaged-up Lee wouldn't hear in the next bed, through her solid sleep.

"A little boy in the Volkswagen your mother crashed into. He's paralyzed, the doctors say. For life. So you, Ann. You must be a good girl now, for her."

I managed to nod. Grandma sighed; a real sigh, quiet and small. My tongue loosened one of my rubber bands. I told myself, Don't swallow.

Grandma's Chiclet-scented breaths rasped into delicate snores. I sucked my rubber band, envying Lee's sleep. Lee, who'd been knocked unconscious instantly in the crash. Hadn't she? Grandma's words were settling inside my chest. A boy, little. Little boy. I wanted to run down the hall and hug Mom hard. But then Mom would know I knew. I spit out my rubber band. I wished I didn't know about the boy. A selfish thought, I told myself. But Mom hadn't wanted me to know. Had she? I sighed loudly, hoping to wake Grandma Healy.

Her snores rasped on. I watched Lee's shrouded body breathe on the other bed. The young, I thought, pressing closer to Grandma. She sighed, too, in her sleep. I sat up. Outside our room, I heard afternoon sounds: pool splashes, TV music. A bar of light guarded my sister's body like the iron bar on her hospital bed. I pulled myself up, barefoot in my denim shorts and girl's undershirt.

I lifted my glinting shoe brace off Lee's bed. My sister stirred, mumbled.

"Lee?" My voice croaked with relief that she'd awakened. That I could—another selfish desire—whisper to her what Grandma'd whispered to me.

"Jell, wan-no," she muttered, sitting up. My throat ached to wake her.

"Who is Victor Newman's archenemy?" I made myself whisper instead.

"Jack Ab-bott," Lee answered in her slow-mo sleep-talk voice.

"Who made Jill pregnant?" I backed up a step like a clever thief.

"Phil. Lip. Two." Lee lay back down, still safely unconscious.

I sank onto my bed, weighted by my shoe brace. As Lee's breaths thickened, I jammed my feet into the shoes. I knotted the laces tight, forgetting socks. Leather chafed my bare ankles. Awkwardly, I straightened my legs. I rolled on my side, one foot jacked up high as if I'd been frozen doing a split. Often I'd wake with my raised leg asleep. Bursting to pee, I'd fumble with my shoes, trapped by them.

In the Ho Jo's room, though, I felt grateful to be anchored. Grateful I hadn't been the one to bang my head against Mom's seat. To glimpse, maybe, the Volkswagen bumper arcing and crumbling like a metal wave. Swallowing a small boy's legs. Bare legs, maybe. Since it had been, only the week before, summer.

I shut my eyes. My feet felt heavy and useless, my right leg already starting to go numb. Paralyzed, I told myself, trying out the word. Was that, I wondered, what Mom had wanted when she'd forced her foot into my shoe?

Not to move again, ever.

When, sleepless shapeless hours later, I heard Dad's knock on our door, Dad's low questioning voice, I pretended to be asleep, like Grandma and Lee. My elevated leg had gone completely numb; my leather-encased feet felt sticky. Under Grandma's snores, Dad's muffled steps began retreating down the hall. My eyes fluttered open. I rolled on my back, lowering my leg like a flag.

Dad's footsteps stopped. Was he lighting a furtive cigarette, not ready to rejoin Mom? Did he need company out there? Someone to hear his low-voiced plans? Tensing my stomach, I sat up. Our room held a more solid darkness now. I untied the shoes that never touched ground. For the first time ever, I realized as I stood up barefoot, I didn't want to know: what next.

101

My teacher told me: First, take off your top.

Standing before her and her husband on cracked brown ground, nothing but Arizona sky stretched all around us, I felt both tall and small. I untucked my sweat-dampened T-shirt from the filmy skirt she and Ray had given me. Veins were swelling inside my sunburnt skin. Giant-sized, our sunset shadows quavered together on the deep-dried mud: Ray's shadow three-legged, because of the cane he leaned on; Alex's square-headed, because of the camera she held; my shadow, because I stood between them, hidden. I eased up my shirt, tucking my elbows under its tight cloth. I was alone with Alex and Ray Kilgore on a playa miles outside Yuma. It was, or so they claimed, the flattest spot in North America.

"Slow down some, hon," Alex instructed me, her Virginia-tinged drawl taking on the cooler teacher tone of Photography 101.

Slow as I could manage with my heart thumping so fast, I tugged my shirt up. Its white sun-struck cloth formed a tent over my face. Blindly, I felt Alex Kilgore take aim. A click; a whir. Hard to hear amidst the dry wind, the shifting grit and lizards. I thrust my elbows straight up, surrendering to Alex.

Her click; her whir. My midriff then my chest were bared; my back was arched; my breasts strained my bra. I yanked the shirt, holding my head in its tight-stretched sack. With a jerk, I broke free, my top half bursting into air. I blinked, abruptly un-blindfolded. *Burning bush,* I thought, fixing first on Alex, her mass of sunlit hair. Her graying ash blond curls glinted with silver and gold. Behind her, the playa horizon vibrated. A sun-shock of flat. I braced for her next flash. All fall, it had felt like—now, out here, it was—only me and them.

They were my first love. Not just Alex Kilgore—my Photography 101 teacher, my ex-mentor—but Alex and Ray Kilgore together.

When, in 1988, in my freshman fall at Arizona State University, I fantasized about Ray Kilgore, I pictured him making love not to me or to Alex but to a combination of me and her. When this gold-and-silver-maned Alex/me embraced my fantasy Ray, my hands were Alex's deft slender hands. Ray lay before me, amazingly naked, his cock long like his face and his body. I caressed him from head to chest to crotch. I massaged the knotted-up muscles of his shattered knee. When (I fast-forwarded over the actual sex act) we lay side-by-side spent, I told him my troubles and he listened, improbably fascinated. He stroked my tangle of curls, telling me I was—he'd say it in witty words I couldn't imagine—everything to him.

Before the shoot, we had walked it, the playa. A mid-December desert day, clear and sunny. We were celebrating the end of my first semester with Alex Kilgore as my teacher. First and last, if New York University accepted my transfer application. On the hardened mud, cracked so deeply it must have been dried for decades, Alex and Ray and I headed off in no direction except away from our cars: the only objects marring the playa's absolute flatness.

I kept sweaty hold of Ray's lean subtly muscular arm. The first time I'd touched him, this man I had adored for months. My heart pumped with each of our shared steps. Most wives, I was thinking, would plant themselves between me and their husbands if their husbands were eying me like Ray Kilgore had been doing all day. But we're not most people, I thought smugly as the Kilgores and I marched forward, Ray in the middle, my shadow the same inflated size as theirs.

"Ray and I walked this playa, too—twenty-some years ago, our big first date."

"Really?" I turned to Ray. His face looked white as ever, too deeply pale to tan. His black and gray hair shone like a thoroughbred's coat. "C'mon," I coaxed him as I'd done in so many candlelit dinners at their table. "Tell all!"

Gamely, panting with the effort of his steps, Ray told me how Alex had been the only girl at Phoenix High to get the jokes on his Existentialist Bulletin Board. How he'd decked it with Sartre quotes and magazine photos of this playa.

"Finally," Alex cut in, "I asked Ray to drive me out there. Told him *I'd* shoot his precious playa." She tossed her head, her hair spectacularly backlit. "We wound up walking and walking like we were exploring some new planet."

"Your own planet," I burst out. Thinking, for today: our own.

"Oh, c'mon," Alex chided me from her side of Ray. "It's just miles and miles of noplace comfortable to sit down. Much less to lie down. How the Hell," she asked Ray, who leaned on her on his bad-leg side, "did we have sex on the ground out here? Couldn't we have just done the deed in your car, like anyone else?"

"Not Mr. Existential. Sex was serious business back then; at least to me."

"I hadn't yet taught Dr. Ray," Alex confided above the wind, "how to play."

I laughed, wondering as we circled back to our cars if that was what she'd teach me, today. In the scant shade of Alex and Ray's Corvette, sitting on a sun-worn unzipped sleeping bag from their Mexico days, we ate the burgers and tacos we'd bought at The Last Stop Diner. It was past four now, the air a perfect mix of warm and cool. What air-conditioning aspires to create, Ray decreed, breathing deep. Alex unpacked her light reflectors and stands from my parents' four-door Buick. As she set up, Ray and I sat leaning on the white Corvette, dusty for once.

The sky was beginning to lose its blue. Ray sipped from a plastic water bottle. When he turned, closer to me than ever, I smelled scotch.

He raised his handlebar brows. "See, *I* never have to worry about driving." He nodded toward his outstretched right leg. I saw clearly through his khaki pants to the bony bulge of his knee, like a gnarled tree knot.

"You think we'll be driving back late, today?"

Ray shrugged. The metal clanks Alex made setting up sounded distant.

"What—" I lowered my voice. "What do you think Alex wants from me?"

Ray Kilgore sipped his scotch, swallowing slow. She knows I'm in love with you, I imagined him saying. Alex knows and she's happy for us; our marriage is *open* again, honey. You've blown it wide wide open.

"You?" Ray studied the horizon. "You're her—you're our—best audience."

"Audience?" I pulled myself up. Is that all? I wondered, dusting off my skirt.

"Ready for you, hon," Alex called out. Blinking, smoothing my straight hair, I stepped around their car into full sunset light, doubly brightened. Alex's foil light reflectors flashed like metal-stemmed outer-space sunflowers.

"Here, hon." Alex straightened from the Corvette's open driver's door. As if presenting an award, she handed me her ostrich-egg candle-holder. I took hold of the brass base. The lacquered egg pulsated with the sun, its dulled brilliance.

"Oh, perfect! You know how I love this egg. You want me to pose with it?"

"And after, hon, keep it. As a present, to remember Ray and me by . . ."

"*Keep* your egg?"

"Sure. But use it—now—to be my Priestess of the Playa."

For Alex's first roll, as Ray stood to one side, I fondled Alex's os-trich egg. I pressed its sun-warmed surface to my cheek; I held it before me like I was about to kiss its featureless face. It felt brass-heavy and eggshell-light, both at once.

"Really," I told Alex as she reloaded, "I shouldn't keep it. I mean, you've done so much for me already." I darted my eyes to Ray; I found myself ending on a flirtatious note. "What can *I* ever do for you two, in return?"

Alex Kilgore looked at me levelly above the blank eye of her camera. That was when she told me to take off my top.

For our opening class, she made us make ourselves cry.

Alex Kilgore had stalked into the high-ceilinged Art Studio classroom like—I'd thought, riveted on her from the start—a lioness with a lion's mane. I sat hunched over the way I'd promised myself I wouldn't do at ASU: still the too-tall girl in the too-small desk. Alex told us all to shut our eyes. Then to picture an image that made us cry. Which was what she wanted our class to do. Cry.

Um—a jock up front had asked, *IS this Photography 101?*

Amidst his fellow jock's snickers, I shut my eyes. I thought first of Bette Davis's nostril hairs, how before big crying scenes she'd pluck one from her nose.

A few girls around me gave stagey sniffles; I put my head down in my folded arms. Then I remembered one of many low-voiced fights I'd overheard between my parents: "*I* bore *you?*" my dad had asked my mom acidly. "When *you* chatter on and on," he informed her, "I only pretend to listen." At that, I stepped forward into the living-room archway as I'd done so often, stopping them midfight with my mere mute presence. Wondering this time if *anyone* cared what anyone else said or if they were all just pretending. Mom twisted her lipsticked lips into a smile. A strained shape like an earthworm crushed underfoot. That was what I pictured in Alex's class, what made me cry. Mom's pink crushed-worm smile.

"You're the only student," Alex would inform me the next week when she asked me to her home for dinner, "who summoned up for me some real tears."

As Alex reloaded again; as the sunset flared, shifting from gold to orange, I hugged myself in my skirt and bra. I didn't look at silent Ray. "You've passed 101." Alex tried a sly grin, a joking tone. "Now you're ready for 102."

"One-oh-two?" I asked stupidly. Behind me, I felt on my bared back the sunset's full slanted heat and weight. In the cooling air, it warmed my skin.

"You *know* I want some shots of you in the skirt alone, hon."

Is this me? I wondered dazedly as I reached behind myself. This half-naked girl? Never had the simple motion of unhooking my bra, my elbows sticking out like water wings, felt so strange. I jolted forward as my bra gave way. My breasts bounced into the air. I dropped my limp bra, noticing my arm lit up with sun, my skin the same lush yet light golden brown as my skirt.

It all made sense for a second: my sunburn flush so deep the sunset seemed to be happening outside and inside my body. I straightened, my pale soft breasts bared to the cool wind. I didn't look down at them. I put my hands on my hips, posing boldly, basking in the afternoon's last warmth.

"Now why not try—" Alex pivoted with her camera. Automatically, I stepped sideways to stay in her lens's eye. Ray must have sidled closer, too; he and I now stood side-by-side. "You two together." Alex darted her eyes between us, including Ray in her next words. "That's what you've been wanting all along, isn't it?"

My first night at the Kilgores' table, I was all eyes. We all seemed all eyes, our gazes aglitter from one candle rising out of the ostrich egg. The egg made a luminous oval glow. I had never seen anything I wanted so much to touch.

"Let's toast what all happened in class today." Alex bent over the candle, carelessly close, and poured me my first-ever glass of wine. Ray raised one hand like a traffic cop, shielding from the flame Alex's combustible-looking curls.

"My hero," she murmured matter-of-factly as she straightened.

I lifted my glass. Already I felt high, invited by my most dazzling ASU professor to this—it seemed to eighteen-year-old me—illicit dinner. Gravely, Alex raised her own glass. Candlelit, she looked with her shadowy fine-boned face and her deep-socketed deeply cynical dark eyes like a gypsy queen, intoning my fortune.

"Today, when I saw this kid's first batch of prints—her parents' swim pool, of all ungodly things, shot like a photo-equivalent of a Hockney painting—I decided we *had* to have her for supper. To declare our own little holiday marking the arrival of a new talent. This kid," Alex added straight to Ray, "is goddamn good."

We clinked glasses, first Alex and me, hard ("You don't know how I envy you," she'd told me in her shiny kitchen, pummeling raw steak with a square spiked hammer); then Alex and Ray, softly so the glass chimed; last, Ray and me, almost missing, our glasses grazing. His eyes dark and sparkly like the wine.

"To the Goddamn Good." Ray downed his whole drink, keeping one-handed hold of his mahogany cane. He'd stayed seated since I'd come in. He was forty or so like Alex, pale like no one in Phoenix, maybe taller than five foot eleven me. Ray had the elongated face of a retired racehorse. His forehead low and bony; his eyes and permanently flared nostrils diamond-shaped. Ray's black-and-white face had made me step back like I'd stepped back from Alex's black-and-white photos, displayed along their condo's white walls. I needed time to take it all in.

"Oops." Withdrawing my glass from Ray's, I bumped the ostrich egg. It wobbled, its flame swelling sideways. Deftly, Alex steadied the candle.

"Y'know, I *saw* that shy l'il smile of triumph you gave in class. Honestly, hon, you're gonna have to be more discreet, if you're gonna be such a—" She aimed the candle flame at my face, a tiny blinding spotlight. "Suc-cess."

I couldn't help smiling again, recalling the Art Studio's hush after Alex delivered her verdict on my photos, the rocket swell inside my chest. "You say that like 'suck-cess.' Like I'll have to—I don't know— suck from a cesspool."

"Or just plain 'suck up.'" Alex righted the candle. "Which you might *also* have a knack for. Christ, hon, you stare at me in class like you worship me."

"I do?" I asked, meaning: I do. Alex grinned from behind the flame flicker, the most flirtatious grin anyone had ever given me. This is my teacher, I reminded myself. Ray raised his brows disapprovingly as if *he* were our teacher.

"Ohh now, Dr. Ray." Alex waved away Ray's unspoken protest like so much cigarette smoke. "See, hon, Ray is a shrink. Allegedly *non*-directive."

"Really? If I didn't so much want to be a photographer, *I'd* want to be a psy-chiatrist, -chologist, whichever one doesn't prescribe pills but just *listens*."

"That's my Ray." Alex pressed her slim hand to the square-knuckled hand he kept curved around his cane's handle. The cane wobbled, supporting Alex, too.

How long had they been together? Twenty years, she answered for both of them. "We got hitched to get away from our screwed-up families."

"Funny thing was," Ray added, his free hand twirling his empty wineglass, "the only people we could talk to about what a mistake our getting married was was each other. Which, at least, was something."

"The best thing," I murmured to my almost drained glass.

Ray nodded; the gently intent *yes-go-on* nod he must use in his practice, curing high-strung girls like me with his slim-Buddha presence.

"Don't know about 'best.'" Alex stood. "Ray and I had lots going on in nonverbal realms, too. See, hon, we had—deep in the late '60s—an open marriage."

She swept off into the kitchen. I coughed, inhaling my last swallow of wine.

Ray passed me his water. "Did she have to wait till your mouth was full?"

One soothing sip and I managed to ask as Alex strode back in, "'Open'?"

"Wide." She set before me a plate of bloody steak. "Any questions?"

As the half-set sun reddened the playa horizon, Ray and I posed for Alex. Face-to-face at arm's length, my bare breasts pointing at him. My nipples pointed, too—which only Alex could see, since Ray kept his eyes locked with mine. His close-up gaze seemed distant, his pupils blurred in his purplish black irises. My fingers trembling—surely he felt that—I held Ray's face. His warm white skin was tinged gold from the sunset. His beard bristle felt dense, a thicket ready to spring up under my fingertips. I breathed the scotch smell of Ray's even breaths; I sealed my own lips against my burger's onions. I wanted to embrace Ray, flatten my breasts against his chest. But he and I stayed planted in place, Ray's cane lying at his side where Alex had set it down after she'd positioned us.

We're only, I reminded my shaky self, posing.

I gaped at my ground-up steak in its pool of blood. "Wow," I found myself saying, not sure Alex Kilgore was serious about letting me ask her any question. "I love meat rare but I've never dared it *this* rare."

"She's never dared it this rare," Alex repeated to Ray in a private-joke tone. And she bent toward me, her chin in her hand. "So this's your first steak tartare?" I nodded. Alex smiled. "I love to watch anyone's first-time anything."

I chewed the cold lusciously rich meat, speechless.

"*Mmmm.*" Alex Kilgore swallowed her own first mouthful.

Beside her, Ray chewed thoughtfully; he did everything thoughtfully. "It's a bit like eating a—poultice. But a classy poultice. Louis the XIV's poultice. . ."

Alex gave her hoot of a laugh, pressing Ray's hand again. As we ate, she coaxed Ray into describing to me his Psychology Master's Thesis on people living and reliving certain central life events. I listened hard and asked smart questions, just as I'd imagined doing someday with the sensitive intelligent man who'd be my first love. I barely noticed Alex whisking away our bloody plates.

Dessert was Grand Marnier liquor for Ray and, for Alex and me, fudge sundaes served in red-striped bowls that looked edible, too. Between spoonfuls, sensing it might be my last chance, I finally ventured a question. "So 'open marriage' means—do *you* mean, I mean— both of you could sleep with other people?"

"Mostly me." Alex sucked hard sauce off her spoon like a greedy girl, her cheeks hollowed out. In her sun-lined face, I glimpsed a waifish twenty-year-old. Ray leaned back on the rear legs of his chair, giving her a bemused half-smile.

"Mostly men I met when Ray and I were driving around Mexican border towns, shooting what became my one and only show. 'Acting out,' Dr. Ray might say. Not that he didn't do his share, back then. By the time we'd settled in Phoenix, we made some rules—no students, no patients—that sorta reformed us."

"Lexie." Ray gave a low warning sound in his throat like a nicker. "That's enough." Alex lifted the wine bottle and rose, a Southern Hostess motion.

"Oh, no no, I think she wants more." She bent over the table, her shirt unbuttoned so low I saw her breasts plumped up into a black bra.

"Alex, your *hair.*" Ray seized the ostrich-egg candle. Its flame knifed up straight. Alex laughed and batted at her scorched curls. The only thing she cooked, I thought; everything else served raw. We breathed the burnt-fur smoke.

"You've wanted all night to do that." Ray set the candle firmly back in place.

"*I've* wanted all night to touch this egg." I pressed my palms around the ostrich egg, feeling through its heated lacquered shell its hollowed inside.

"*I've* wanted to touch this egg-*head.*" Stepping behind her husband, Alex sunk her thumbs into his coarse black and gray hair. She curved her long fingers around his long face. Ray heaved a sigh that sounded both exasperated and supremely content. Alex began massaging his temples.

"I'd best get home to Mom and Dad." I rose, unfolding my stork legs.

"Don't let Lexie scare you away." Ray leaned back, his head pillowed by his wife's breasts. Under his straight unmoving brows, he rolled his eyes up at her.

"Ohhh, I think we'll be seeing a lot of this one," Alex told him languidly, bowing over him. Her silver- and gold-glinting hair tickled his face. I edged out the door, wondering if they'd pull off each other's clothes as soon as I left.

In my car's rearview mirror, I looked with my wine-stained lips like a happy vampire. I began driving back to my parents' house as I did every Friday night. I felt floaty, like the time I'd filched my mom's Valium. But not, like then, numb. The opposite of numb. In my parents' boat of a Buick, I whizzed along at the speed limit—fast, for me— picturing Ray and Alex. Alex climbing onto Ray's lap; Alex straddling Ray as he rocked his chair, rocked the two of them slower and harder.

I pressed my thighs together. I fingered the scalloped edges of the photos I'd so triumphantly presented in class. My glossy tickets to— what? My heart pumped with half-imagined hopes. Once a marriage was open, could it ever really be closed? Was an open marriage like an open house? Come in; try my husband on for size. My hair blew back in the desert-night wind so it felt fuller, like hers.

I approached an intersection, poising my foot over my brake, thinking the way my dad had taught me, *Stop, Stop, Stop,* then, as the light stayed yellow and I floored the gas, *Go no matter what.*

Alex clicked and whirred; I shifted my gaze to Ray's close-up mouth, his lower lip moist as always. My mouth watered behind my sunburnt lips. What if I pulled his face forward and kissed him? How far would Alex let our pose go?

As if in answer, Alex told us both, "Now maybe a few shots lying down? The Priestess of the Playa meets Mr. Existential. Over here on our—sleeping bag?"

Ray and I turned away from each other to face her, dumbfounded.

She lowered her camera. Wind blew her loose hair over her mouth, a desert woman's veil. Through her hair, she spoke to Ray sharply and quietly, like a wife. "Don't think I haven't noticed how you've been watching her."

"Watching her?" Ray echoed Alex, sounding as incredulous as I felt.

Instinctively, the way I used to do when my parents would begin one of their quiet fights, I backed up a few steps, the playa ground flat as concrete. I hugged my plush breasts, feeling exposed without Alex's camera flashes. She was stepping up to Ray, answering him in a whisper; she was bending to hand him his cane.

Was it possible he wanted me, for real? *Wasn't* that what I'd been wanting all along? I slid my feet back ten steps, my sandals scraping grit. I stopped at their sleeping bag. I was still feeling like a kid, eager to distract my parents with my good-girl obedience. So I lay down on the sleeping bag, just as Alex had asked.

Certain chemicals turn color when light hits them. This Alex explained to me in the ASU darkroom, the week after our first dinner together. She'd pulled me from Photography 101, signed me up for a Directed Study with her alone.

"Photography, hon, is a whole technology built around letting light hit film. Then *not* letting light hit it while you, first, wash out the part that *didn't* change—" Alex waved that timid part away with one hand, "and, second, fix the part that *did* change to make good 'n sure it stays changed." She stepped next to me in the red-lit dark, her breath smelling of the orange slices she'd been sucking. I looked down at her, a head taller. She held up a long folded sack.

"This here's called a Changing Bag. Double-zipped to keep out all light. You do your own developing inside this bag. Feel it. See how many layers it has?"

I slipped my hand into one of the Changing Bag's accordion sleeves.

"You'll need both hands, actually." Alex slid her hand inside the crackly bag so it brushed my hand. "What I sense about you," she told me as if I'd just asked, "is that you've got an eye like my eye, but also something I—being my mama's daughter—never had." Inside the bag, Alex's hand clasped mine. "Discipline."

"But I—I've only done a few shoots." My hand felt limp in Alex's, mine as hot and sweaty as hers was cool and dry. "I hope I can—live up to what you want."

"You're the one's gotta want it, hon." Alex released my hand, pulling hers out briskly. The Changing Bag hung from my arm, one oversized sleeve.

"I do," I told Alex, trying like a bride to sound sure. Were the rotten-egg fixer fumes going to my head? It's too hot in here, I started to say.

And a bull-necked young man thrust open the curtains covering the darkroom's door.

"You're here," he told Alex. "I left messages. At your office, on your car."

"Listen, hon," Alex began, and I wasn't sure if she meant me or him. "I'd like to talk but you've caught me in the middle of a class session—"

"'Caught you'; that's right."

He took another step, leaving the curtains half-open behind him. In the crack of light, his blandly tan face looked so similar to other ASU jocks that—I found myself thinking—I'd never be able to identify him in a police lineup.

"C'mon, hon." This time, Alex meant me. She turned her back on him; she took firm hold of my arm. "You need air and I need a smoke."

He tensed gamely as if to block us; Alex bulled her way past him. She and I slipped down the hall, ducked through a side entrance of the Humanities Building. We stepped straight into the September midday, its punishing sun. Leggy blonds on bikes whizzed by along the blindingly white sidewalks.

"Who was that?" I asked Alex, sun-dazzles bobbing in my eyes.

"Oh, another student. Ex-, I mean, student." She glanced back at the side door; she fished a Camel pack from her pocket. "Don't *you* keep staring at me."

"I'm your student, too. I'm studying you."

"Ha." With a flourish, Alex struck her match, its flame upstaged by the all-surrounding sunlight. "Just don't ask me what I'd do for a Camel. These days I only light up away from Ray. He's always after me to quit something or other . . ."

"Like seducing students?" I asked back, light-headed from that darkroom.

Alex hooted with laughter, falling onto a concrete bench under a grapefruit tree. "You oughtn't talk to your teacher that way." She crossed her legs. Even in the heat, she wore black jeans and a man's white pressed shirt. "Y'know hon, I think Dr. Ray might be due to break a few rules himself soon."

With me? I wasn't bold enough to say. Feeling my giveaway face flush, I stepped up to a water fountain, salmon pink like the Humanities Building. I splashed my face hard then settled on the bench beside Alex, my bangs damp.

"Let your face show." Turning to me, side-blowing smoke, Alex smoothed my bangs against my head. "It's distinctive. Which lasts way longer than pretty."

"'Distinctive'? Don't think anyone else sees me that way."

Only, I didn't add, my mirror self. Alone in my bedroom at home, I had admired how my too-prominent bones stood out under my too-thin skin, how my starey eyes shone with the hyper green of traffic lights signaling GO.

"No one around here would 'get' a face like yours." Alex flicked an ash at two shirtless expressionless jocks sunning themselves on the Humanities' front steps. "But *I'd* like to—shoot it. Your face. A tutorial of sorts, it'll be, for you to watch me do—I haven't done near enough lately—a real shoot. Tomorrow afternoon at our place." Alex stood, adding, "I know Ray would *love* to see you, too."

Love? As I made my giddy way back to my dorm, I felt my heartbeat jack up and up. If Alex had been having her own affairs, breaking their rules, did she now owe Ray a fling? Was that how it worked? I walked faster. Toward them, away from them. We have—I thought, green diamonds of sun flashing above me between spikey interlocked palm fronds—a date.

The nylon sleeping bag barely cushioned my head from the hard ground. Ray and Alex were exchanging murmurs—hers slow, maybe coaxing; his curt, questioning. I was lying on my back, my breasts half-flattened. The gold- and orange- and red-streaked sky arched above and around me, stunningly uncluttered. It hurt my eyes and ears, so much wide-open space. Wind stirred my airy skirt. I remembered the distant bitter kick of Mom's Valium on my tongue, my limbs growing logy as I waited for it to work. To relax me, for once. What would my parents think if they saw me lying here? Their gawky daughter.

Maybe inside I'm like Alex, I told myself as Alex and Ray approached. An adventuress; willing to try everything. Ray's cane tapped the hardened dirt like a blind man's. My bare-chested body stiffened as they loomed above me: tall unsteady uncertain-looking Ray; short smiling determined-looking Alex.

"What—what's going on here?" I asked the sky-space between their heads.

"What do you want to go on here, hon? We're open to suggestions."

"Open?" I blinked, dizzy from all the sky, all the windy empty space.

"Look." Alex took Ray's arm as firmly as she'd taken mine to lead me out of the darkroom. "Let's try a few sleeping-bag shots. Let's see what happens."

I snapped my gaze to Ray, his impassive face. "I guess we can—see."

He jerked his chin slightly. His *yes-go-on* nod. I rolled on my side, hugging myself again, harder. The air was fast losing its perfect mix of warm and cool.

At the door, Alex told me Ray wanted to watch our shoot. And she led me into their condo for my second visit. Ray needs, she informed me, his entertainment. Awaiting Ray, I sat at their butcher-block counter chopping scallions for salsa. Alex stood before me ironing white button-down shirts. Her hair was pulled into a ponytail, steam dampening her tendrils. "See, I'm just another Valley of the Sun matron." Alex licked her finger and touched the iron's tip, a spark snapping. "Haven't had a show in years. But maybe you'll inspire me, hon." She folded the shirts she and Ray wore into one pile. "How'd you wind up out here? You don't belong here anymore'n I do. You look like the sun alone would kill you."

Dipping chips in the salsa, Alex and I traded childhoods. Mine solitary at grade school in Kansas and high school here, but cocooned at home with my mom and dad, who—agreeing on one thing, that I was gifted—framed the photos I shot each summer of my flocks of cousins. The closest I came to having friends.

Alex was the opposite: a bold popular cutup amongst her Phoenix High friends and boyfriends; a brooder and pacer of empty rooms in the sparsely furnished Spanish-tiled mansion her thrice-married Southern Belle Mama couldn't afford to maintain. Its kidney-shaped swim pool visibly reeked.

"So after Ray and I moved to this condo—after Mexico and Ray's accident—I made Ray *change* the kidney shape of our little pool to an oval, my blue egg."

What kind of accident? I was working up the nerve to ask when Ray rattled the front door. Leaning on his cane, he crossed the living room in jerky up-and-down steps.

"Hey, Dr. Ray." Alex filled his glass. "Can we borrow this?" She bent over him, unknotted his tie. First she slipped onto me one of the freshly pressed shirts. Their uniform, I decided, straightening like a new recruit as she buttoned me up.

"When Ray was at Harvard—*where*, I'll have you know, he spent most of his time writing lovesick letters to little ol' me back in Phoenix— the guys in his dorm were still required to wear *ties* at dinner." Alex draped Ray's tie around my neck.

"One night—" Ray swallowed half his wine. "I came in wearing the skin of a Biology lab rat around my neck. Questioning, I claimed, the whole nature of 'tie.'"

I laughed louder than Alex. Ray granted me his bemused smile. I flushed.

"Now don't get all hot and bothered; I need you cool and kinda blank." Alex lined me up against her living room's wall. "You know: your Young Nun look—"

"Sometimes I feel like I *oughta* be some kind of nun," I told Ray while Alex tilted her lights. And I described my one date at Phoenix High. The boy I'd imagined to be bookish drove me to Camelback Mountain for attempted necking. I chewed my cinnamon gum all the way up; I was still chewing it when he stuck his tongue in my mouth. Didn't I, he asked, know what a date is supposed to *be?*

"Hey, that can work." Alex focused her lens. "Repressed Sexy is the best sexy, to a certain kind of—sensitive guy." Beyond her shoulder, Ray nodded.

I swallowed, Ray's tie tightly knotted at my throat. "Just the kind of guy I'll never meet here in the Valley of the Sun-tanned."

"Which's one reason I'm helping you get transferred outa ASU. Till then—" Alex aimed her Nikon. "You might as well stick with Ray and me."

"Lexie, c'mon," Ray protested from the shadows. "This is pearls before swine. Poor kid doesn't want to spend all her weekends hanging out here with us."

I faced Alex's rapid-fire flash flash flash: *I do; I do; I do.*

Alex helped Ray down onto the sleeping bag. Changing bag, I told myself. I remembered the darkroom jock, remembered Alex telling Ray as I'd left our first dinner, *I think we'll be seeing a lot of this one.* Ray blocked my sky now, rolling onto his side so he faced me. *This one, this one,* I thought as Alex bent and pulled the sleeping bag around us. She zipped up one side so it wrapped Ray and me. She loved, she'd told me that first night, to watch anyone's first-time anything.

I met Ray's blurred-black eyes, unblinking like a lizard's. Inching forward, hiding my face, I burrowed into Ray's reassuringly solid shoulder. I breathed in. Through his cotton shirt, his sweatless skin smelled pickled by liquor.

Ray maneuvered his arms around me, steering the small of my back. Our crotches aligned. Through the rough cloth of his khakis and the gauzy cloth of my skirt, I pressed my hips to his. Was Ray hard? Wouldn't I feel that through his pants? Or was the dense fleshy mass behind his zipper as hard as men got?

"Re-lax," Alex was instructing from above, far above it seemed, her voice muffled as Ray rolled on top of me, heavily. God; had he passed out?

My breasts were flattened, my ribs crowded close to my heart. How had women through the ages managed to breathe under men? I tensed my limbs, half-wanting to heave Ray off of me. Half-wondering if Alex might then turn on me. Revoking her letter, snatching back the future she'd invented for me?

"Don't be afraid t' move, you two. Just act like no one is watch-ing—"

What turns her on, I felt sure as she drew out that word. Alex Kilgore wants to watch my first time. To shoot it. I began stiffening up again, my eyes squeezed shut against Ray's scotch smell. Gently, he rubbed my thighs up and down as if to warm me through my skirt. Did it look, from outside the bag, like he had his hands on my skin? Like he was unzipping his pants? I still didn't feel Ray hardening behind his still-zipped zipper. Because he was too drunk? Or because it hadn't been real at all, his seeming attraction to me?

Ray began to grind his big-boned hips against mine. I gasped because it grated through my thin skirt, thin skin. Bone against bone.

Ray nuzzled my shoulder. *"Pretend,"* he breathed into my ear.

"Rain! We have to *cel*-ebrate that, too, tonight!"

Grandly, as raindrops dotted the oval pool, Alex slid open the glass door to the patio. Lounging on the couch, breathing wet sage— delicious to us parched Phoenicians—she and I watched the late-November downpour spatter their pool. Skating back and forth in the breeze on their glass coffee table: the letter of recommendation Alex had written for my application as a transfer student to NYU.

"Oh, to go to New York at your age!" Alex paced her white flickering room. She paused at each of her Mexico photos, their lavish blacks undimmed. "'Inside Out,' I called my Mexico show—such a '70s title. But that's how *I* felt, at twenty."

"So that's why all the photos go back and forth between inside and—?"

"Right again, Miss Straight-A. See, the people I shot didn't give a hoot what their houses looked like outside—tin roofs and unpainted wood. But the *insides*: every inch so fancifully decorated, so fucking year-round *festive.*" She studied an overhead shot of a family sharing a fringed blanket, their three bent bodies picking up its zigzag pattern. The young father, whose mustache seemed painted on his pretty-boy face, curled around his pregnant wife who in turn curled around their sleeping sons. "I felt way, way outside of all that. And I tried, with this little *familia,* all the wrong ways to get, y'know, in."

"So what did happen down there, with Ray and his leg and all. . .?"

"Ask Ray, hon. It's his story to tell. How he rescued me."

In a fight, with knives? Alex and I snapped our heads around as Ray's airport cab pulled up. He'd spent a week at a therapist's conference in San Francisco.

"Home, I'm Honey." At the door, he dropped his travel bag, keeping hold of his cane. I tensed, wanting to rush over to him with Alex, like a second wife.

I waited till Alex was in the kitchen dishing up our enchiladas to tell Ray that I'd been asking her about Mexico, his accident. "She says you rescued her. . . ?"

"She *would* put it that way. Lexie needs her little dramas." Ray downed a long swallow of wine. "We were just tequila-drunk kids. Her last man in Mexico, see, was this choirboy, this teenage daddy. Didn't let on how furious he felt—at Lexie for sleeping with him and at me for letting her—till we were crammed in his VW bug. He was driving and yelling in Spanish, both at seventy miles per hour. I grabbed the wheel. I wound up the only one injured when the bug rolled over."

"We all might've died if you hadn't taken that wheel." Alex appeared in the kitchen archway, her rainy-day hair buoyant, her voice raised as if onstage.

"Sure, sure." Ray rolled his eyes, something only I saw. "It took Lexie and poor praying Alfredo hours to pry my leg loose. Lexie and I flew back to the States, to a Phoenix hospital so my dad the doctor could treat me. Could gloat over the hippie-dippie mess we'd made; could trundle me off to med school—"

"It wasn't *just* a mess. I don't regret one minute of Mexico."

Bet Ray does, I answered Alex silently. Ray shrugged. "Lexie likes to see me—she's the only one; my family thinks I'm a first-class fool—as some sort of hero."

"You are," she insisted, sullenly setting down our enchiladas. "Mine."

After we ate, Alex opened a San Francisco present from Ray. When she lifted from its nest of tissue the hand-painted skirt, she declared it all wrong for her.

He must've been thinking, she told me, of you. She tossed me the skirt.

It fit. I stepped from their bathroom, my long knob-kneed legs fluidly draped. The net cloth, nearly see-through, was painted with shades of sienna that matched highlights I thought no one noticed in my light brown hair.

"It suits her," Ray agreed with Alex, sounding unsurprised.

"Then she oughta keep it. *If* she lets me shoot her in it. And I know the perfect *place* to shoot her." Alex turned to Ray, locking eyes with him, all at once intently intimate. "Our favorite place. The playa!"

"The opposite of *No Exit*," Ray explained to me, his voice wine-slowed. "That's what I told Alex years ago, back in Phoenix High. The playa is nothing *but* Exits."

"The perfect backdrop for her look—so goddamn grandly blank."

"It's a deal!" I twirled on tiptoe in my weightless new skirt, wondering as I spun what might happen between me and them in the land of All Exits.

Pretend? Had I heard right? Ray nuzzled my other ear.

"Please," he breathed, so raggedly low I knew he didn't want Alex to hear.

"C'mon now, Dr. Ray," Alex was crooning from above us as if she were directing us in a scene. "Isn't this what every man wants? To be a girl's first . . ."

So maybe she did know that nothing was happening inide our bag. Was she, I couldn't not wonder, disappointed in Ray, in me? Roughly, as if he'd prove something for both of us, Ray held me tighter and pumped his hips harder against mine. Alex clicked and whirred faster. I gripped Ray's shoulders, his big shoulder blades rotating under his skin. I writhed against him, straining to match his rhythm.

"Good," he mumbled in my ear. Good acting? Or did it feel good to him?

Clicks, whirs. I stroked his back, feeling as numb and clumsy as I'd felt high on Mom's Valium, wearing three-fingered Minnie Mouse gloves. Clicks, whirs.

"*Ohh*—" I burst out, realizing this alone might make them—make the whole game—stop. I snapped open my eyes, meeting Alex's glassy lens eye over Ray's suddenly tensed-up shoulder. And I threw back my head, hitting through the puffy nylon bag hard-mud ground. I squeezed shut my eyes at that pain, wondering if Alex thought it the first-time pain of her husband thrusting into me.

"Oh, God," I gasped for good measure. Then I let myself go limp.

"Good," Alex told us, all husky-voiced. Ray collapsed onto me with a gusty dead-drunk sigh of relief, exhaustion. I kept my eyes shut, kept my body stiff and still under his. Spent, yes: but not at all in the way I'd imagined.

"Good," Alex repeated like she couldn't stop herself. "Good good good good."

Object # 1: My Buick's heat-blistered steering wheel, its blue-plastic skin peeling like blighted tree bark, scarred by tiny burst bubbles.

At our last one-on-one session, Alex Kilgore handed me my portfolio, my cover sheet scrawled with a lipstick-red Magic-Marker "A." She told me she'd submit my Object Studies to her old editor at *Southwest Photographer*. Really? I asked, the rocket in my chest jolting into liftoff position.

Object #2: My windshield shield, pleated cardboard, one side painted turquoise; the other displaying silvery block letters, SEND HELP.

We strolled into the bright December afternoon, chatting about the playa trip we'd take that weekend, Alex smoking a Camel. As she strode off, she pulled an orange from her purse. She'd eat it to hide from Ray her smoky breath, I guessed, feeling privileged to know all of Alex Kilgore's little secrets.

Object #3: An apple left behind on my unshaded front seat at highest noon, half-baked, its thinnest skin half smooth and red, half brown and deflated.

The playa was not as far away driving out as it had seemed driving in. No intersections and road lines marked my progress. I drove bare-breasted into a dusky dark that made the desert feel like a huge deserted theater, minus seats and stage. No one is watching you, I kept reminding myself. And I kept darting glances at my rearview, half-hoping to see their headlights behind me.

After I had struggled out from under Ray, out of the bag—he rolled on his back with his eyes shut—after Alex declared, as if she and I were the ones in cahoots, "That's just what I wanted, hon," I had bent and grabbed the ostrich-egg candleholder by its brass base. I swung it up like a weapon; I pictured shattering the hollow egg over Alex's head, her fake-playful grin frozen on her face. "C'mon now, hon." She reached toward me like a grade-school teacher disarming a little girl.

"You didn't either get what you want," I whined, clutching the egg to my breasts. "That wasn't my first time! And we didn't even do anything just then," I rushed to add because I saw in her face she knew already. "But we've been—Ray and me—seeing each other almost all summer—"

"Oh c'mon." Alex shook back her hair as if merely impatient. She shot a glance at Ray, lying too still to be asleep. Ray not denying what I'd just wildly improvised. "If only that *were* true." Alex snapped her eyes back to me alone, though she raised her voice enough above the wind for Ray to hear. "At least *somebody* would be getting some action from him."

Then Alex broke our locked gaze, looking down—giving in, it felt like—first.

I took a barefoot step back, watching her hair blow over her face again like a transparent veil, feeling satisfied that I'd hurt her. I'd made her admit to me, her best audience, the real state of her marriage.

So I turned my bare back. So I ran, my breasts jiggling hard with each step.

"Nothing *hap*-pened," I shouted to Alex as I jerked open my Buick's door.

"Sure—" Alex hollered, seizing the last word. "We were just *play*-ing!"

I hurled the candleholder onto my front seat. The egg cracked; I scrambled in, too. Pulling out with a lurch, I glimpsed them in my rearview: Ray still lying in the sleeping bag; Alex calling my name, waving my T-shirt like a white flag.

As the dark thickened, I tightened my grip on my wheel; I fought the urge to spin it, turn around, rescue my photos. Not Ray and me grappling in the bag, but the ones from before, from sunset. Had I ever felt so nearly beautiful?

I did spin the wheel. My Buick bumped round on the hardened ground to face where I'd been. Where I thought I'd been. In the new darkness, I circled and circled as if on a rotary with no signs or streets to choose. *Pretend,* Ray had begged me. All so he could put on some show for Alex, so he could pretend to be his younger self; all so she could keep staging these games she needed to stay entertained. And me? Did this prove what I'd do for a Camel?

"But nothing *hap*-pened—" I repeated out loud, not believing it this time. And hadn't Dr. Ray warned me that certain events keep happening to a person, inside them, over and over? I banged my hands on the wheel, braking the car. Then I lifted the candleholder beside me, its ostrich egg jaggedly cracked. I broke off one curved shard. Keeping hold of that, I shoved open my door, dumped the candleholder onto the playa. A heap of metal and shell. I slammed my door, noticing distant pinpoint lights. Before heading toward them, I ripped my skirt into strips; I wrapped my breasts, toga style. I pictured Alex and Ray's dark bright gazes, candlelit, intently fixed on me. If Ray hadn't been too drunk, I might have given him—him and Alex, my best audience—my virginity. I shivered in my torn-up skirt. How far I was willing to go: just to be seen the way they saw me.

All through my drive back to Phoenix, I kept holding my ostrich-egg shard, fingering it as I sensed I'd do for years. Its two layers: the cool white lacquer thick yet hollow-feeling; the inner curve of eggshell thin yet dense, pearly.

Warm to my fingertip touch, that shell still holding a trace of life.

Celebration

July 10, 1998

Cracking an egg for her husband's birthday cake, Sarah spread her thumb and index finger so the white stretched. The yolk plopped into the bowl. Her doctor had spread his gloved fingers that way—only wider, Sarah watching from between her own knees—to demonstrate the thickness and stretchiness of Sarah's mucus. No reason, Dr. Hess had decreed, for no baby. At least not from what he called Sarah's end. Deftly, Sarah whisked the egg into a golden froth. She raised her wrists like a magician, pouring in milk and canola oil. Both low-fat, for Paul's heart. Then she lifted the whole bowl of wet ingredients. These she dribbled in extravagant satiny streams over the dry.

"One, two, three—" She counted the strokes of her wooden spoon, not wanting to count and light Paul's fifty-two candles. Each year, Sarah dreaded this day.

BIRTHDAY CAKE BLAZE IGNITES HOME, she'd once clipped from the paper. What are the odds of that? she wondered now the way she often wondered about their hypothetical child. Its chances of inheriting the talent Sarah's mother still insisted Sarah had or the dark moods Paul's father always denied. Paul's dad was Manic-Depressive; Paul was,

161

Paul joked, Depressive-Depressive. At one hundred, Sarah stopped her spoon. Then added a hundred and first stroke, for luck.

She wiped her eggy hands on her flour-powdered denim shorts. Fingers still sticky, she swept back her long damp hair. Shampooed, for once, but tangled. She was sloppy as a teenager, Paul liked to say. Or "lazy as" or "sweet as" or "supple as"; it still turned them on: the sixteen years between them. Sarah, at thirty-five, still Paul's Child Bride; his, he once murmured, Personal Virgin.

Snock. She unscrewed the maraschino cherry jar. Popping her cherry: had it really felt like that? she remembered asking Paul. From, he'd known she'd meant, his end. She mixed the cherry juice with milk. Bright red streaked the white, blending into an aggressively cheerful pink. Would this cake, this celebration she was making, come on too strong? Would it, after his long day at the Center, turn Paul off rather than on?

Pinky-pink! Sarah remembered Tim T. chanting in her own days at the Center. She set aside some extra cherry milk, deciding she'd stop by Tim's Mildly/ Moderately Retarded Room today on her way to pick up Paul.

"Mmmhmm," she hummed as she poured the remaining plain milk into a saucer. The metal slot on the front door clanked. Sarah kept pouring, humming as loud as Tim T. did when he imitated his beloved vacuum cleaner. Pretending she didn't know it had arrived: the mail.

"Here, puss." Sarah eased up the window and set the saucer on the brick sill. As if at a secret lover, she smiled at the upstairs tenant's tom-cat, sunning himself on the leaf-strewn fire escape. A lucky sign; a sign that the sperm-count results they awaited wouldn't come today of all days. Although that was exactly the kind of trick pulled by what Paul's racetrack-addict Dad called the Odds Gods. The tom stropped Sarah's hand, his hot fur aglow in the hazy sun.

Paul loved cats as much as she did, but Sarah didn't want them lavishing a babyless couple's love on an animal. Didn't—this was the reason she said aloud—want any other creature sharing their nest above the trees.

"OK, cat. Enjoy." She relatched the screen, old paint flaking on the sill. Suspiciously, the tom circled the milk. Like Paul, he thought he couldn't be led. Sarah fingered a grainy paint chip, turning her back to grant the cat privacy.

She and Paul had bought this 1950s apartment five years before, with the assumption—uneasy, on both ends—that they'd soon have a baby. Only last year, after Sarah quit her stressful Center job, had they begun seeing Dr. Hess, tracking Sarah's ovulations. Taking in, one week ago, Paul's semen sample.

Under leaf rustle, the cat lapped the milk. As he licked the china clean—rougher, sexier sounds—Sarah imagined circling her tongue around Paul's nipples. How long had it been since they'd had sex for sex's sake? She turned to glimpse the black streak of cat, rushing off on urgent business.

"OK," she told herself. Meaning: OK, wimp; check that mail.

First, she lifted her bowl, noticing on the table a spill of white powder. *That might be all the baking soda,* her worrywart mom would point out. As sloppy compensation for any baking mistakes, Sarah stirred in an extra cup of walnuts, Paul's favorite. Carefully, she slid her overfilled pans into the oven.

She padded across their tidied-up living room, past the overloaded bookshelves and the coffee table piled with newspapers. Dispatches from the distant-seeming outside world. Kneeling by the front door's mail slot, Sarah set aside a birthday card from her mother, who counted Sarah's childlessness, not to mention Sarah's careerlessness, among her life's disappointments.

Drawing a breath, Sarah lifted a thin envelope from the hospital Urology Lab. She remembered her sisters' college-application replies. Thick meant yes; thin, no. She carried the envelope unopened into the cave of a bedroom, flipping on the nightstand lamp. It glinted off Paul's blood-pressure pill bottles and, on her side, the ovulation thermometer. Today fell on an off-week.

"Fuck fertility," Sarah murmured aloud. As if to Paul, tonight.

Spread open on Paul's pillow was *The Journal of Psychological Disorders.* In one issue, Sarah had read that women failing to conceive showed as high a depression rate as AIDS patients. What did it mean about her that she still savored like an unearned reward her days alone? Days she had imagined to be numbered. Picking halfheartedly at the letter's seal, Sarah studied the poster tacked above their bed. A Vermeer milkmaid; a gracefully arced stream of milk that always looked warm. Reassured, Sarah turned her back on the bed.

She opened their closet; she slipped Paul's sealed sperm count into her empty artist's portfolio. For now, she told herself. Then she bundled up the construction paper and glue and homemade birthday cards stacked beneath the portfolio. Arms full, she shuffled out to the cherry- and vanilla-scented kitchen.

Half an hour left. Sarah flipped fast through her sketch pad: line drawings of her husband's bearded face, of the tomcat's fluid poses. Years before, her sisters had tried to talk Sarah into going to Art School as their mother had longed to do. *I just think you could do better,* they'd kept remarking about her Center job as a teacher's aide. Later, her sisters had said the same thing about Paul, back when he'd seemed a first lover Sarah would outgrow.

All Sarah wanted—or so she'd told her oldest sister Sibyl, the still-single corporate lawyer—was to have a happy home. "All?" skeptical Sibyl had repeated. *But Sarah, sweetie, that's what's hardest to make. And to keep.*

Sarah lifted the dozen cardboard cards Paul would lay end-to-end on their floor tonight: one for each year of marriage. The only artworks she actually enjoyed making. Cartoon sketches of her and Paul—his hairline receding; her waistline expanding—captioned by newspaper headlines. MAY-DECEMBER ROMANCE BLOSSOMS FOR RUTHLESS DICTATOR, in 1986, the year they wed.

Last year, 1997, she'd dared a reference to their baby plan— PROSPECT OF ALIEN INVADER THREATENS SMALL-TOWN PEACE—and Paul's laugh had sounded forced. As Sarah pulled out the 1998 headlines she'd clipped by whim, the phone rang. That shattering sound. On tape, Paul's deep, forbidding voice recited their number, offering no incentive for the caller to disrupt them.

Happy one, Saint Paul. It IS today, isn't it? Sarah drew a sharp cake-scented breath. The long-distance rasp of Paul's seventy-year-old dad.

—Found myself back down here in Florida. Friend of mine from my old Pimlico days has a horse here at the Gulf Stream track he wants me to size up. . . And now I'm hoping my Saint Paul might wire me some cash to—see me on home, son. And 'course I'm hoping you two—a crackly pause, implying there should be three or more—*make yourselves as big a celebration as—you can.* On your small-time salary, Sarah filled in. The Dad heaved a rough exhale—a chain-smoker who'd live forever—and hung up.

Briskly, Sarah shuffled her '98 headlines, making sure they were all here. During his last visit, Paul's dad had filched money from Paul's wallet. Tall as Paul, he'd paced their small apartment restlessly in his big-shouldered sports jacket. "Sizing up" their home; asking Sarah when he'd "get" his grandson.

Paul's mood would deflate if he heard that fake-fatherly voice. So, Sarah decided, she'd make him forget to ask about phone messages or mail. Forget—what they did best—the outside world. SAINT PAUL BEDEVILED BY BLIZZARD. She considered cutting off *Blizzard* and substituting—what? *Babylessness?* Everyone outside them would assume that must bedevil Paul. Everyone who'd be shocked by how little they'd done all these years to cure their infertility.

As she smelled her cake solidifying, Sarah pulled a headline that could send a different—a defiant—message. Microscopic newsprint shreds stuck to her finger as she pasted the headline onto her square of cardboard. Below it, she pasted her '98 sketch. Her ink belly too rounded, like she *was* pregnant.

The oven buzzed. Quarter till four. Fifteen minutes left to dress and—shouldn't she?—read Paul's long-delayed sperm count. Sarah shut off the buzzer, her gluey fingers sticking to its knob. She flung open the oven. The cake layers bulged with walnuts, bumpy like two halves of a cherry-speckled brain. Bending into the sweet heat, Sarah vowed to make Paul's birthday—no matter the number of candles or of sperm—perfectly damn happy.

She clutched the wheel, approaching the Merritt Parkway turnoff. Locked now in 5 P.M. traffic, shaken now from having read the sperm count, Sarah felt more timid than ever about merging. As her car queued up, she fiddled with the radio, trying to find music she wouldn't mind dying to.

Paul's ex-shrink, who'd prescribed the Zoloft Paul still took, viewed that sort of thought as a symptom. Scanning for Disaster, he'd call it. *No Matter What,* Sarah and Paul had engraved inside their wedding rings.

She skimmed past grunge rock, settled on Stevie Wonder. Then floored the gas. *Yester-you, Yester-me, Yester-day.* Dodging and weaving on the Merritt, Sarah wondered: *Was* everything going to change, now? Last week, in their wild ride to the hospital, she had clutched to her breast the plastic cup of still-warm semen they had to deliver within an hour. She'd raced through the hospital corridors, forgetting which floor the Urology Lab was on. The nurse she'd asked had smirked. Finally, Sarah had burst through the lab doors, hating more than the smirking nurse the bored lab technician who'd recorded the exact time when Paul had ejaculated.

Hadn't she sensed then, Sarah thought, what the test would reveal?

She swung into the Center lot, parked in the ASSTNT PRINC. slot. She ducked past the vans and the waiting throng of wheelchairs, bowing her head in the cinder-block halls. Hidden, as always, behind her swinging dark hair.

"Gen-tle, Gen-*tull,*" witchy Maritza Juarez mimicked. She was wheeled out of the Severe Retardation corridor, her big flat face purply bruised. Avoiding Ritza's hex stare, Sarah darted into the sunny Mildly/ Moderately classroom.

"*Pink milk,*" she announced above Tim T.'s vacuum. "Look, Mr. T.!"

Tim kept inching his vacuum's snout over his carpet square, plump and methodical as an elderly janitor. Another Downs kid who never seemed to change. The tube attachment bobbed around his thick neck like a tamed snake.

"He earned a big *ten* today," Mrs. Bell called from across the emptied-out classroom. Meaning, Sarah knew, minutes of vacuuming.

"Way to go!" She stepped onto Tim's sucked-clean square of pink shag. Besides the vacuum cleaner he earned every afternoon, Tim T. loved Easter candy and all things pink or green. "So did your *Mom* send you that?" Nodding at his new-looking Celtics sweatshirt, Sarah held out her milk carton.

"Mom-*not!*" he shouted above his vacuum. And Sarah nodded again, not believing him. His mother in Boston never visited but constantly sent clothes that matched her son's jade green eyes. Sarah thumbed open the milk carton.

"Look—" She tilted its triangle mouth toward Tim. "Pink *milk!*"

"*Pinky*-pink?" He switched off the vacuum hum he imitated all day. Still slow and fussy, he parked his Hoover. Then he bounded up to Sarah. Throwing back his crew-cut head so his neck creased, he gulped the cherry milk.

"Slow down, T'n T—" Mrs. Bell lumbered over, brandishing Kleenex. "All smiles t'day, aren't ya?" She shook her head of dreadlocks, wiped Tim's pink-smeared grin. "I think, for some of 'em, 'Downs' oughta be called 'Ups.'"

Sarah laughed uneasily. Even with mellow-voiced Ma Bell, she felt shy. "I've gotta go get Principal Paul," she told Tim, backing toward the door.

"Tall Paul!" Tim straightened up as if Paul were here. Sarah always admired how Paul talked to students in the same level tone he used with staff. She nodded. Tim T. cupped his pointed ears, resuming his happy hum. Sarah slipped into the hall. What were—would've been— the odds of her copping out as a mom, like Tim's? Something not to worry about anymore, maybe.

"Touch gen-TULL!" Maritza hollered down the hall. How crucial, Sarah thought, were those few IQ points that separated high-functioning Moderatelies from low-functioning Severelies. Just like the few statistical degrees between a low sperm count and a borderline. Crucial and cruel, she told herself, halting at Paul's office. Feeling oddly—inappropriately, they'd say here—lighthearted.

Through her husband's half-open door, she glimpsed his slumped shoulders. A bad day or only average? How did stoic Paul measure that?

167

Sarah smoothed her new olive dress, stained now with dribbles of pink. This office had seemed huge to her years before but sadly small today. She crept up behind Paul and kissed his saucer-sized bald spot.

"Sare?—" He swiveled his chair, his forehead lined from brooding. Spread across his desk was an Incident Report: 2 HEAD-BUTT/ 1 TIME-OUT.

"Asleep on the job?" Sarah asked. And she quoted from a vampire movie they'd seen. "I know how you love your naps, those 'little slices of death.'"

"Right." Paul finger-combed his wiry Fidel Castro beard. "It's those big slices of life that give me trouble."

"Not today, I hope. You didn't forget your birthday, did you?"

"Till you got here." Ruefully, he scanned her new dress. "But my time is up, huh?" He pulled himself to his feet. Sarah raised her gaze, reassured as always by his height. Had she expected him to be shorter now, somehow?

"Foolish mortal, you can't escape me." She took his elbow. Outside the door, Maritza moaned. *Male staff!* voices would shout if Ritza began to Go Off.

"What'll you do if I resist? Wrestle me into four-point restraint?"

"Whatever—" Sarah stood on tiptoe. "You want." She kissed him, his beard pleasantly scratchy. His lips tasted of daylong black coffee.

"I'm shocked, doll," he told her, Bogart-style. "It's not Fertility Week."

She made her voice half-mocking, like his. "Fuck fertility."

Paul's smile spread out crooked and slow. Tightening her grip on his arm, Sarah steered him toward the rear exit. Would he be secretly relieved by the news she decided—now that she'd faced him—she'd have to tell him tonight?

Jittery-fingered, Sarah iced his cake—thickly, to hide its nut-riddled surface—and stabbed it with fifty-two candles. Surer-fingered, she slipped off her bra and rebuttoned her low-cut dress. Then—one superstition she'd invented that he'd never noticed—she cut a flat square of cardboard for next year's birthday card. This she slipped onto the bottom of the card stack.

Meanwhile, Paul had been showering and changing into his home clothes, a worn shirt and khaki shorts. So Sarah felt, as she stepped into the living room with his cards and his beribboned bottle of wine, too dressed-up.

He was lying on the couch, his long feet hanging off. The air conditioner vibrated above him, cooling from across the room Sarah's flushed face. She spoke his name quietly above its contained roar. Paul sat up. She walked toward him. They tended to be awkward with celebrations; they did better with everyday life, padding around each other, savoring their shared quiet. That's what we'll celebrate tonight, Sarah reminded herself as she stopped before him. Our life as it is. She set down the cards, staying bent so he'd see her breasts.

"Like your birthday clothes," he murmured. She settled close beside him. He shot her a let's-take-this-slow look, pouring the wine. "Any news today?"

"Well. No." She took a big first sip. As of now, lying to Paul. "Except—your dad called. Off on some racetrack trip; God, won't he ever *retire?*"

"From being Manic-Depressive? Nope. It's a life sentence."

"Speaking of manic, Saint Paul, you should've seen Tim T. today. I brought him some pink cherry milk and he gave me his vacuum hum of joy."

"'Joy'?" Paul asked skeptically. Sarah downed more wine.

"Joy." She slid off the couch to her knees, lifted his birthday cards.

"Don't suppose, Sare, we could skip laying our life across the floor?"

She stared up, trying not to sound hurt. "You don't *like* 'This's Our Life?'"

"Sure I like it. I always like your drawings. But Christ, Sarah. I'd just as soon ignore this birthday. So let's not make such a big production out of it."

"OK then, Saint Paul. We'll forget all about '87—" She tossed that early card over her shoulder. A silly headline playing on their sex-talk: PEAK YEAR FOR VOLVOS. "'93, too—" Sarah flashed him that year's headline: RIVAL TWITS. (The original had been RIVAL TWITS NEW CHAMPION; with a scissor-slice she'd made the verb a noun.) "Forget especially '96, the year we maybe *shouldn't* have started 'trying'—" She whizzed '96 hard, a wobbly square Frisbee. It clunked their stereo. "I mean: does the world need one more of *us*?"

With a flourish, Sarah raised the new 1998 card. Her ink cartoon of them, the cartoon-colored *USA Today* headline pasted above it: U.S. IS #1.

"'Number One' what?" Paul asked, gamely grinning now.

"That's what *I* wondered. There *was* something in small letters specifying whatever the Bar Graph thingy was supposed to show. But at first I thought *USA Today* was simply declaring 'the U.S.' to be The Best, period. Only on my card, 'US' is us, you twit. Us two."

"We two," he corrected, mock-teacherly. But he eyed her as if distrusting her antic mood. "What's up with you tonight, Sare?"

"I'm just—" She set the '98 card down over the blank '99 card. "Just 'up.' Up for no reason, like a Downs kid." She pulled herself to her feet.

Breathlessly, her braless breasts jiggling, Sarah fetched his cherry nut cake. Its fifty-two unlit candles vibrated as she carried it out to him. She set the cake plate on the couch end table. "So what're you gonna wish for?"

"Nothing," Paul answered firmly, like he expected a fight. "Just— for things to go on as they are. I'm feeling too old to want anything more."

"Oh?" Sarah bent and kissed him, rubbing into his bristly beard. Her lips, as she pulled back, burned. "The last thing I want you to feel tonight, Saint Paul—" reaching down, she unzipped his khaki shorts, "—Is old."

Paul closed his heavy hand over both her poised hands. "Look." His features were morphing toward his darkest-eyed melancholy face. "Of course I'm feeling old this week, what with today, with waiting to hear my goddamn—"

"Count." Sarah straightened up. Paul raised one brow. Before he could ask, she burst out, "Listen, OK; your sperm count came today. And it is—like we'd expected—low. 'Borderline-low,' the letter said." Above his dark beard, Paul's darker eyes were unreadable, unchanged. "So the doctor says we oughta go back to the hospital and discuss further treatment, 'options.' But y'know what *I* wish?" Paul shook his head stiffly. "That we could just—not."

He waited a beat. His voice came out lower and slower than ever. "C'mon now, Sare. You don't have to pretend you're not disappointed in this, in me—"

"I'm not." Unsteadily, she stepped back. She fished from her pocket a matchbook. She struck one match, its tiny heat pulsing above her fingertips as she bent over his cake. "See, I'm thinking now that maybe we've had so much trouble making a baby because we *shouldn't*." She dipped the pulsing light: wick to dry wick. "Maybe it's all a sign from the—Odds Gods."

She shook out the match. Fifty-two bright hyper flames quivered. Sarah knelt again before Paul. By cake-light, his end-of-the-day eyes glinted. He smoothed Sarah's hair behind her ears, schoolgirl style. She reached into his pants. This's me, he'd whispered to her the first time she'd touched his cock.

"I'm gonna make your birthday happy whether you like it or not." Keeping her eyes on his face, she moved her fingers in slow sure circles. Tense creases disappeared from Paul's forehead. As if they were everywhere on him, her soothing hands. His face seemed to turn younger by the second.

"Shouldn't I—blow that out?" he managed to ask, half-choked.

"Not if we're both wishing for nothing."

His cake pulsated, fitful candles sinking into thick icing. It's in our hands, Sarah told herself. If they decided not to want a baby, their life could go on like before. Couldn't it?

More slowly than Sarah, Paul sank to his knees. He kissed her, eased her onto the wood floor. She kissed back hard, burrowing into his beard. His spine tightened. Had he hurt his back? Too old, Sarah thought, to fuck on the floor.

Over Paul's shoulders, his cake vibrated wildly: its remaining brightness doubled by the wax and sugar glaze puddled on its top, oozing down its sides. As Sarah wrapped her thighs around Paul's hips, she saw his big feet disrupt his new cards. '98 and the unmarked unnoticed '99 card. She stretched one leg, calibrating her movement so Paul didn't feel it. He was nuzzling her neck, burying his face in her long hair. Hard as she could, Sarah kicked it far under the couch: the blank card that would be filled, next year, by who knew what.

———

July 10, 1999

Waiting inside her new hypersensitized skin for a crack of lightning, Sarah spread her suddenly puffed-up fingers. She lowered her eyes from storm clouds roiling over the ocean. "God," she mumbled, remembering "swollen hands" listed in one of the baby books as a sign of something dangerous.

"'God' what?" Paul sat up straighter in his deck chair. Ever since they'd left home—this was their third motel—he had held himself subtly on alert.

Sarah met his narrowed ready-for-disaster gaze, keeping her new worry to herself. Instead, to lighten the tension building between them in the muzzy electrically charged heat, "God, do you know what *day* this is?"

"For starters, Day Ten of De-Leading-Gate."

Paul's tanned hands, Sarah noticed, were still blistered from all the furniture he'd moved to prepare their apartment for having its lead paint stripped off. Normally, Paul and Sarah never took—never wanted—vacations away from home. Now, they weren't allowed back until their apartment passed the inspection it had flunked twice, so far. Sarah was trying not to see this as a bad sign: their home deemed unsafe for the baby they'd been stunned to conceive mere months after they'd officially, last July, stopped trying.

She rested her swollen hands—why didn't Paul notice?—on the firm swell of her belly. Big for four months. Sarah had always imagined pregnancy couldn't feel as uncomfortable as it looked. These days, on and off, the ache of her stretching skin amazed her.

"Guess again." She gazed out toward the busy beach road that separated them from the darkening ocean. On the balcony opposite theirs, an unabashedly fat bikini-clad mom strode up to her wood rail. The balconies here all faced each other, as if designed for lack of privacy.

"Todd—" the mom called down to her morose-looking son. He sat digging in the permanently dirty sand below.

"Well," Paul was going on, "there *is* something else. I hadn't wanted to bring it up myself, hadn't wanted to upset you, but—"

"It's gonna *storm!*" the mom hollered at little Todd as if this were his fault.

"'But' what?"

"—But you do remember, Sare, that today's Friday. The last day we're allowed to call and make an appointment for the—the amnio—"

"Please." Sarah held up one puffy hand. "Can we not talk about that *quite* yet?" She hugged her new belly. The lower half of her T-shirt felt sticky from salt water she'd let dry. Although it was early afternoon, she hadn't changed.

Hours before, in the cooler morning light, she'd waded into the surf as Paul watched her from the shore. He'd sat in the sand, unshaded and uncomfortable looking. Hulking gulls circled him. She splashed up to her thighs, bellying the clean green underside of the waves, feeling big in the oversized red T-shirt she wore at his request, so he couldn't lose sight of her.

Sarah squinted toward the fogged-over Atlantic, its surf too distant to hear. This morning's sparkly water had been replaced by a choppy olive-gray surface. The ocean's true color, minus its gloss of sun? Todd's mom's balcony door slid shut. In the courtyard, boys wrestled a Frisbee into the rising wind.

Weeks before, in the ultrasound monitor, Sarah and Paul had glimpsed their fuzzy fierce-looking son. The blood tests Sarah had taken set the odds of her having a Downs baby at one in eighty, higher than normal for a thirty-six-year-old woman. An amnio was strongly recommended—was routine, Paul kept saying—but was not, Sarah had been relieved to learn, required.

"Why're you so eager to stick a dangerous needle in my belly?" she asked now, adding: "Why *de-lead* if we're not going through with this?"

Paul sighed, exaggeratedly patient. "You're the one, Sarah, who set up that de-leading the minute you entered your fourth month. . ."

"Which is supposed to be the 'safe' month. Past the miscarriage zone." Sarah wiped her sweaty forehead. "But, of course, *you're* the one," she went on as she'd stopped herself from doing before, "who thinks Tim T. can't feel joy."

"What?" Paul shot her his You're-A-Hormone-Crazed-Pregnant-Lady stare. His beard glittered with sweat. "What's that got to do with anything?"

"It's got everything to do with anything!" Sarah heaved herself up. "Whether or not *you'd* consider a Downs life worth saving, living. Because if Tim T. *can* feel joy, when he vacuums or when-ever—"

"When he vacuums, right. Poor kid lives in a vacuum. Look, you don't need to explain Tim T. to me. I help *keep* him safe in that damn vacuum."

"And what's *wrong* with living like that? Safe from the world! Some people'd say that's how *we* goddamn live!" Sarah shuffled to their sliding door, her bare feet swollen like they'd been for weeks, bread loaves.

"C'mon now, Sare," Paul began again in his maddeningly level voice. "Calm down. Stay out here with me. We always watch storms together—"

"Yeah? Well, this storm hasn't even *started* yet." She slid the glass open, stepped into their room, slid it shut hard. In the stale comforting quiet, she crouched by her beach bag. Panting, she dug out her sandiest, most dog-eared pregnancy book, the one her big sisters had given her at Easter.

Sarah had taken her Home Pregnancy Test in March, alone at the apartment while Paul visited his suddenly sick dad in Florida. Their last visit together, it turned out. Pulling herself up, Sarah remembered for a dizzy second the sweep of pink on the Test strip. Shocking pink; aptly named. She'd watched the strip turn color so close-up it filled her sight like a sunrise sky.

Minutes past midnight, she'd phoned Paul in Florida.

"I just took a Home Pregnancy Test. And it came out a *big fat yes!*"

Paul was so groggy at the other end she'd had to repeat her news. But once he'd understood, he'd told her: "If that's right, that's stupendous."

Gratefully, Sarah hugged her copy of *What to Expect.* Even sleepy and ambivalent, Paul had come up with the perfect word. Stupendous. Wasn't it, to be carrying a baby? She settled heavily onto the bed. And wasn't it understandable that Paul might still feel overwhelmed? After all, her pregnancy news had been followed within a week by the death of his dad.

He'd had a heart attack at the Gulf Stream track, telling his favorite story: how he'd seen Secretariat win the Belmont. How "Big Red" had surged so far ahead of the other horses, so indisputably Number One.

Sarah thumbed the index. *Hands, swollen. p. 128.* She flipped back pages curdled from an old ginger-ale spill. First trimester, she'd carried ginger ale and this damn book everywhere. Paul had been carefully kind to her, cooking when she couldn't stand the smell of raw meat. After dinner, he'd napped on their couch for hours. Sleep, his old favorite drug. Only now—at the end of her fourth month, both of them worn down by this trip—did Sarah sense in Paul what she'd suspected all along: his resistance to the new life they awaited.

EDEMA (SWELLING). Sarah skimmed the bold-faced paragraph. She marched back onto the sultry porch. Paul sat facing the storm clouds, his bald spot sunburnt. Would it be a relief when he, like the clouds, simply burst?

"'If your hands become puffy, notify your doctor,'" she read into the wind. "'Such swelling may be insignificant or—if accompanied by a rise in blood pressure—it could signify the onset of a dangerous condition: pregnancy-induced hypertension.' Doesn't that sound like me? 'Hypertense'?"

"Jesus, Sare." Paul stared at her hands holding the book. "How long have they been like that, like your feet get? Why didn't you tell me?"

"Why didn't you notice?" Sarah dropped *What to Expect* onto the table.

"Christ," Paul was saying as if to himself. "My last night in Florida, when I shook my dad's hand good-bye. Only days before his heart attack? I noticed *his* hands seemed swollen. Seemed, for the first time in years, bigger than *my* hands. But I didn't say anything, didn't even think of it again till now—"

"Stop—" Sarah cut him short, a puffy-handed karate chop, "scaring me."

"Sorry." Paul tugged from under *What to Expect* the AAA map they'd used to chart their way to cheaper and cheaper motels. "You lie down and I'll—"

"Find yourself some route to escape?" she asked, attempting a joke. But it came out as hostile-sounding as everything else she'd found herself saying. Electric pre-storm wind blew her hair. She met her husband's wearily patient stare, feeling as wicked as Medusa, snake curls flying around her head. "Maybe you want that amnio because you think *it* would wind up being your escape."

"What?" Paul gaped at her over his half-unfolded map.

"I've been thinking about your dad, too," she pushed on recklessly. "How he died telling that Secretariat story, how he was always ranking and rating everything, everyone. Do you—do we—have to rate our baby like that? Like one life's worth having and another's not?"

"Look," Paul told her, coldly calm. "We see this—see lots of things— differently. One time, back before the Zoloft, my shrink asked me if I'd rather not have been born. I said yes. And I was surprised—this's what it's like to be depressed—I was *surprised* when he said most people would say no."

"Which—I bet—is what most Downs kids would say. I mean you know how—God, Paul—how sweet and cheerful almost all those Downs kids are—"

"*You* damn well know how much I like those kids. Better'n I like almost anyone." Paul pulled himself up, too. "But, long as we're talking 'what-ifs': a kid of ours might not turn out so cheerful. You keep forgetting what genes he might get from me, from my dad." Paul's thinning hair thickened in the wind. "Hell, I can see the headline: WORLD'S FIRST DEPRESSIVE DOWNS BABY—"

Sarah pivoted, jerked the glass door open. "You never *did* want our baby!" She lurched into the room. With a clack meant to be heard, she locked the door.

Because misty rain began to fleck the glass doors, Sarah didn't see at first that Paul was gone. She had turned her back, dialing and redialing Dr. Hess's New Haven number. She wanted to ask about hypertension, to find out if she should get her blood pressure taken today. But she'd heard only static.

"Paul?" Sarah unlocked the sliding door, stepped onto the empty balcony. Drizzle stung her face. *Crack*: distant lightning flashed, illuminating the ocean horizon. For comfort, Sarah rested her hand on her belly's solid curve.

"One, two, three," she began to count, the way she and Paul did when they cuddled on their couch at home, listening to a storm approach.

"Hey: you couldn't be timin' con-*trac*-tions yet?" Still bulging from her bikini, Todd's mom gathered Barney dinosaur towels off her balcony rail.

Sarah lowered her hand from her belly. Thunder rumbled, approximately four miles away. "No, no—I'm timing the *storm*, how many *miles* away it is."

"Just saw your *hus*-band headin' out into it." Todd's mom plodded toward her open door, damp shocking purple towels wadded in her arms.

"Where?" Sarah felt embarrassed to shout. "Where was he heading?"

"That'r way." Todd's mom pointed stoutly toward the motel office, the parking lot. "Better track him down, hon. He might come in *handy*—"

With a broad sympathetic smirk, she barreled into her room. The drizzle was thickening. Sarah backed into her own room. Her sister Sandi, an architect and divorced mom, had warned: don't get pregnant unless you could go it alone. *However safe you feel, little sister, you may have to.*

Me and my Depressive-Downs baby, Sarah thought, shaking out

her damp hair. At the next lightning crack, closer each time, she covered her ears. If she were left all alone, would she have the amnio? *Would* she abort a Downs baby? Sarah's stomach muscles tightened protectively. Maybe yes, she couldn't stop herself from thinking. Pressing her ears harder, humming like Tim T., she paced in small circles. Hypertension setting in now, for real?

PREGNANT MOM PERISHES WHEN PHONE LINES FAIL & HUBBY FLEES.

Inside her, either her stomach or her fetus—she still couldn't distinguish—gave a light flutter. Sarah stopped pacing. Apologetically, she pressed her hand to her belly, the skin there sturdy now. An oversized thickened orange rind. Under her hand, nothing stirred. When pregnant women are distressed, Sarah remembered reading, fetuses fall into "anxious stillness."

Bending fast, she groped in her beach bag again. Dizzily, she rose, clutching her wallet. Her clumsy fingers inched out a small glossy fax-paper square, a frozen image from their ultrasound. Afloat in grainy grays that had shifted like surf-pounded sand, their shrimplike fetus gave an anxious—an anguished-looking—scream. Hadn't Paul felt what she still felt, seeing its face?

I want that one; that one's mine.

Salty wind blew through the door, drops speckling the ghost image. Frantically, Sarah blew onto the wet darkened fax-paper. What if she could never see it again, that face? In the next gust of wind, her fingers lost hold of the ultrasound picture. It fluttered under their unmade bed. Ruined anyway, Sarah thought as she sank back onto the mattress. She wished she could sketch the tiny face, while she still remembered it. You can if you try, her mother always told Sarah plaintively back when Sarah struggled over her never-good-enough drawings. I won't push mine to be anything he's not, Sarah vowed, clenching her swollen hands. If only I can have him. She reached again for the phone, but her right hand stayed clenched. She gripped her stiffened puffy fingers. Slowly, she unbent her right fingers, one by one.

"Hello, hello—" she barked into the dead phone. Slamming it

down, she bent for her sandals. She would head out into the rain, find a doctor for herself. For—she thought, meaning the baby and herself—*us*.

As if this were a magic word, Sarah heard her name called outside the door.

They both—when Paul stepped into the sliding-glass doorway, his hair wetted down so he looked bald—spoke at once.

"I tried to call Dr. Hess but I couldn't get through—"

"The hospital; the local hospital; I know how to drive there—"

Sarah sat up straight. "Hospital?" She stood unsteadily in her sandals.

"You'd locked the damn door, Sare, and I didn't want to waste time. So I asked the old lady at the lobby desk where's this—" he held up the dripping AAA map, "—Groton *Hospital*. So we can get your blood pressure checked—"

New strong wind whirled up behind Paul, whipping away the map. It wheeled off the balcony, end over end. Sarah stepped into the doorway beside him. In the courtyard below, their map plastered itself against a hammock post. Boys—one plump, two skinny—were riding the hammock, whooping.

"So let's get going, Sare. Get you checked out. Just in case."

Sarah drew a steadying breath of salt wind. The ocean was submerged under steamy low-hung clouds. Turning to Paul, she shot a side-glance at the room, its lit-up clock. Nearly four-thirty. Half an hour left till their deadline to schedule an amnio passed. Hadn't Paul noticed the time?

"C'mon." Firmly, he took hold of her arm. A tall nervous man with big calm hands. That had been her first impression of him. She let him lead her down the wobbly wood steps. Thunder sounded above them as they started across the concrete courtyard. A giant's rumbling stomach.

Inside Sarah something fluttered again. Like the thunder, moving closer. "Hey. I feel him. Least I think that must be him, moving. Oh

180

Paul," she half-shouted in the wind. "Don't you ever—since our ultra-sound—picture him?"

"Sure I do. I picture him happy." Paul halted near the hammock, letting go of her arm. Drizzle blew harder onto their faces. "He's asleep in his beautiful room. Maybe the one place he'll ever feel so comfortable."

"*Bum*-mer—" The plump boy, grinning as widely as Tim T., fell off the hammock. Or was pushed, the other boys whooping louder. But the fallen boy jumped up and hurled himself back on the hammock, overturning it.

Paul stepped past the happily entangled boys. Sarah watched him peel the tattered map off the post. Would it tear like thick wet paper—a Downs fetus, pulled from her womb? Sarah answered the question: I don't want to know.

"Now—" an older mom than Todd's hollered. "You boys come in now—"

Paul gripped Sarah's arm again, the map pinned under his elbow. Boys brushed past them, each galloping in a different direction toward their families. The hammock twisted loose, half-unhooked. The one place *I* felt comfortable, Sarah thought, remembering her afternoon swinging in that hammock. Held safe in its rope mesh; yet weightless for a change, afloat.

Rain pelted down at last, exhilaratingly cold and hard. Goose bumps popped up all over Sarah's tender receptive skin. Intact flesh-droplets. Paul steered her past the green-lit VACANCY sign, toward the parking lot. Rain drenched Sarah's face, her salt-sticky hair. Bent in the wind, Paul unlocked their car.

He all but shoved Sarah into her side. She fell onto her seat in sudden quiet. The storm's roar was reduced to rhythmic drumming on the car roof.

Outside, Paul's large dark figure fought its way around to the driver's door. By shifting gray-white light, Sarah studied her hands. Somewhat less swollen in this cooler air. So maybe the swelling had simply been caused by heat?

"Alone at last." Paul slammed his door. Sarah breathed the wet-nickel tang of the wind he'd let in. "Christ, it's gotten late." He pointed to the car clock. Then, abruptly, faced her. "Fifteen minutes, and the amnio office'll close."

She faced her door, took hold of its handle. "Yeah, OK," she bluffed, hoping he didn't realize the phone lines were down. "Do you want us to run back to our room? Call and schedule that test? And if it comes out bad, I guess you'd want to break into *his* room—his beautiful room—and pull him out?"

"I wouldn't want to want that," Paul protested. Neither would I, Sarah thought. Sure that, nevertheless, she might. If they knew.

"Look," Paul began again as she let go of the door. "The final decision's yours, Sarah. But even if we agree we'd do nothing to the baby, shouldn't we—" he nodded at the streaming windshield, "—*see* what's goddamn coming?"

Through the rain, miniaturized headlights on the beach road wavered like the flames on Paul's cake. Those spluttering candles he never did blow out.

"No," Sarah told him, eyes on the lights. "God. If we both *want* the same thing—to do nothing, no matter what—I say we might's well skip the amnio."

"You say," Paul repeated as if he agreed with that part, at least. Don't put all this on me, she drew breath to reply. But Paul was starting the car, sounding more resigned than anything. "So I guess we're going to—fly blind."

Sarah's heartbeat sped up as if at danger. Paul jerked the car into gear. Lightning illuminated his hands. Bigger, now? Pre–heart-attack swollen? No. Sarah squinted at his bony blistered hands. Not yet. Final-sounding thunder cracked above and around them. "Happy birthday," was all she told Paul as he backed up the car, crunching crushed oyster shells under the wheels.

"You got me." He kept his eyes on the rearview, his bearded profile grimly determined. Sooner or later he'll want you, too, Sarah assured their baby.

Already trying to sound, to the baby, surer than she felt.

Paul flipped on the wipers. At the first slow swipe, the beach-road headlights washed away. Sarah faced only silver quivering space. What the baby might see, afloat in his own sealed-off world. Already, she promised him, loved by one person, no matter what. Was that enough to live on? The car lurched forward, the two wipers thumping like one pulse.

Why, Sarah asked herself, want anything more?

About the Author

Elizabeth Searle is the author of *A Four-Sided Bed*, a novel, and *My Body to You*, a collection of stories that won the Iowa Short Fiction Prize. Her short stories have appeared in magazines such as *Ploughshares, Redbook*, the *Kenyon Review, Five Points, Boulevard*, and *Michigan Quarterly Review* and in anthologies such as *Lovers* and *American Fiction*. She earned an M.A. from Brown University, where she studied with John Hawkes. A former Special Education teacher, she has taught fiction writing at Brown, Oberlin, and Emerson College. She is on the Literacy Committee and Executive Board of PEN/NEW England. She lives with her husband and baby son in Arlington, Massachusetts, where she is at work on another novel.

This book was designed by Wendy Holdman.
It is set in Concorde type by Stanton Publication Services, Inc.,
and manufactured by Bang Printing on acid-free paper.